BENEATH
THE ICE

LAKESHORE U

BENEATH THE ICE

LAKESHORE U

L A COTTON

Published by Delesty Books

Beneath the Ice
Copyright © L. A. Cotton 2023
All rights reserved.

This book is a work of fiction. Names, characters, places, and events are the product of the author's imagination or used in a fictitious manner. Any resemblance to actual persons or events is purely coincidental.

No part of this book may be reproduced or used in any manner without the written permission of the publisher, except by a reviewer who may quote brief passages for review purposes only.

Edited by Kate Newman
Proofread by Sisters Get Lit.erary Author Services
Image: Wander Aguiar Photography

LAKESHORE U

Bite the Ice
A Lakeshore U Prequel Story

Ice Burn
A Lakeshore U Story

Break the Ice
A Lakeshore U Story

On Thin Ice
A Lakeshore U Story

Beneath the Ice
A Lakeshore U Story

Cold As Ice
A Lakeshore U Story

For all the Connor Morgan fans...

CHAPTER 1

CONNOR

I was a lucky motherfucker.

That was the only thought circling my mind as I watched my girlfriend go through her morning routine.

"What?" Ella asked with a hint of amusement as she flashed me a demure smile over her shoulder.

"Just thinking…"

"Care to share those thoughts?"

"Unless you want to end up late to class… again." My brows waggled. "I should probably keep them to myself."

"Horndog," she chuckled, returning her focus to her skincare routine.

Toner. Moisturizer. Some funky-looking shit that she swore kept her skin smooth and wrinkle-free.

It shouldn't have been so sexy watching a girl rub

and massage cream into her face, but every single thing about Ella Henshaw turned me on.

A year in, and I wanted her as much, if not more, as I did at the beginning of our relationship.

She was everything I'd ever wanted. It had just taken me a while to realize it.

But when you were a freshman playing for one of the best damn hockey teams in the NCAA, a relationship was the last thing on your mind.

At least, that's what I'd told myself back then, when I got Ella in my bed the first time around. I was a nineteen-year-old idiot who thought he knew better.

When I'd finally pulled my head out of my ass last year and made my move to win back the girl I'd let slip through my fingers freshman year; luck had been on my side. Ella agreed to give me another chance, and the rest, as they say, was history.

I couldn't imagine life without her now.

My best friend. My biggest supporter. The love of my life.

Ella was perfect for me, and one day she would—

"Connor!" She let out an exasperated breath. "You're distracting me."

"Stop being so fucking beautiful then, kitten."

A dreamy look churned in her dark brown eyes as she stared at me through the mirror.

"Love you, El."

"Love you too, you big goofball. Now go do something productive so I can finish getting ready. I promised the girls I'd meet them at Roast 'n' Go before my first class."

"Yeah." I dragged my ass out of bed and pulled on some sweats. "I need to hit the gym."

"Mm-hmm," she murmured, eyes fixed on my torso.

"See something you like?" I smirked, loving the feel of her eyes on my body. But not half as much as I loved the feel of her hands, her tongue trailing down my—

"Shower. Now, Morgan."

"Yes, ma'am."

Ella's laughter followed me out of my bedroom.

More often than not, we stayed here, at the house I shared with my teammates, Austin and Noah. The guys made her feel more than welcome, and it helped that Noah's girlfriend Aurora was over a lot.

Besides, with Austin and I being seniors, our house wasn't party central anymore. The guys saved that for Lakers House—the team's frat house.

I'd never quite understood the frat connection personally, but some of the guys dug that shit.

Downstairs, I found Austin nursing a coffee. "Hey," I said. "Rough night?"

"You wouldn't believe me if I told you."

"Hot date?"

"Booty call."

"Nice." I grinned. "Fallon?"

He nodded, clearly unwilling to share the finer details of his off-on friends-with-benefits arrangement with a girl in our class.

"You know, you can talk to me about this stuff. I'm pretty good at—"

The chair legs scraped across the linoleum as he shot up out of his seat. "I'm heading in. I'll see you there."

"If you wait—"

But he was already gone, the front door slamming a few seconds later.

"Good morning to you, too," I murmured as I hit the button on the coffee maker.

Austin was a hard ass. I'd thought having his little sister start her freshman year here would soften his jagged edges. But if anything, he'd only become more and more withdrawn since Aurora arrived at LU.

I wasn't going to let our goalie's bad mood ruin my morning, though.

Life was good.

No, scrap that. Life was fucking fantastic.

I had the girl of my dreams in my bed every night. I played for one of the best damn NCAA hockey teams in the country. I had the best friends a guy could ever wish for. And a future playing in the NHL was so close I could almost taste it.

It didn't get any better than that.

I was on fire.

Which was a strange fucking thing considering Ellet Arena was a cool fifteen degrees. But I felt good, strong. I felt like I could take on any team in the division and win.

And I had no doubts that the Lakeshore U Lakers would make the Frozen Four their bitch next spring.

One last time before I graduated.

Fuck yeah.

My mouth twitched as I glided across the ice, marking the puck with keen eyes as my teammates executed the play with well-rehearsed perfection.

But it was our left-winger Mason Steele who got the praise as he lined up the shot.

"Looking good, son," Assistant Coach Dixon called as the puck sailed into the net.

Noah skated over to Mase and clapped him on the shoulder. "You'll be gunning for my record soon," he smirked.

"Okay, bring it in." Coach Tucker hollered, and we all rushed over to the benches. "You're looking good out there. Strong. Mason, nice slap shot. Maybe Coach Dixon is onto something. Maybe we should be using you more in the attacking zone."

We all glanced at him, waiting for his reply, but his stunned ass only managed a muttered, "Thanks, Coach."

I got it. Mason wasn't used to the spotlight. In fact, he preferred to stay out of it as much as possible. But since the arrival of the new assistant coach—Coach

Dixon—he'd had a fire lit under his ass and was killing it on the ice. He was looking real fucking good taking the shot too. But Mason never talked about turning pro. He hadn't entered the draft, and he had a bunch of responsibilities back home that made chasing his own dreams difficult.

Coach dismissed us, and my mind turned to other things. Mainly, getting my hands on my girl for a little post-practice rub down.

It was one of my favorite things in the world. Ella. Some scented oils. And a little naked skin-on-skin time.

"I wonder how Harper is," Noah said to no one in particular as we filed into the locker room. "She wasn't in class again," he added, this time aiming his words right at Mason.

I smirked to myself. Dude wasn't fooling anyone.

Harper was Coach Dixon's daughter, a little fact none of us had realized at first. It meant she was off-limits, but it didn't stop the tension between her and Mason from spilling over every time they were in the same space.

As far as I was aware, nothing had happened between them.

Yet.

Mason let out a heavy sigh. "If you've got something to say, Holden, just say it."

"Who, me?" Noah smirked. "I don't have anything to say."

"You're an ass."

"Takes one to know one."

I left them to it, making a beeline for my bench, stripping out of my kit and down to my boxer briefs.

I was ready to hit the showers and get out of here, but Mason was all alone now, wearing a miserable as fuck expression.

"You need to get laid," I said, dropping down beside him. "Get rid of some of that tension you're carrying around with you."

"Is that what you do?" He gave me a sideways glance, his brow quirked.

"Damn right. Ella is like my own personal therapist." I grinned. "You should have taken my advice at the party."

"Nah, she's Coach D's daughter," he said, but his expression was saying otherwise. "You never shit where you eat."

"Unless your name's Holden." I held out my hand, and he low-fived me.

When Noah had gone after Austin's little sister, Austin hadn't handled it well. But things were pretty chill now.

"I think a few of us are heading to Millers after here," I said. "If you want to tag along."

"Don't tell me you're going to start migrating there."

"What's wrong with Millers?" I asked. "The girls like that there are no bunnies, and Harper is working again, so it's a two-birds-one-stone situation."

Mason's expression soured. "I think I'm going to

head home and cram in some reading. I can't afford to fall behind."

My brows pinched as I studied him. Something was off, but I didn't know if he was pissed that Noah kept pushing the Harper thing or whether something else was on his mind. "What's going on with you?"

"Nothing. Why?"

"It's okay to let us in, you know," I said quietly, aware that he wouldn't appreciate the others overhearing our conversation. "It doesn't have to be me, Austin, Aiden, or even Noah. But any one of us would gladly listen."

"Do me a favor, Morgan." A weary sigh rolled through him. "Save the heart-to-hearts for Noah." With a little tap on my cheek, he got up and grabbed his shower bag.

"One day, Mase," I called after him, failing to keep the laughter out of my voice. "One day, you'll understand."

"You think Mase didn't come because of Harper?" I asked Noah as we sipped our beers while the girls chatted happily with Harper.

Millers was a bar and grill downtown where she worked. Mason had been a little too quick to turn down the invite earlier, which only fueled my suspicions that there was more going on there than he was willing to admit.

"Yes, now we're talking." Noah fist-pumped the air, pulling out his cell phone as he slung his arm around my neck and started belting out the team's anthem: Nickelback's *Saturday Night's Alright for Fighting*.

I joined in, giving the camera all my best moves. Noah panned his phone around the bar, capturing Ella and Rory before moving to where one of the rookies was busy chatting away to Harper.

"Who's that?" I asked, noticing him texting someone.

He grinned. "Who do you think?"

"Holden, what did you do?"

"Sent him a little motivation, didn't I?"

I leaned over and read the texts.

Mase: Should Harper be working? She still looks a bit pale.

Noah: She's fine. At least, she says she is.

His fingers flew over the screen, and I chuckled. "Don't push him too hard."

"A little friendly nudge never hurt anyone. Besides, it would do him good to get out of his head for once."

"What's he saying?"

"Being typical aloof Mase. But he's only fooling himself."

I got up and squeezed Noah's shoulder. "Go easy on him."

"I will."

I moved a couple of seats down the bar to where Harper now stood alone. "What's up, Dixie?" I asked, noticing her glum expression as she stared at her cell phone.

"Nothing." She pasted on a smile, but she wasn't fooling me. I saw the cracks.

After typing out a reply to whoever she was texting, she pocketed her cell.

"Another drink?" she asked.

"Sure thing. Got a lot to celebrate tonight."

"Oh yeah?"

"Got my girl. My team. A future with the Philadelphia Flyers. Life is good, baby. Damn fucking good."

She chuckled, "I could do with some of that Connor Morgan positivity."

"Hey, I've got enough to go around." I winked, leaving her to get on with her job.

"What was all that about?" Ella asked, coming up to me.

"Just checking in on Harper."

"Does she seem okay to you tonight?"

"Cutler probably traumatized her with his lame-ass pick-up lines." I kissed her head. "How's my girl doing?"

"I'm good."

"Happy?"

"The happiest." She flashed me a bright smile. "I can't believe we're already a third of the way through senior year."

"Believe it, kitten. Then the world is our oyster."

She tensed a little, the way she did whenever I brought up the future.

I knew Ella wanted a life with me, but I also knew she was holding back.

I didn't blame her, though. If everything went to plan, come graduation, I'd be training with the Flyers.

It was my dream come true—the end goal for as long as I could remember. But somewhere along the way, my dream had expanded to include Ella.

So I'd do whatever it took to get her to follow me to Philadelphia.

"Con—"

Grabbing the back of Ella's neck, I nuzzled her shoulder, cutting off whatever she was about to say.

I didn't want to hear it, not tonight.

"Connor!"

"Can't get enough of you, baby." I trailed tiny kisses along the curve of her shoulder.

"We're in public, you big oaf."

"You think I care?" Pulling back, I touched my head to hers, breathing her in. "It's you, kitten. Always has been."

"You know you say things like that, and I almost believe it." A teasing smile played on her lips.

"Almost, huh? Maybe I need to up my game."

Ella laid a hand on my chest, gazing up at me like I hung the fucking moon.

I wanted to tell her she was it for me. She was the woman I was going to marry. The future Mrs. Morgan. The mother of my kids. The only person I wanted to grow old with.

But I didn't.

Because sometimes words weren't enough, and I wanted to be enough. I wanted every milestone in our lives together to be one she remembered.

So I swallowed the words and fixed my mouth over hers, kissing her deeply. Pouring everything I wouldn't yet say into every tease of my tongue and slide of my lips.

Ella Henshaw was mine.

And no matter what the future held, I never planned on letting her go.

CHAPTER 2

ELLA

I watched Ward Cutler flirt shamelessly with Harper. She seemed to be into it, which surprised me. Because I was sure I'd picked up on a vibe between her and Mason a couple of times.

But then, Mason wasn't the kind of guy to play outside the rules. And most of these guys had one rule they followed.

No relationships.

Connor was the exception. Well, he and Lakers captain Aiden Dumfries and star right-winger Noah Holden.

But three out of twenty-seven wasn't exactly the norm. Still, it made going to games and hanging out with the team a little bit easier.

Last year, it was a lot. Being around Connor and his teammates, constantly fighting off the puck bunnies who followed wherever they went. Now with my girls by my side—Aiden's girlfriend, Dayna, and Noah's girlfriend, Aurora—it was easier to ignore them. And if I was feeling particularly bitchy, easier to piss them off.

When we hung out at Millers, we didn't have that problem, though. It wasn't a team hangout which meant here; we were just another group of college students.

"You think she's into him?" I asked Rory as we sipped our cocktails.

"Who, Ward?" She glanced over at them. "I'm not sure. Maybe. She definitely has a type."

"She does?"

"Yeah, unavailable," I chuckled, but Rory wasn't laughing. "She deserves to meet someone who sees how great she is."

"Yeah. Uh-oh," I said, noticing Harper tense at whatever Ward said to her.

From over here, I saw Ward laugh it off, but Harper looked a mix of hurt and pissed.

"Maybe we should intervene," I suggested. "She looks ready to beat him with that bottle.

"I'll go," Aurora said.

I nodded, leaving her to it. She said something to Harper, but Harper hurried away, disappearing through the staff door.

"What was all that about?" Connor and the guys came over and took up the various seats around the table.

"I'm not sure. I think Ward said something—"

"It was a joke." He appeared, looking sheepish. "We were talking about her old man, and I think I hit a nerve."

"Way to go, rookie," Noah teased. "You really wooed her."

Ward flipped him off. "Think I'm going to head back to the house. They're having an Xbox tournament. You guys in?"

"Something tells me Rory will stick around until she knows Harper's okay, so I'm in." Noah got up. "Let me go say bye to her."

I looked at Connor and smiled. "Go. You know you want to. I have a ton of assignments to get through anyway."

"I'll walk you home, then head over." Connor placed a kiss on my lips.

"Pussy-whipped," Ward coughed under his breath.

"And proud." Connor grinned, tightening his arm around me.

I loved that about him. That he wasn't afraid to show me how he felt no matter who we were around. He was always holding my hand, kissing me, finding ways to touch me.

"Okay," Noah said, rejoining us. "Rory is going to

stay here for a little bit and make sure Harper is okay. We ready to roll?"

"Sounds good to me." Ward seemed a little too eager to leave.

"Ready, kitten?" Connor nuzzled my neck.

"You're going to the house with the guys, remember."

"We might have time for a quick—"

"No can do, big guy." I shoved his chest gently, stepping around him.

"Wait up for me then?" he pouted, giving me big puppy dog eyes. The ones he knew I found hard to resist.

"Depends on how late you are."

"Fine, go to sleep." He slid his arm around my waist and drilled his mouth to my ear. "I'm sure I can find a way to wake you up when I slide into bed with you."

"Mmm, is that a promise?" I asked, a little breathless as we headed out of the bar.

"Always, kitten. Always."

The perks of having a boyfriend who played for the Lakeshore U Lakers?

Front-row seats at Ellet Arena.

Excitement buzzed in the air as we watched the

team warm up on the ice, waiting for the visiting team to appear.

"Go, Lakers," Dayna yelled. "Let's go, guys."

"Okay, you. Let's try and rein it in a little," Harper said. "They haven't even faced off yet."

She gave a little shrug, her cheeks flushed, but when Aiden glided past our section, flashing her a cocky wink, she went wild.

But it wasn't Aiden who had my attention. It was Mason.

He looked over at Harper, and I shot Rory a questioning look. The tension was so freaking obvious between them. I was dying for one of them to make the first move—if they hadn't already.

It wouldn't surprise me in the least.

He zipped past us, and Rory leaned into Harper. "Okay, that was a little weird," she said.

"Yeah." Harper gave her a tight smile, but I missed their next words because Dayna squeezed my arm.

"Oh, here they come."

The other team filed onto the ice, and the announcements started while both teams huddled around their benches for the pregame pep talk.

By the time the captains got ready for the face-off, I was a bag of nerves. It was Connor's final season with the team, and I knew what it meant for him to go all the way and win the Frozen Four.

The team had missed out last year. It would crush him and the other senior players to miss out again.

The game started, and Ellet Arena broke out in a victorious roar as Aiden won the puck, passing it across the ice to Noah, who flew down the right wing.

"Crap," Rory grabbed Harper's hand as a defenseman from the Bulldogs checked Noah with such force he went slamming into the boards. But he shook it off and got straight back into the game.

"It's okay, Lakers." Dayna cupped her hand around her mouth. "Win it back. Let's go."

A wave of cyan and indigo players raced toward the defensive zone, trying to block the Bulldog's breakout. Connor moved in to check their attacker, but a Bulldog player came out of nowhere, slamming into him and knocking him clean off his skates.

"Oh God," I gasped as the rest of the crowd took a collective inhale as he went down like a sack of bricks.

"He's okay." Dayna wrapped her arm around me. "He'll be fine."

But my man didn't get to his feet and shake it off.

He didn't move.

"Get up, get up," I murmured, worrying my bottom lip as he lay there.

Another second passed, and another. And I was ready to scale the plexiglass and go check on him myself, but finally, the linesman noticed, signaling for the game to cease play.

Noah reached him first, crouching over his friend as the referee made his way over.

"Please be okay. God, please be okay." I gnawed my thumb, hardly able to believe my eyes.

I knew the risks. Everyone did. Hockey was a fast-paced game, and it wasn't uncommon for players to sustain a myriad of injuries. But time seemed to stop as I watched the people gather around him.

The man I loved more than anything.

"He isn't moving. Why isn't he—"

Connor thumped a glove down on the ice and slowly pushed himself up, talking to the referee.

The roar of the crowd made pride and relief reverberate inside me. When Connor put on his number twenty-three jersey, he belonged to them, the fans. But his heart, the man underneath the jersey, was mine.

"See, he's fine." Dayna hugged me tighter as we cheered right along with them. But after that scare, my heart rate would take a while to slow down.

Once on his feet, Connor conferred with the referee before skating right up to the plexiglass glass in front of us. He pressed his hand against it, and I laid my hand there, swallowing down the tears gathered in the corner of my eyes.

Thank God he was okay.

I knew what hockey meant to him—what his dream of going pro meant.

"Fucking love you, kitten," he mouthed.

"Love you too," I sniffled. "Please don't do that again."

He chuckled before tapping his stick on the glass and skating back to the Lakers bench to be assessed by the medic.

"This game will be the death of me," I murmured.

"Yep. I have a real love-and-hate relationship with it," Rory said, offering me a sympathetic smile.

"But if you're going to love a Laker, you have to love the game," I said, unsure who I was trying to remind more—her or myself.

Of course, it was the first rule of being a hockey girlfriend.

These guys didn't just play hockey; they *lived* it. *Breathed* it. Throw in a guy with a real shot at going pro, and sometimes, it felt like being second best. But you couldn't think like that if you wanted your relationship to work. You had to support your man. Cheer him on from the sidelines. Watch as he made his dreams come true. And hope like hell that he would make room for you in his life when he became an NHL star.

Because I had no doubts, Connor could go all the way.

And I could only hope our relationship would survive that.

After the game, the guys headed to The Penalty Box, the team's favorite bar, while the girls and I headed for dinner.

But one phone call had abruptly ended our plans, and we ended up at the bar, minus Dayna.

I spotted Connor and the guys the second we entered. Unsurprisingly, they were surrounded by a horde of puck bunnies, all hoping to score with a Laker.

"I really hate this place," Rory muttered.

"It's not so bad. Come on," I said, grabbing her hand.

Harper hesitated, though.

"You good?" I asked her.

"Maybe this was a bad idea." Her gaze flicked over to where the guys were—more specifically, where Mason was.

"If he doesn't like it, he can leave." I made a beeline for their booth.

"Where's Dayna?" Aiden asked, his brows crinkled with concern.

"She called you a bunch of times. She got a call from her mom."

"Shit?" He shot up and dug out his cell phone. "Is everything—fuck, my battery is dead. Where is she now?"

"At your place," I said. "I think her dad is sick, and her mom is worried."

"I've got to go," he said.

"Keep us updated." Noah pulled Rory between his legs. "And if there's anything we can do…"

"Thanks. Hopefully, it's nothing too serious. She'll be devastated if—"

"Go, be with your girl," Connor said reassuringly.

Aiden dipped his head before hightailing it out of there.

"Shit, I hope Dayna's old man is okay." Noah dropped his chin on Rory's shoulder, sliding his hands under her baggy hoodie.

"I'm going to get a drink," Mason said to no one in particular, sending an icy ripple through the air.

Harper pretended not to watch him, but we all saw her gaze follow him to the bar.

"I'm sad for Dayna and her parents, but I'm really fucking happy you're here, kitten." Connor pulled me onto his lap, kissing the back of my neck. "I like this dress. I'd like you better out of it, though."

"Behave." I twisted around to look at him. There was a shadow in his eyes that worried me. Smoothing my thumb over his brow, I asked, "Are you sure you're okay?"

"Doc gave me the all-clear."

"I don't care about the doctor." I fisted his sweater, leaning into him. "I care about you."

"I haven't taken a hit like that for a while," he admitted. "Reminded me how quickly everything can go to shit. But I'm fine, baby. I promise."

"Good, because I've got plans for you later."

"Oh yeah?" The heat in his gaze burned away some of the shadows.

"Yup. Consider it your prize."

"Prize, huh? I like the sound of that."

I scraped my nails along his jaw and smirked. "You should."

"How long do we need to stay?" He grinned.

"Heard that, Morgan," Noah piped up. "And you're not leaving until we've sunk at least three more beers. We're supposed to be celebrating."

"I can think of about six ways of celebrating that don't require beer or your pretty face, Holden."

"Connor!" I swatted his chest, but it only gave him an excuse to grab my arm and loop it around his neck.

"Love you, kitten." He flashed me a mischievous grin. One that made it impossible to stay mad at him.

"What am I going to do with you?" I said.

"How about loving me forever?"

"Forever sounds kind of serious."

"Oh, it is." he pecked my lips. "Deadly serious. I'm talking the big white wedding. Little picket fence. A heap of dark-haired little babies running around."

"You really want all that, don't you?"

"Want it, kitten? I intend on making it all happen. Just you wait."

God, when he said things like that, it made my heart fit to burst.

"You're a good man, Connor Morgan," I said, not really sure of what else to say.

I wanted it all too. I did. But we were in a bar surrounded by our friends. It didn't seem like a good time to talk about the future.

"Yours, Ella. I'm yours."

He meant it. Every word.

There was just one small problem.

Part of Connor would never be mine.

Not while he played hockey.

CHAPTER 3

CONNOR

"We could have gone to the bar," Ella said as I unlocked the door and let us into the house.

After back-to-back games, I was more than happy to come home and get my girl naked.

"Got better plans for you, kitten."

"You mean you didn't get enough last night?"

"Let's get one thing straight." I slung my duffel bag down and stalked toward her. Ella smirked, backing up as I advanced. Her thighs hit the sideboard, and she had nowhere else to go.

"Con," she breathed as I pinned her there, caging her in, my hands planted on the sideboard.

"No amount of time with you is ever enough, El." Leaning in, I ran my nose down the side of her neck, breathing her in.

Home.

She smelled like home.

And I fucking loved it.

"The minute I get done fucking you, I'm already thinking about the next time. I want you morning, noon, and night, baby. So stop sassing me, get naked, and spread those beautiful legs for me."

"Here?" She arched a brow. "What if the guys come home early?"

"Noah is out with Mase and his family. Austin is at the bar. We have the house to ourselves for at least the next couple of hours."

"You don't know that." Her hands slipped to her Lakers hoodie. The one with my number on the breast. Right over her heart.

Right where it belonged.

"They could come home any minute. You wouldn't want them to see me naked, would you? Your mouth on my pussy?"

Fuck.

Heat shot through me like lightning. "Is that what you want, kitten? You want me to drop to my knees and taste you?"

"It wouldn't hurt," she chuckled, slamming her hand into my stomach. "But let's move this upstairs, Romeo."

"Jesus." I stumbled forward as she slipped out from between me and the sideboard, my dick rock hard and aching in my sweats.

"You want a drink?" Ella called from the kitchen.

I wanted a lot of things, but it looked like I wasn't getting them anytime soon, at least not in the hall.

"Water," I replied, taking my bag upstairs.

It had been a good weekend; two wins in the bag. The team looked strong, well-organized, and sharp on the attack. Between Noah, Aiden, and now Mason, the Lakers were set, a force to be reckoned with this season. There was still a way to go, but dreams of making it to the Frozen Four were beginning to taste a whole lot more like reality.

I shouldered the door to my room and went inside. This house had been home since sophomore year when Austin and I decided to move out of Lakers House and get our own place. A lot of good memories were housed in these four walls. And more of them than not included Ella.

After dumping my bag, I wasted no time stripping down to my boxer briefs. By the time Ella joined me, I had stretched out on my king-size, watching the ESPN highlights.

"I brought snacks."

"The only snack I need is you." I waggled my brows, failing to keep the humor out of my voice.

"You are such a goofball."

"Come over here, and I'll show you exactly how goofy my balls can be."

Pure laughter pealed out of her. "God, I love you."

Ella went through her nighttime routine. Teasing

me with the odd seductive smile as she removed her makeup and slowly undressed. It was the best kind of foreplay. Knowing that only I got to see her like this. So natural and uninhibited.

"What do you make of Harper and Mason?" she asked me, slowly undressing.

"You want to talk about Harper and Mason... *now*?" I palmed my dick. I was still semi-hard from the kiss downstairs. But seeing Ella work her pants down her toned legs, revealing her black lacy panties, had me flying at full mast again.

"So needy," she teased, crawling on the bed toward me.

She looked fucking edible. All that soft skin was still sun-kissed from the summer, just begging to be touched. Tasted. Cherished.

I couldn't resist reaching for her, clamping my hand around her waist and pulling her atop of me.

"So what do you think?"

"About..." I ran my eyes over her body. Her magnificent tits, the tempting curve of her hips, her long slim legs that always looked so fucking good wrapped around me.

"Harper and Mason."

"Babe," I groaned, dropping my head to her shoulder. "You're killing me here. I'm trying to seduce you, and you're more interested in talking about our friends."

Ella grinned, sliding her fingers into my hair and

tugging my head back a little so I had no choice but to look her in the eye. "I'm here, aren't I? Naked and on top of you."

"You're wearing too many clothes, and I'm not inside you yet."

"So much for seduction." Challenge lit up her eyes.

Oh, it was on.

So fucking on.

In one smooth, well-rehearsed move, I flipped Ella onto her back and gazed down at her with a smug smile. "Better?"

"It's a start," she chuckled.

"You know, I keep wondering when this will wear off."

"This?"

"You. Us. The way I want you every second of every single day. It's my favorite thing in the world."

"Sex is your favorite thing? How dreadfully predictable, Mr. Morgan."

"Not sex, smartass. You." I slid my hand underneath Ella and squeezed her ass. "I love your smile and your heart. I love your laugh and the fact you don't take any of my bullshit. I love your tits and your ass. But most of all, I love that you get me, El."

"Connor," she whispered, a little choked up. "I love you too. You know that, right?"

"I know, kitten. I just look at you sometimes, and I can't believe how lucky I got."

"I am pretty amazing."

"Damn right." I brushed my mouth over hers. Once. Twice. Letting my tongue run along the seam, teasing her.

Ella opened up for me, tangling her tongue with mine, and a deep sense of rightness went through me.

Guys grew up thinking sex was only exciting when it was no strings. But fuck that. Sex had never been so good as it was with Ella. I knew every inch of her body. I knew how to get her off every damn time. And she knew exactly how to reciprocate. There wasn't a position we hadn't tried or a part of her body I hadn't mapped with my hands or lips, tongue or teeth.

There was an intimacy in that level of knowing someone that just didn't come with a casual hook-up.

It didn't hurt that after we got done rocking each other's worlds, we could hang out and watch movies or play video games or hit the bar.

The kiss turned hungry as my hands roamed over her body, dipping between us to cup her pussy.

"Con," she breathed, arching into my touch.

"Should have taken these off," I said, unable to break the kiss, to stop touching her for even a second.

Hooking them aside, I plunged two fingers into her. "So wet for me, kitten."

"Yes... God, yes."

I curled them deep, rubbing her G-spot. "I want you to come hard and fast," I said.

Ella nodded, pressing her lips together, trapping the nonsensical moans falling off her tongue.

My thumb pressed down on her clit with just the right amount of pressure to make her shatter. "Fuck yeah," I grinned, sucking a path of kisses down her throat as she cried out.

Shoving my boxer briefs down my thighs, I didn't bother stopping to get them all the way off. I needed inside her.

Now.

Leveraging my hands under Ella's ass, I nudged up against her before thrusting inside. "Fuck, baby." I kissed her deeply, finding a slow grind that had Ella panting and moaning my name over and over.

"Connor, more... I need... ah."

I swallowed her cries, licking my tongue into her mouth.

Fuck, she was perfect. Rolling her hips to match my thrusts, rippling around me in a way that had my eyes rolling into my head.

"Your pussy was made for me," I crooned, picking up the pace.

Sliding one hand under her knee, I spread her open, changing the angle to let me go deeper.

"Fuck, Connor," she breathed, her entire body coiling tight, the air crackling around us.

I ran my hand up her stomach and over her tit, squeezing gently before collaring her throat as I pounded into her. "So fucking perfect."

She stared up at me, all dreamy-eyed and heavy-lidded. "Harder... harder."

"Your wish is my command, kitten."

My world narrowed down to her, pleasure splintering inside me as I raced toward the edge.

"You think you can come again for me?" I asked, and she nodded, grabbing my hand and shoving it between our bodies.

"Greedy girl," I chuckled, working her clit. "Do you have any idea how much I love you, El?" I rasped. "You fucking own me, baby. Own." I kissed her. "Me."

"Yes... *Yes*." Ella trembled beneath me as she came, clenched around my dick.

"Hold on, baby," I urged, riding her harder... faster. She began sucking on my neck and my shoulder, grazing her teeth right over my pulse. It was so fucking good; pleasure raced down my spine and barreled into me as I came with a roar.

We lay there, breathless and sated. Basking in the afterglow.

"Mmm, I love you." Ella trailed her fingers over my face.

"Love you too, kitten." I pressed a lingering kiss to her brow.

"That was nice."

"Nice?" My brows pinched. "Babe, if it was only nice, I wasn't doing it right."

She ran a hand up my chest. "You know what I mean."

"The only words I want to hear coming from your pretty mouth after sex are that I rocked your world."

Rolling off her, I tucked my arm under my head and inhaled a deep breath. "So, Harper and Mason, what are you thinking?"

"Oh my God, Con! I literally have your cum leaking out of me, and now, you want to talk about them?"

My laughter filled the room. "Like you aren't dying to tell me what you think."

Ella nestled into my side and laid her hand on my stomach. "I think they're sleeping together."

"Nah, no way. Mase would tell me." She arched her brow at that, and I chuckled. "Okay, he'd tell Noah, and Noah would tell me."

"Well, if they aren't sleeping together yet, it's going to happen."

"Don't get too excited, kitten. You know Mase. He doesn't do serious."

"Says every hockey player before he meets the right girl. I need to go clean up." Ella pressed a kiss to my chest, but it wasn't enough, so I gently gripped her chin and angled her face to mine, kissing her deeply.

"I'd say give me five, and we'll go again, but full transparency, I feel like I could sleep for a week."

"Don't worry, stud. If I get needy, I'll break out Mr. BOB." Ella headed into the bathroom, but I called after her.

"Don't you dare play with BOB without me."

Her muted laughter was the only response I heard before I crashed.

"Mmm, there she is." I hooked my arm around Ella's waist and pulled her back into me.

"I wasn't expecting you home so soon."

Home.

That word on her lips did things to me. Pure animalistic neanderthal things. Like my soul knew she was the one, and it wanted to bind her to us in any way possible.

We really needed our own place. Stat. But it hadn't seemed necessary until recently, and now it was senior year, and the months were ticking by. It hardly seemed worth it when come spring—after graduation—we'd be moving to Philly.

At least, that was the plan.

"How was it?" she asked.

"Scottie had the time of his life."

Mason had arranged to give his younger brother a tour of Ellet Arena and a little session on the ice with a few of the guys.

"Harper managed to get him out on the ice."

"Oh my God, that's amazing."

Scottie was autistic and a Lakers superfan. But he'd never braved the ice before.

"She's so good with him," Ella added.

"She is. Caught some serious tension between her

and Mase again. But then Coach Dixon turned up, and she took off."

"Oh."

"Yeah, something is going on there. I just can't figure out what."

"Maybe we should stay out of it this time," she said. "Look what happened when we tried to help Noah."

"Worked out in the end, didn't it?" I shrugged.

"But it almost didn't."

"We were only trying to protect them."

Noah and Rory had been sneaking around behind Austin's back—behind our back. It had the potential to blow up and cause problems for the team. How was I to know Noah would get all up in his head and call things off with her?

We were guys.

Guys did dumb shit all the time.

"I'm just saying that maybe we should let them figure it out themselves."

"Mase and Harper... I don't see it," I mused.

"Oh, I don't know. I didn't see myself falling for a hockey player either." A teasing smile ghosted Ella's lips.

"Oh, you didn't, huh?"

"Nope."

"And now?"

"Now, I'm pretty damn proud to call myself a Lakers girl."

"Fuck yeah." I picked her up and sat her on the

counter, pushing her thighs wide to accommodate me. "It's you and me, kitten. You and me against the world."

"You make it sound so simple, Connor."

"Because it is simple. So long as we've got each other, the rest will follow. I just need you to trust me, okay?"

"The NHL is going to be different. You might not want—"

"Don't." I dropped my head to hers. "Don't you dare fucking say it. Going pro doesn't change anything. Not for me."

"Connor—"

"No, El. We're not having this conversation. Not now. Not ever. You're mine, kitten. Forever."

"Bold promises." Her brow lifted, and I didn't like the skepticism in her eyes.

"You need me to put a ring on it and show you just how bold I can be?" I stared down at her, and she paled.

"Don't joke about that."

Shit, I shouldn't have said that. But it was so tempting to just do it. Get down on my knee and ask her for forever.

"I know you think everything will change after we graduate, but it doesn't have to be that way. Not if we don't let it."

"Okay." She nodded, but I saw the uncertainty still lingering there.

But it was okay. I had a plan.

Ella loved me. I knew that.
And I was fucking gone for her.
I just needed to show her.

CHAPTER 4

ELLA

"You seem distracted," my friend Jordan asked as we studied in the library.

"I'm fine."

"Says everyone who isn't fine." She kept her voice low enough to meet the building's noise regulations.

When I didn't offer a reply, she rolled her eyes. "Let me guess. You're worried you can't do the whole being with a professional hockey player."

"How do you do that?" I asked.

She was like the people whisperer. It was weird, especially for someone who generally didn't like people.

Jordan was very particular about the people she let into her life. I knew I was an odd exception, given the fact she loathed hockey players after an incident during her sophomore year that she refused to talk about. But she and Connor had an amicable relationship. She gave him shit, and he threw it right back at her. By Jordan's standards, that practically made them besties.

"Call it intuition." She shrugged.

"Fine. I'm a little worried."

"Because you think he'll fall victim to the lure of fame, fortune, and fucking his way across the country?"

"Nice, Jordan. Real nice."

"Come on, El. I'm joking. Connor is crazy about you. I'm surprised he hasn't put a ring on it already."

My heart flipped in my chest.

"We've only been together a little over a year."

"So? When you know, you know."

"Jordan Fontain, I didn't have you down as a romantic," I said, deflecting the fact her words made my heart beat wildly in my chest.

"I'm not," she scoffed, "and I'd appreciate it if you never repeat those words to Noelle."

"Trouble in paradise?" Noelle was Jordan's girlfriend. They reminded me of sunshine and rain clouds.

"No, but I have a certain image to uphold."

"You're right. Cold-hearted bitch does suit you." I fought a smile, and she flipped me off. "Behave, or Mrs. Cadger will throw us out."

"Dramatic much? You work here. She won't throw you out."

"No, but she'll chew me out for cavorting with the

'Idiots who can't abide by the library's most sacred rule.'"

"Mrs. C needs to get laid."

"You're telling me."

"But going back to Morgan. You guys are okay, right?"

"We're good. It's just hard not to look past graduation and wonder, you know."

"Yeah, I get that, but none of us know what's around the corner, El. You shouldn't let that stop you from enjoying each day until you get there."

"Are you feeling okay?" I gawked at her, and she scowled.

"Oh, fuck off."

"You and Noelle still coming tonight?" We'd planned some girls' time with Harper and Rory.

"We'll be there," she said. "Maybe this time we can keep it girls only."

"I can't be held responsible for what my boyfriend and his friends decide to do."

So they had a tendency to gatecrash girls' night. They were kind of needy like that.

"I still can't believe you went to the dark side," Jordan muttered.

I couldn't either.

But Connor had charmed the crap out of me during Halloween of junior year, and the sex had been life-altering. Besides, the stubborn ass wouldn't take no for an answer.

Sometimes I couldn't believe it had been a year, and then other times, it felt like we'd always been together. I guess that's what finding the love of your life did to you.

"Ugh." Jordan gave me a little shake of her head, and I frowned.

"What?"

"You've got that look."

"What look?"

"Like you're only just realizing your boyfriend is a Laker, and you're wondering how to get yourself out of it."

"Bitch."

"Puck bunny." Jordan smirked.

"How dare you." I clutched my chest dramatically.

She knew how much I hated that particular taunt.

Being with a Laker wasn't always easy. Especially being the first official girlfriend on campus. I'd spent months being subject to scrutiny, bitchy comments, judgmental stares, and online trolls.

Girls constantly talked about lifting each other up and straightening each other's crowns, but the minute a guy was involved, girl code went out of the window.

"In all seriousness, El, if anyone will go the distance, it's you and Morgan. It pains me to admit it because he's a Laker, but he's one of the good ones."

"Yeah, I know."

And he was mine.

I just didn't know for how long.

"Where is this place again?" I asked Jordan as we followed her and Noelle down the street.

It was a part of town we didn't come to very often, but Jordan was from Lakeshore, so she knew all the local hotspots, especially all the Laker-free places.

I loved Connor and our life together, but having an identity outside of being Connor Morgan's girlfriend was still nice. And I cherished my time with the girls in places where I wasn't constantly being scrutinized by the puck bunnies.

"It's a cute little bar on the edge of town. They do the best sliders you'll ever taste. Seriously, foodgasmic." Jordan glanced over her shoulder, winking.

"But are the cocktails good?" Dayna asked and Rory snickered.

"They do this house special daiquiri that is to die for," Noelle replied.

"Now we're talking."

"Hey, you okay?" I asked Harper as Jordan, Noelle, and Dayna went on ahead. "You're quiet tonight."

"I'm good. Actually, there's something I've wanted to talk to you both about."

We reached the bar and followed the girls inside. It was a trendy little place, all industrial fittings. Wood and steel and brick blended together in perfect synchrony.

"Does this have to do with a certain brooding hockey player?" Rory asked.

But Harper wasn't looking at her; she was looking across the room at...

"Mason," I murmured.

He wasn't alone, sitting with a girl I vaguely recognized.

Harper pushed past us and marched over to them, the girl with Mason looking at her with a mix of confusion and disbelief.

"Isn't that the new server at Millers?" Rory said.

"What's she doing here with Mason, and why does Harper look like someone just ripped her heart out of her chest?"

"Our table is ready," Jordan said. "Where's Harper?"

"She's uh... she'll be over soon." Rory gave me a helpless look, and I shrugged.

Clearly, something was going on. And from the tension bracketing Mason's mouth as he glanced between the two girls glaring daggers at him, it wasn't anything good.

"Is that Mason Steele?" Jordan asked as we all slid into the booth.

"It would appear so."

"Are he and Harper...?"

"Honestly, we don't know," Rory said. "She's been

really tight-lipped about him, but they have some serious tension going on."

"Jesus, what did they put in the water over at Ellet Arena? First Morgan, then Dumfries and Holden. If Steele hangs up his playboy badge too, the puck bunnies will go into meltdown mode."

"Better hold that thought. Harper is heading this way."

"Hey," Rory said. "Is everything okay?"

"I... I need to leave. Now."

"Okay, sure. Whatever you need." Rory stood, giving us an apologetic look.

"Go, it's fine," I said. "Just let me know if everything is okay later."

She nodded, wrapping her arm around Harper and leading her out of the bar.

"What are we going to do about him?" Jordan tipped her head toward where Mason sat, staring at the door Harper and Rory had just left through.

"Rain check on dinner?" I said.

"Sure." Jordan smiled. "Go play Cupid."

"Sorry," I mouthed, sliding out of the booth. But I couldn't just leave Mason sitting there all alone. He looked so... so lost.

He spotted me approaching and dragged a hand down his face. "What do you want, El?"

"Actually," I said, sitting opposite him. "I wanted to see if you're okay."

"What do you think?"

"Honestly, I'm not sure."

"So Harper didn't tell you?"

"No, actually, she didn't. But I'm listening…"

"Fuck." He curled his fist on the table. "I really fucked up."

"You and Harper?" I deduced.

I'd suspected, but it wasn't until watching Harper spot him across the bar with another girl that the final pieces fell into place.

Mason shut down, staring down at the table.

"How long have you two been—"

"Don't, okay. I get what you're doing, and I appreciate it. I do. But I can't do… this."

"You can't talk? I know I'm not Connor or Noah or one of the guys, but I'm pretty good at listening, Mase."

"I didn't mean for this to happen."

"You didn't mean to get involved with Harper, or you didn't mean to hurt her?"

"Both. Any of it. I don't even know how the fuck I ended up here." A frustrated sigh rolled through him.

"But…"

"But she's everything I never knew I needed, El. And I just fucking ruined everything."

"So fix it."

"Yeah," he snorted, "because it's that simple."

"Sure it is. If you like her, and you're sorry, tell her that."

His brows crinkled as he rubbed his jaw,

considering my words. "And if it's not enough?" he asked, a hint of vulnerability in his voice.

Wow. Mason didn't just like Harper; he *really* liked her.

"You won't know unless you try."

It was obvious he wasn't going to tell me what exactly had gone down, but I couldn't leave without offering him some words of advice.

He got up and gave me a stiff nod. "Thanks," he said.

"Go get her, tiger." I smiled, but he stared blankly at me. "Just go," I murmured, feeling like an idiot.

Mason took off like a man on a mission, and I pulled out my cell phone.

> Ella: The weirdest thing just happened…

> Connor: You decided you want to try anal again?

> Ella: Connor Morgan!!!

> Connor: Come on, babe. It was worth a shot.

My mouth twitched. He was unbelievable. And never getting near my ass again after the first and only time we'd tried that.

> Ella: Mason was at the bar… with a girl.

Connor: Harper?!

Ella: No, but Harper was with us and looked like he'd ripped her heart out when she spotted them.

Connor: No shit.

Ella: He wouldn't fess up to me, but he's gone to try and 'fix things.'

Connor: Babe, I thought we decided to stay out of it…

Ella: I did, mostly.

Connor: Does that mean girls' night is off? Because I have something you can snack on if you're hungry.

Ella: You did not just say that!

Connor: I'm home alone, kitten. And I saw how fucking hot you looked before you left for dinner.

Ella: I'll call an Uber.

Connor: Better yet, I'll come pick you up. I feel like a late night drive.

Sometimes, I couldn't believe this was my life. Parking down by the beach with my hockey star boyfriend, his face buried between my thighs as he licked me toward sheer ecstasy.

"Fuck, you taste so good, kitten." He pushed my knees higher, contorting my body to near-impossible angles.

"Shit, Con," I breathed, pleasure firing off around my body as he speared his tongue inside me while rolling his thumb over my clit.

It was quick and dirty, and I loved every freaking second.

"You want my cock, kitten?"

"Yes... yes," I chanted, desperate for more.

"Such a needy little thing," Connor chuckled, leaning up to kiss me. There was hardly any room in his truck, but somehow, he managed to cram his big body against mine and fill me with all eight inches of his glorious dick.

"Jesus, kitten." He started rocking back and forth, one of his hands banded around my back and the other high around my hip. "You take me so well."

"Con," I cried, pinned there and completely at his mercy. The pressure built inside me until I could barely stand it any longer. "I'm going to come," I whimpered, biting down on my own lip as my entire body started trembling.

"I'm almost there... together," he panted. "I want to go together."

"I don't think I can hold— ah." Pleasure crashed over me as he started fucking into me like a man possessed. "Oh my God."

"Fuck, El. Fuck, fuck, *fuuuck*." He collapsed on top of me. "You are amazing." Connor pressed a sloppy kiss to my lips.

"That was fun." I gently shoved him off me, needing to catch my breath.

"What, no snuggling?" he chuckled, pulling up his sweats and dropping down into the driver's seat.

"You can take me home to snuggle."

"You need some tissues?" he asked.

"I've got it."

We had sex, a lot of sex. I was used to cleaning myself up in strange places.

"I'll miss this, you know," he said.

"Miss what?"

"Late-night truck sex. When we graduate and move to Philly, and I'm halfway across the country every other weekend, there'll be no time for this."

"And there goes my happy bubble," I murmured, my heart sinking.

"Shit, El. I didn't—"

"It's fine." I gave him a weak smile. "But we should probably go before the cops show up."

Connor fired up the truck and backed out of the rest area. As he pulled onto the road, he reached over and pulled my hand onto his thigh. "I love you, kitten."

"I know. I love you too."

We drove in silence for a little while, then he said, "My mom called. She invited us for Thanksgiving."

"Don't you have a game that weekend?"

"Only on Saturday. So we could head down Wednesday night and come back Friday."

"Sure."

"We don't have to—"

"No, no. We should go." Lord knows I'd been putting it off for long enough.

"She's excited to see you."

Mrs. Morgan was a sweetheart—an older lady with a penchant for baking and gardening. The first time I'd stayed with them, I gained four pounds thanks to all the cookies she fed me.

Mr. Morgan, however, was a different story altogether. He loved his son. Loved his wife and their family. He just wasn't so keen on the girl who had stolen his son's heart—and focus away from hockey, as he constantly liked to remind me.

"It'll be nice," I said with zero enthusiasm.

"I know my old man can be a little prickly."

"Prickly?" I scoffed. "Is that what we're calling it?"

"El, come on. He's just protective."

"We've been together for a year, and the last time we saw him, which I might add was only a month ago, he asked me what I planned to do since our relationship was on borrowed time. His words, not mine."

"He's a stubborn old fool. It isn't personal." Connor

shrugged, but it did little to ease the tightness in my chest. "He's just always been focused on the end goal."

"And he thinks our 'little relationship'"—I air quote the words—"is a distraction you don't need."

"Babe," Connor squeezed my hand. "I explained how it is to him. He understands, and he knows you're not going anywhere."

I wasn't convinced, but I didn't have the energy to argue.

"It's fine."

I'd do it for him because family was important to Connor. And I knew that, deep down, his dad only wanted the best for him.

I'd just need one or two glasses of wine to get through it.

CHAPTER 5

CONNOR

"You going to answer that?" Ella asked as my cell rang for the third time since we left the rest area.

"It's just Noah. He probably—"

Her phone vibrated, and she dug it out of her purse and frowned. "It's Rory. She says, 'Noah says tell Connor to answer his damn phone.'"

"Tell her I'm driving."

"She says, 'Our bad. Noah just wanted to let you know we're at Zest with Mason and Harper if you want to stop by. I think Aiden and Dayna are coming too.' Oh my God, he did it." Ella smiled.

"So when you told him to fix it..."

"I guess he did."

"You wanna go torture him a bit more?" I grinned

over at her, and she flashed me a bright smile, her soft laughter filling the truck.

"If we go, you have to behave. I remember what it's like to be the new girlfriend."

"Fine," I grumbled. "I promise I'll behave."

"You think they'll tell us the truth about what happened?"

"I'm guessing she took Mase's stick for a ride and decided it was worth sticking around for."

"Oh my God," she burst into laughter. "I'm sure you weren't this goofy last year when you were trying to convince me to give you another shot."

"What can I say, kitten? You make me happy." I lifted her hand to my mouth and kissed her knuckles. "Can you see a parking spot?"

"Just down there." She pointed down the street, and I parked. "Oh, there's Aiden and Dayna." She waved at them as they climbed out of Aiden's car.

"Hey," I said as they came over to us.

"Mason and Harper, I can't believe it," Dayna laced her arm through Ella's, and the two of them headed toward the bar.

"I can't believe she dragged me out for this shit."

"You're our captain." I clapped him on the shoulder. "It's only right you're here to welcome Mase over to the dark side."

"I need a fucking drink," he muttered, entering the bar after the girls.

I followed him inside, grinning the second I spotted Noah and Mason with their girlfriends. "Lovers," I said as I slid in next to Noah and Rory's side. "Isn't this cozy."

"Don't be an ass, Con," Rory said.

"Sorry, Rory, baby. I'm only busting Mase's balls. I see you two figured your shit out." I wagged my finger between Mason and Harper.

"Don't start," he murmured.

"Relax, I'm happy for you. Even if she's way out of your league." I gave Harper a playful wink as I pulled Ella down onto my knee.

"Hi, guys," Dayna said. "Sorry to gate-crash. Noah said—"

"It's fine." Mason tugged Harper further along the banquette to make room for Aiden and Dayna.

"So you two are what exactly?" Aiden asked.

"What do you think they are, Cap?" Noah snorted. "Joined the dark side, didn't he?"

"About fucking time, too," I added, holding out my fist to Noah.

"You guys are so weird." Ella rolled her eyes.

"How is your Dad feeling now?" Harper asked Dayna.

"He's feeling a lot better, thanks. Thankfully, it was nothing serious."

"That's good."

"Our numbers are growing," Ella said, stroking her hand along the back of my neck. "This is a good thing. Soon we'll outnumber the bunnies."

"Kitten, you'll never outnumber the bunnies," I scoffed. "Two disappear, and four more pop up."

"There's plenty of guys left to go around," Noah said, and Rory elbowed him in the ribs. "Come on, shortcake. I didn't mean—"

"Quit while you're ahead, bro." I smirked.

"What are you doing this weekend, Harper? We're trying to talk Rory into girls' night. While the guys are away, the girls will play."

"Are you trying to give me a heart attack?" Noah massaged his temples.

"Relax, we won't do anything too crazy." Ella grinned, and I did not like the look she was wearing. "It'll be fun. Please come, and then Rory will come."

"I'm up for girls' night," Harper replied.

"Yay." Ella clapped. "I've invited Jordan and Noelle too. I'm thinking drinks and dancing. Maybe a strip cl—"

"Okay, kitten. Enough of that." I pressed my hand to her mouth. "Noah and Mason are new to this game. You can't be planting those kinds of seeds of doubt before a big weekend of games."

"Pretty sure she's joking," Rory said.

"Don't be so sure, Rory, baby. I've seen how wet my girl gets when she watches Magic Mike."

"Connor Morgan!" Ella snatched my hand away. "You did not just say that in front of all our friends."

I shrugged, barely hiding my amusement. "We don't keep secrets."

"That's... I... ugh. You're such an asshole at times."

"But I'm your asshole, kitten. And you wouldn't have me any other way." I nuzzled her neck, and she melted against me.

"Please don't maul Ella at the table," Rory said.

"Jealous, shortcake?" Noah teased. "Because that can—"

"Don't you dare." She held up her hand and pinned Noah with a hard look.

I looped my arm around Ella and gently grazed my teeth over her ear. "This is fun," I whispered.

"They're so cute together. Look." Ella nudged my cheek a little.

Harper and Mason were huddled close, whispering to one another.

"He's got it bad," I said.

He couldn't take his eyes off Harper, and I knew exactly how he felt. How much of a rush those early days could be.

Mason deserved to be happy. The guy gave everything to his family; it was about time he had someone in his corner. And I knew we'd all seen how amazing Harper was with Scottie.

She'd won the hearts of both the Steele boys, and I couldn't be happier for them.

"Life is good, kitten." I pressed a lingering kiss to Ella's neck, smiling to myself.

Life was so fucking good.

"Still no sign of Coach Dixon?" I asked Mason as I joined him on the bus.

"Nope."

"Should we be worried?" He'd been MIA for a few days now. Coach Tucker kept telling us it was business as usual. But it was Harper's dad. The same Harper he was now banging on the regular.

It was a whole shit show waiting to happen if you asked me. But Mason couldn't fess up to her father if he was missing.

"Okay, listen up." Coach Walsh swiped his ball cap off and ran his fingers through his hair. "Coach Tucker and I know things are a little weird with Coach Dixon being absent, but we can't afford to be distracted. We've got two big games ahead of us, and the Mavericks won't go easy on us just because we've got some in-house problems. So we go out there and show them that we've got our shit together."

I glanced over at Mason, who was sitting with Austin. He's got his eyes closed, but I saw the tension bracketing his features.

"We go there, do our jobs, and represent yourselves and the team the best you can."

A chorus of 'Yes, Coach' rumbled through the bus.

Coach Carson joined Coach Tucker up front, and

then we were off. It was a ten-hour drive to Rochester, so we were flying out of Cleveland Hopkins to cut down the travel time.

"Got any plans for Thanksgiving?" I asked Noah.

It was still a couple of weeks away, but with the team's busy schedule and senior year classes in full swing, it would be here in a blink.

"Well, seeing as Rory and I can't rustle up a decent parent between the two of us, probably just do something at the house with Austin. If he can quit being an asshole." Noah raised his voice a little to catch his attention. Austin glowered at him, flipping him off.

"That's going well," I said, and Noah chuckled.

"He loves me. Really."

"Just waiting for you to slip up, Holden," Austin murmured.

"Not going to happen, bro. Me and Rory are endgame."

"Who says that a few weeks in?"

"I can count at least two guys on the bus. Myself included." Noah grinned at me and then leaned over the seat to ruffle Aiden's hair. "What says you, Cap?"

"I say. Sit the fuck down and quit being a jackass."

"Sounds like you need to get laid more, Cap. Work off some of that tension," Ward chimed in.

"Want to say that again, rookie?"

"Don't piss him off, Cutler. Or you'll end up on the bench."

"He doesn't get to make that call."

"Care to wager that?" Aiden pinned the rookie with a withering look. Anyone who truly knew Aiden knew it wasn't legit, but Ward sunk down in his seat a little.

"Sorry, Cap."

"Thought so."

"Don't let the power go to your head," Noah whispered between the small gap in the two front seats.

"It'll be the holidays before we know it, and then it's straight to the playoffs."

"If we make it," Noah said.

"Of course, we'll make it. We're going all the way."

"It'd be a pretty cool way to end your college career."

"The best fucking way." I grinned.

"Can't believe you, Aiden, and Austin will be gone next season."

"All good things come to an end, Holden."

"True. But it won't be the same."

"At least you'll have Mase."

"Say what now?" he said.

"Holden's getting all emotional because he doesn't want to lose his besties next season."

"I thought I was your bestie," Mason deadpanned.

"I hate to break it to you, Mase, baby, but you're back up."

"Fucking idiot," he mumbled, folding his arms over his chest and closing his eyes again.

"I think you hurt his feelings," Noah said.

"He's a big boy. He can handle it. You heard about the girls' big plans tomorrow night?"

"Yeah." The muscle in his jaw twitched.

"It'll do Rory good to go out with the girls; get away from your suffocating ass."

"I don't suffocate her."

"I'm joking. But she needs to learn to spread her wings a little and not hide behind you or all those literary quote hoodies."

"I happen to like her hoodies."

"Only because they swamp her figure."

"Not true."

"Yeah, yeah." I smirked. But I didn't blame him. The thought of another guy hitting on Ella or even leering at her made me want to hurt something.

I'd had longer to get used to the separation than these assholes, though. Same with the puck bunny drama. Didn't matter how obvious you made it that you had a girlfriend. There was always one or two bunnies willing to brave the odds and try and make a move.

Thankfully, I'd never gotten caught in one of their traps. But it happened from time to time.

"Can I tell you a secret?" I blurted, quickly glancing at the seats around us. But everyone was either listening to their AirPods or deep in their own conversations.

"If it's about the kinky shit you and El—"

"Asshole," I hissed. "If I tell you, you can't tell anyone."

"Who am I going to tell?"

"Seriously?" I gawked at him.

"Fine. I swear on Rory's life, your secret's safe with me."

"I'm going to ask El to marry me."

"The fuck?" He practically yelled it. "Shit, sorry. I just... Wow, that's... Wow."

"Yeah, I know." I ran a hand down my face, suddenly feeling a little vulnerable that I'd told him.

I'd been thinking about it for a little while. We were only a year in, but I knew. There wasn't a single doubt in my mind that Ella was it for me. The sooner I could make that official, the better.

But I hadn't told anyone yet. Well, until now.

"Say something then," I said.

"I... Shit, that's a pretty big deal."

"It is. But when you know, you know. And everything will change once I join the Flyers. I want El to know I'm serious about her, about us."

"You got a ring?"

"Not yet. I was hoping you might come shopping with me soon."

"For real?"

"Yeah. You and maybe Austin, if I pluck up the courage to tell him."

"You should. Aww, shit, man. I'm happy for you. Even if she turns you down, I'm—"

"What? Why the fuck would you say that? Now you've probably jinxed it."

"I haven't jinxed it."

"You don't know that." I sank back into my chair and blew out a frustrated breath.

I was being ridiculous. I knew that. But this was a big deal to me.

I wanted everything to be perfect.

"Do you know when you're going to do it?" Noah asked.

"Over the holidays, I think. Maybe Christmas Day." Surrounded by our families. Or maybe I'd take her somewhere super romantic and shower her with love and attention, then get down on one knee.

"I really am happy for you, Con. And you know she'll say yes. Ella loves you, man." He grinned. "You two are the real deal."

"I fucking hope so," I whispered.

Because I needed her.

I needed Ella like I needed hockey.

They were the two most important things in my life.

CHAPTER 6

ELLA

"Yummy." Dayna plucked her cocktail off the tray. "I am so looking forward to this."

"To the guys." I held up my glass. "Another win and another step closer to the playoffs."

"Mason looked a little off tonight," Harper said, sipping her margarita.

Sadness radiated from her, and I leaned over, covering her hand with mine. "Everything will work out. It was one loss. They turned it around tonight."

"Yeah, I guess. I don't want my dad to ruin things for him or the team."

"The team has never looked better," I said with a reassuring smile. "You have nothing to worry about there."

One loss didn't define a season; the important thing

was they'd gone out there tonight and turned it around against the Rochester Mavericks.

Now we could celebrate and enjoy some girls' time before they got back tomorrow.

"I'd like to make a toast to us," Dayna said. "It's not easy loving a Laker, but it's definitely made it a bit easier that we have each other to lean on."

"Hear, hear." Rory smiled, downing half her drink.

"Easy, girl," I chuckled. "We want to go dancing. Pace yourself."

"Sorry." She blushed. "I'm a little nervous."

"Babe, you look gorgeous. Doesn't she look gorgeous?" I looked at Harper and Dayna, and they both nodded.

"So hot." Harper winked. "We'll be fighting off the guys later."

"Oh God, no."

"Relax," I said, noticing how uncomfortable she looked. "We'll look out for you."

"And at least there won't be any bunnies at Zest."

"I'll drink to that," Dayna lifted her glass again. "I'm going to need another one of these. So yummy."

I arched a brow. "Pace yourself, remember."

Dayna poked her tongue out at me, and we all laughed.

"So Harper... is it true?" she asked.

"Is what true?"

"Oh, come on. Don't play dumb. Is it true what they say about Mason?"

"I'm not answering that." She went all coy, busying herself with her drink.

"Babe, we're all friends. You can tell us."

"Dayna," Rory said with a little shake of her head.

"No, it's fine." Harper smiled. "I just... it's really new, and I... I really like him."

"Well, yeah. It's Mason freaking Steele. The guy is untouchable."

"Was... he *was* untouchable," I pointed out. "It's obvious he's completely smitten with you, Harper."

Her cheeks burned even darker. "Do we have to talk about this?"

"Uh, yes." I nodded. "Do you have any idea how exciting it is when another girl joins our circle? I spent almost ten months being the only Laker girlfriend. It was a lonely time."

"Now all we need is to find somebody for Austin," Dayna said.

Aurora almost spat out her drink. "Fat chance of that happening. You've met my brother."

"I thought he and Fallon had a thing going on?"

"I think she thinks they've got a thing," she corrected. "But he won't commit."

"Maybe he just hasn't met the right girl," Harper said.

Aurora didn't look convinced.

"She has a point," I added. "Look at Noah and Mason. And let's not forget Mr. Grumpy himself, Aiden."

Dayna snickered. "He never stood a chance."

"I guess," Aurora said. "But I think Austin needs to deal with some stuff first."

"How is that going?" Dayna asked.

Aurora's arrival at LU, and her subsequent relationship with Noah, had been rough on him. But it was finding out the truth about Rory's eating disorder that broke something inside him.

Connor and I had talked about it and figured that he blamed himself for a lot of what she'd been through at the hands of their mother. But Austin wouldn't talk to anyone about it, and we all saw the strain between him and Aurora.

"It's a work in progress. But we'll get there."

"Well, I have news," I said. "I get to spend Thanksgiving with Connor and his family. Yay me."

"What's wrong with Connor's family?" Rory asked.

"His mom? Nothing, she's a sweetheart. But his dad... that's a whole other story."

"I find it hard to believe you haven't won him over. You're one of the nicest people I know." Dayna gave me a warm smile.

"He thinks I'm a 'distraction.'" I air-quoted the word.

"Ah, he's one of those."

"Yep. He wants to see Connor go all the way."

"Well, I hope Connor sets him straight."

"It's fine"—I waved them off—"I get it. Hockey is

everything to Connor and his dad. I wasn't part of the plan."

"Plans change, babe," Dayna said. "And you know Connor is going to do something crazy like propose before you graduate. He's always talking about the future."

"No one knows what the future holds," I murmured.

"No. Nope." Dayna slid another drink in front of me. "We are not doing that tonight. Connor loves you. You're going to get married and have cute little Connor Morgan babies. And you'll take them to all his games, and he'll be that adorable dad who comes up to the boards and kisses them through the plexiglass."

The girls all swooned.

"Oh my God, stop," I let out a strangled laugh. Even though the dream she painted was one I'd imagined more than once.

It was hard not to let my mind wander to the future when Connor made me feel like the most beautiful girl in the world.

There wasn't a single day he didn't tell me how much he loved me. But a tiny part of me couldn't help but wonder if his father was right—if I was a distraction. One he'd come to resent once his career in the NHL really took off.

"Okay," Dayna clapped her hands together. "Enough talk. I want to dance."

"Oh, I don't know—"

"Come on, Rory. It'll be fun," I said, draining the rest of my sugary sweet margarita.

More than ready to put the serious talk behind us.

"Connor?" I murmured as his bed dipped and a warm naked body pressed up close to me.

"Shh, go back to sleep, kitten."

"What time is it?"

"Early. Sleep." He brushed a kiss to my hair before pulling my body back into his. Anchoring his arm around my waist, he let out a soft sigh. "Home, sweet home."

God, when he said things like that.

"You played well," I murmured, patting his forearm, still half-asleep.

"I'm glad I got your approval."

"Mm-hmm." I snuggled closer to him.

"Fuck, kitten. Try not to do that too much." Connor's chuckle fluttered over the back of my neck, sending a ripple of awareness through me.

I turned in his arms and gazed up at him. "Hi."

"Hi." Connor leaned in, sliding his mouth over mine. "I missed you." Grabbing my leg, he hiked it over his waist.

"Is that a pistol you're packing, or are you just pleased to see me?" I fought a smile.

"I'm always happy to see you, kitten." Connor rolled his hips a little, creating the most delicious friction between us.

"Tease," I scolded.

"Hey, if you want to hop on and ride my dick all the way to orgasm town, I won't—"

"Babe, you've got to stop it with the sex humor."

"What, why?" He droned, genuinely offended.

"Because... it's a little weird."

"My girl thinks I'm weird," he pouted, flashing me those big puppy dog eyes of his. "Say it ain't so, Toto."

"I thought we were sleeping."

"We were until I realized how beautiful my woman is and couldn't resist copping a feel."

"Okay. I'm getting up."

"What? No!" He tried to pull me back down, but I'd already sat up, kicking my legs over the edge of the bed.

"I'm going for a run. You need to rest." I leaned over him and kissed his forehead. "When I'm back, I'll make us breakfast."

"You're really going to leave me in this state?" His eyes flicked to the obvious tent in his black boxer briefs.

"If you promise to get some sleep, I promise to make it worth your while later."

"You drive a hard bargain, woman."

Giving him a little wink, I pulled on my leggings and one of his LU hoodies and shoved my feet in sneakers.

I didn't make a habit of running every day, but it

was either put some space between us and hope Connor got some rest or end up underneath or on top of him and feel guilty for the rest of the day.

Although Mr. Morgan was most definitely not on Team Connor and Ella, I didn't wholly disagree with him. I could be a distraction for Connor, especially when he needed to rest.

Between practice and games, the team's schedule was intense.

"I won't be—"

My expression softened. Hand tucked under his pillow, brows furrowed a little in contemplation; Connor was already fast asleep.

I slipped out of there quietly and headed downstairs.

The house was quiet, but I suspected Austin would be asleep, and Noah would have headed straight to Rory's place. He stayed there almost as much as I stayed here. I wouldn't be surprised if he made it official soon, and moved out of the guys' house and in with her.

Sometimes, I wondered why Connor hadn't suggested I move in with him and the guys. It seemed the next logical step. But then, I also knew he wanted to start our life together, officially, once we'd graduated.

There was no rush. At least, that's what I kept telling myself.

So why did it sometimes feel like there was an invisible clock ticking down around us?

Shaking off the unwanted thoughts, I grabbed a

bottle of water from the refrigerator, had a little drink, set my smartwatch to workout mode, and slipped out of the house.

Hoping the early morning run would chase away the lingering notes of desire...

And the niggling little seeds of doubt.

When I got back to the house, I was a sweaty mess.

"Sexy," Austin said as I slouched against the kitchen counter in a breathless heap.

"I pushed a little harder than usual."

Once my feet had hit the asphalt, the adrenaline had become addictive. I hadn't meant to run halfway across town, but that's exactly what had happened.

"Give me five, and I'll make you guys breakfast. Where's Con?" I asked.

"On the phone with his old man, I think."

"Lovely," I mumbled under my breath, helping myself to a glass of water. My stomach growled, and Austin arched a brow.

"What?" I shrugged. "I've worked up an appetite. Congrats on the win this weekend."

"Should have been two wins."

"Well, nobody's perfect."

After washing my hands, I got to collecting the ingredients I needed to make pancakes and bacon. The guys were supposed to stick to a strict diet, but a little treat never hurt now and again.

Besides, between practice, conditioning, and game time, they worked off the extra calories and then some.

Austin didn't reply, but he was like that sometimes. He didn't go out of his way to make me feel uncomfortable, but he also didn't hide the fact he was a little pissed that his friends had caught the *love bug*, as they liked to put it.

"How are classes?" I asked, attempting small talk.

"Fine."

"And Fallon? You know you could always ask—"

"Not up for discussion, Henshaw."

I brushed off his dismissal, offering him a megawatt smile. "So what about Harper and Mason?"

"What about them?" He shrugged.

"You have nothing to say on the matter? I find that hard to believe."

"What's to say? My friends are all fucking idiots, apparently."

Ouch.

"Or maybe they're onto something."

His bitter laughter filled the kitchen. "Yeah, onto a boatload of disappointment and drama. No thanks." He got up and headed for the door.

"Where are you going? I'm going to make breakfast."

"I'll grab something on my way in."

"Austin, wait—"

But he was already gone.

"What was that all about?" Connor appeared a few seconds later.

"I think I upset him."

"Not possible, kitten." He came over and pulled me into his arms, gazing down at me. "Austin is going through some stuff."

"Maybe you should talk to him. He's so... angry."

"Austin will figure it out. He's had a lot to deal with since Rory arrived."

"Yeah, I know." I hugged him tighter. "Did you get some rest?"

"I had an extra hour. But I would have rather spent it inside you."

"Horndog." I rolled my eyes. "Are you hungry?"

"I'm hungry for something." He started peppering my neck with kisses.

"Connor, be serious."

"Fine, feed me, woman." He grabbed my ass and squeezed hard.

Connor sat down at the table while I started making the pancake batter. "What did your dad want?" I asked.

"Oh, you know. Just checking in after the weekend."

"You mean he wanted to give you his opinion on your performance."

"Come on, kitten," he chuckled. "That's not... yeah, okay. He wanted to give me his opinion. But he means well."

Oh, I was sure he did.

I was also sure he'd thrown in a dig or two about me. But I didn't ask. I was in a relationship with Connor, not his father. His opinion of things wasn't important.

At least, that's what I tried to tell myself.

"They're looking forward to seeing us over Thanksgiving."

"Great." I hid my grimace as I mixed the batter before adding it to the pan.

"Babe, come on, don't be like that. Mom loves you, and my old man is just... well, you know how he is."

Did I ever.

"It's fine," I said.

Connor got up and came over to me again. "Don't be mad, kitten. I know he's a lot. But he's family, and he only wants the best for me. He doesn't know what's best for me, though. I do." He took the spatula from my hand, placed it down on the counter, and turned me in his arms. "It's you and me, El. You hear me?"

I nodded, emotion swelling in my chest.

"I love my dad," he went on. "He's always been my biggest supporter. But you, you're my girl."

"I know."

"Yeah?" His eyes twinkled.

"Connor..."

"He'll come around, I promise."

"Connor, it's been a year."

"Yeah, and we're in college. He doesn't think it'll go

the distance." I paled, and he stuttered, "Shit, babe. I didn't mean—"

"It's fine." I pulled away from him, trying to mask some of the hurt twisting around my heart. "I get it. He doesn't think I'm the one."

"Whoa, whoa, whoa, babe. That is not it."

"Connor, you literally just said—"

"Fuck, I know. I didn't mean it like that." He dragged a hand down his face, blowing out an exasperated breath. "Look, babe. I love you. You. Nothing my dad says is ever going to change that."

"Okay," I said, conceding because this was one argument I wasn't going to win. I couldn't make Ted like me. But I didn't want to lose Connor over it.

"Yeah?"

"Yeah." I nodded around a small smile.

"Good. Now, feed me, woman. I'm starving." He pecked my lips. "And then afterward, I might eat you."

CHAPTER 7

CONNOR

Ella and I spent the rest of Sunday together. After the fraught conversation this morning, I didn't want to let her go.

She had to know that my old man's opinion on our relationship didn't matter to me. He was old school. He wanted me to focus on my hockey career, not girlfriends. But that was all going to change when I told him and Mom about my plans to propose.

I planned to wait until we visited over Thanksgiving to tell him. I wanted to look him in the eye and have that conversation so that he could see how serious I was.

And if he couldn't accept that... Well, that was on him.

Ella was it for me. And I couldn't fucking wait for the whole world to know it.

My cell phone vibrated, and I leaned over Ella to grab it off the coffee table.

> Noah: Shit hit the fan with Coach D at Millers.

"Fuck," I breathed.

"What's wrong?" Concern pinched Ella's features.

"Something went down with Harper's dad."

"Oh God, I hope she's okay."

I read Noah's next text and said, "Mase took her to see his mom and Scottie. Coach Tucker and Coach Carson had to escort him out of Millers."

"Wow."

I quickly texted Noah back and threw my cell down. "Come here."

Ella snuggled back into my side, laying her hand on my chest. "I hope they figure it out."

"Mase will look after her. Something tells me he's in deep."

"Yeah. I'm so happy for them. We just need to find Austin someone now."

I scoffed at that.

"Connor..."

"Austin is like Mase on crack, kitten. It's going to take a special girl to change his ways."

"Stranger things have happened," she murmured, poking me in the ribs.

"You mean like me watching you across campus for two years before plucking up the courage to make my move?"

"Connor Morgan"—she arched a dubious brow—"we both know you did not watch me for two years."

"Maybe not full-on creepy stalker mode, but I saw you, El. And I knew I'd messed up freshman year. I knew I'd let something amazing slip through my fingers."

"Taking my virginity and then ghosting me," Ella tsked.

"Hey, I left a note."

"Connor!" She smacked me in the chest, but I caught her wrist, bringing her hand to my mouth to kiss her knuckles.

"I was young and naïve, baby. I'm not that boy anymore." I pulled her arms up, hooking them around my neck.

"No, you are not." Ella smirked, her eyes twinkling with love and lust and so much adoration I felt like a motherfucking king.

"I love you so fucking much, Ella Henshaw. I hope you know that."

"I do. I love you too, Connor Morgan. More than I ever thought possible."

"Wanna get down on your knees and show me?" I wagged my brows suggestively.

"Oh my God," she snorted. "Can you ever just be serious?"

"You know me, kitten. Besides, you kind of left me hanging this morning."

"I left so you could rest. You know that thing athletes need to do after a heavy weekend of games."

"The house is empty, babe. We're alone. I'm horny. And you look fucking delicious in my jersey. In fact"—I anchored my arms around her and stood—"movie time is over."

"Connor!" Ella's shriek filled the house, making me grin like a fool.

God, I would never tire of that sound.

I wanted to spend the rest of my life giving her reasons to smile.

I just wanted her.

By my side. In my life.

Forever.

Monday morning in the media room, the mood was tense. News had traveled fast about Coach Tucker and Coach Carson dragging Harper's dad out of Millers' Bar and Grill yesterday.

Mason looked about as pissed as Coach as he waited for the last few stragglers to file in and take their seats.

"Okay," he said, failing to disguise his grim expression. "I'm not going to sugarcoat it. I know you've probably all heard the news. Effective immediately, Coach Dixon will no longer be working with the team. There will be an official statement issued by the college later today, but James breached the terms of his contract. Regardless of what went down, James is a friend with personal ties to the team." His eyes landed on Mason. "All you need to know is that he won't be coming back, and he's getting the help he needs. The story ends there. Should anyone approach you for information, you direct them to me or Emerson."

At the mention of the team's PR manager, a couple of the guys shared knowing looks. Emerson had quite the reputation around Ellet Arena. Elusive. Ruthless. And drop-dead gorgeous. She also had a very strict rule about mixing business with pleasure if the rumors were to be believed.

"Anything you want to add, Mason?"

Holy shit. My eyes flew to Noah, who looked as surprised as I felt.

Mase cleared his throat. "As most of you know by now, Harper and I are... together." Someone snorted, and he pinned them with a murderous look. "I'd appreciate it if you could all keep a lid on this Coach Dixon thing. She's been through enough."

Pride swelled in my chest. Mason kept his cards close to his chest. Even after two years of knowing him and playing on the team together, I barely knew anything about his life. His childhood. So the fact he was standing up for Harper, declaring her his in front of the entire team, was a magical fucking thing.

Noah smirked, clearly thinking exactly the same thing.

"Proud of you, Mase," he mouthed around a grin, and Mason flipped him off.

"Okay, okay. Enough of that," Coach said. "We have a big weekend coming up. I expect one hundred and ten percent from everyone. No distractions. No drama. Let's get the job done, okay?"

A murmur of 'Yes, Coach' went around the room.

"Good. I want to see you out on the ice in ten."

Everyone began filing out of the room. But I lingered behind with Noah and Mason.

"How's Harper?" I asked.

"She'll be okay."

"You did good back there," Noah added.

"It was the least I could do after what he did to her yesterday."

"That bad?"

"Yeah." Mason's expression darkened, anger radiating from him. "I'm thinking of doing something nice for her. But honestly, I'm fucking clueless."

"That's what friends are for." Noah flashed him a knowing grin. "You need to Darcy the shit out of her."

"Don't start with that Darcy bullshit."

"Harper studies English," he added. "I'm telling you, Mase. It's the way to go."

"What about you?" Mason swung his gaze to me. "You got any better ideas than this idiot?"

"Keep it simple. Dinner, a movie, a stroll on the beach under the stars."

"On second thought, I'll figure it out myself." He shook his head as we made our way down the hall toward the locker room.

"What did I say?" I looked at Noah with a frown. "I thought they were pretty solid ideas."

"Dinner and a movie? Ella's a lucky girl," he snorted.

"Fuck you, Holden. Fuck. You."

"Let's just hope for her sake the proposal is better."

"Keep your voice down."

"Relax, no one's listening. So what is the plan?"

"I'm not entirely sure yet," I said. "I have some ideas. But I need to get it right."

"Well, yeah. It isn't every day you propose to the woman of your dreams."

"He's... what?" Austin appeared.

We hadn't noticed him come in.

Fuck.

"Nothing," I said. "Just shooting the shit."

"Tell me you're not seriously going to do it."

"And if I am?"

"I'd call you a fucking idiot."

"Nice, man," I scoffed. "Real fucking nice."

"You're still in college. What's the rush?"

"I'm not rushing. I just know. Ella is it for me, Aus. I want her to know that. I want the world to know that."

He studied me; his brows pinched in contemplation. I braced myself for whatever stupid thing was about to come out of his mouth. But he surprised me.

"Well, good luck, I guess. If Ella knows what's good for her, she'll tell you where to stick your ring."

Laughter bubbled inside me. All things considered, it was as good a blessing as I would get from Austin.

"Love you too," I said with a shit-eating grin. "But listen, I'm not telling anyone else. So keep it to yourself, okay?"

I knew I could trust them both.

"Of course," Noah said, and Austin nodded.

"I'll take it to the grave." He strolled off as if I hadn't just confessed I was going to propose to my girlfriend. "Asshole," I muttered.

"He's only busting your balls." Noah smiled.

"Yeah, I know."

"So." He waggled his brows. "When are we shopping for rings?"

Practice was intense. I don't know if Coach Tucker was working off some of his frustration or what, but by the time we got off the ice, there wasn't a muscle inside me that didn't ache.

"What's wrong?" Ella asked as I approached the library counter. She'd worked part-time here since freshman year.

"Practice was a bitch."

"Poor baby. You need one of my special massages later?"

"How about now? We could sneak behind the stacks and—"

"Shh. Mrs. Cadger is—"

"Mr. Morgan," the old hag appeared. "I thought I'd politely requested that you didn't come around here accosting your girlfriend during her shift."

"Sorry, Mrs. C. I was actually here to check out a book."

"Connor Morgan, Lakers hockey player, and mediocre student is here to check out a book... hmm," she scoffed, making me flinch. "I'd almost believe it if it wasn't so unbelievable."

"Geraldine, you wound me." I clutched my chest.

"Two minutes, and it's Mrs. Cadger to you." She gave Ella and me a stern look before disappearing into her office.

"She hates me," I said.

"She doesn't hate you. She's just... cranky."

"She needs to get laid."

"Connor!" Ella chided, but I saw the amusement dancing in her eyes. "Did you want something, or was this just a social visit? I need to work."

"Just came by to see my girl and give you this." I pulled the little brown bag out of my rucksack.

"Hmm, and what do we have in here?" She opened it and peered inside. "Is that a purple velvet cupcake?"

"Got you the last one."

"My hero." She leaned over the counter and fisted my hoodie, smacking a kiss on my lips. "Now, get out of here before *Geraldine* issues you an infraction." Her lips curved in amusement.

"She wouldn't." I feigned surprise because the old hag definitely would.

"Care to test that theory?" Ella smirked.

Hands in the air, I backed away from the desk. "I'll see you later."

She nodded, mouthing, "I love you."

"Love you too. Bye, Mrs. C."

A muted grumble drifted from the office as I turned and headed out of the library, only to walk straight into Rory.

"Little Hart," I grinned. "Fancy seeing you here."

"You know I'm an English major, right? What are you doing here?"

"Ella's working a shift."

"Ah."

"Actually"—an idea sprang into my head—"do you have time to talk?"

"Talk about what?"

"Come on, Rory, baby." I grabbed her arm and laced it through mine. "Take a walk with me."

"Okay, you're being weird... More weird than usual."

"Rude," I chuckled. "How are things with lover boy?"

"We're good."

"Good?" I arched a brow, a hint of a smile playing on my lips. "You can talk to me, you know."

"I am not talking to you about my relationship with Noah."

"What, why not? I just so happen to be an excellent giver of advice."

"Because you're one of Noah's best friends. It's weird."

"So I guess it's going to be a bit weird if I want advice about mine and Ella's relationship then."

"I..." She got all wide-eyed and tongue-tied. "You want *my* advice?"

"Well yeah, if you don't mind."

"I mean, I guess I can try and help. Oh God, you're not breaking up with her, are you? Because she'll be—"

"Breathe, Rory, baby. I'm not breaking up with anyone."

"Oh, thank God for that. Because I love you, Connor, you know that. But if you guys split up, I'll have to pick Ella. Sorry."

"Good to know you've given this some thought." I ran a hand over my jaw, suddenly feeling nervous.

Maybe this was a bad idea.

Maybe I needed to keep my plans to myself and avoid anyone else's opinions or advice.

It was Aurora, though. She was like the little sister I'd never had. I valued her friendship, and I knew she would help a guy out.

I spotted a quiet bench up ahead and headed toward it.

"Connor, what are—"

"Come on, let's sit." I dropped down and patted the space beside me. Her brows crinkled, a mix of humor and confusion in her eyes.

"You really want to talk, huh?"

"I need your help."

"Is this about"—she glanced around, checking we were alone—"sex? Because I'm not sure—"

Laughter pealed out of me. Fuck, she was cute. In a totally naïve sisterly kind of way.

"You think I'm asking you for sex advice? That is the funniest fucking thing I've heard all day."

"Connor!"

"Sorry, but... jeez, Rory. I'm pretty confident in my ability to make my girl—"

"Okay." She slapped her hand over my mouth. "Enough of that."

"You're blushing." It came out garbled as Rory slid her hand away.

"I can't talk to you about that stuff, Connor."

"Don't be so shy. Unless my boy Noah isn't satisfy—"

"Do not finish that sentence," she practically growled the words. "What did you want advice on?"

"So I have this plan."

"Plan?"

"Yeah. But I..." Fuck, this was harder than I anticipated. Telling my friends was one thing. But telling Ella's friend—that was a whole other ball game.

"Connor, what is it?"

"I... shit, little Hart. I'm going to ask Ella to marry me," I blurted out in one breath.

"Oh my God, you are? Oh, Con. That's wonderful news." She threw her arms around me, hugging me tight.

And just like that, little Aurora Hart gave me all the confidence I needed.

CHAPTER 8

ELLA

The next couple of weeks flew by. Between classes, my shifts at the library, spending time with the girls, and supporting the team in their next round of home games, there was hardly time to catch my breath.

"I can't believe you're going out of town for Thanksgiving," Rory said as we sipped our pumpkin spice lattes in Joe's.

"Don't remind me," I murmured.

"I think it's kind of cute that Connor wants you to go home with him."

"Definitely not cute, babe. I heard Mason's mom decided to invite you all."

"Yeah, but Austin won't come. He said, and I quote, 'I'd rather stick pins in my eyes than spend the weekend surrounded by a bunch of lovesick puppies.'"

"Yep. That sounds like Austin," I chuckled. "So he's staying at the house alone?"

"'Maybe he'll invite Fallon to keep him company."

"Don't you think it's a bit weird he sleeps with her but never brings her around the guys or us?"

"They're not in a relationship." She shrugged.

"Yeah, I know that's what he says, but surely she wants more? I wouldn't appreciate being someone's dirty little secret."

"Maybe she likes their arrangement."

"Said no sane girl ever," I scoffed. "Women always want more. Oh, here's Harper."

We waved her over, and she joined us, slipping off her knitted scarf. "It's getting cold out there," she said. "Do you want another drink?"

"I'm good, thanks."

"Rory?"

"I wouldn't mind another pumpkin spice latte. Thanks."

We watched her join the line. "She's got that annoying glow," I said.

"Glow?"

"Yeah, you know that honeymoon phase glow where everything's still exciting and new."

"You think? She just looks like Harper to me."

"That's because you've also got the glow," I explained.

"I have?"

"Yep, and it's annoying."

"Sorry?" Rory frowned, and I chuckled.

"Oh, don't be. It's great... for you guys. I just miss those days. When everything was simple."

When Connor and I first got together last Halloween, everything had been intense and all-consuming. We hadn't been worried about anything but the next time we were together. The next time we could get our hands on each other.

Now, we had an entire future to worry about.

And I wanted it.

I did.

But sometimes, I didn't want to have to deal with all that stuff. I didn't want to worry about going to his parents' house for Thanksgiving and saying the wrong thing or crossing Mr. Morgan. I didn't want to worry about what happened when we graduated and Connor turned pro.

I wanted time to slow down; I wanted to savor these moments before we lost ourselves to the demands of adult life.

The truth was, I was scared.

Scared of everything changing.

Scared of what our relationship might look like beyond college.

"One pumpkin spice latte," Harper said, holding a tray. "I don't know how you drink that stuff. I can't stand it."

"Oh, it's yummy. What you got in the bag?"

"Some gluten-free brownies. You want?"

"I won't say no." I dipped my hand into the bag and took one, popping it into my mouth. "Mmm, this is pretty good."

"So good." Harper savored a square. "Rory, you want?"

"Oh no, I'm good, thanks."

"You could try. Just a small piece," Harper suggested.

"I... okay." Rory took a piece, breaking off a tiny morsel. She popped it into her mouth and looked down at her lap as she chewed it.

She was working hard on eating in front of us, but it was baby steps.

"It is good." Her smile was infectious.

"So good. I swear Mase buys me at least a bag a day. I'll gain the freshman fifteen in no time." Harper paled, guilt washing over her expression. "Shit, Rory, I didn't... I'm—"

"Relax," Rory chuckled. "It's fine. You can talk about this stuff around me. In fact, I need you to, okay? I'm in a much better place, but it's going to take time."

"Well, I think you're both gorgeous," I said. "Noah and Mason are lucky to have you."

"Connor didn't do too badly either," Harper smiled, and I smiled right back.

"You're right," I said despite the little squeeze in my chest. "He didn't, did he?

"You okay over there?" Connor asked me as we headed to Dayton. It was a four-hour ride which gave us plenty of time to talk.

Plenty of time to avoid the hard topics.

"I'm fine," I said around a small smile.

"Thanks for doing this."

"Of course."

Besides, it was either survive his dad or survive my mom and my sister. At this point, I didn't know what was worse.

It wasn't that I didn't love my mom and sister. I did.

Until Margo met her husband, Jonah, it had always been the three of us against the world. But I was the baby of the family, and with that came a certain amount of coddling. Being around them for any length of time was like being slowly suffocated to death.

It's probably why I rarely went home. My life was in Lakeshore now with Connor and our friends. I had no intention of returning to Ann Arbor after graduation. I wanted to get a job in the city and spend my days surrounded by language and literature.

I hadn't quite narrowed down what I wanted to do with my life, but I was hoping to apply to intern programs with a few publishing companies.

"So... I think my folks have invited Sara and Émile for Thanksgiving."

"Lovely." I barely hid my disdain.

"Come on, babe. Sara is like a sister to me."

"A sister who you dated for almost a year."

"Yeah, when we were fifteen."

"Connor, you lost your virginity to her."

"I... yeah, but we've all got a first, kitten. You can't hold that against me."

"No, but I would rather not have to spend Thanksgiving with her." Or ever see her again.

The first time was bad enough. The way she'd smiled at Connor was like they were sharing some big secret.

"She's engaged," he added, leaning over to grab my hand.

"That doesn't stop a lot of people." I shrugged.

"Stop them from doing what?"

"Come on. You can't deny it's a little bit weird that she comes around your parents so much still."

"She's been friends with my family for years. Our parents used to hang out all the time."

"Yeah, I know."

It didn't mean that I had to like it.

"El, she doesn't have anyone else since her parents died."

"She has Émile, her fiancé." I gave him an incredulous look.

"Yeah, but he doesn't know her like my folks do."

"Okay." I pressed my head against the glass, done with this conversation.

I didn't want to sound like the jealous girlfriend, but it was impossible not to get a little green when the first and only time I'd met her, Connor's dad had made it more than obvious that he thought Connor and Sara were perfect for one other.

"It won't be like last time," Connor said. "I promise."

I nodded, too weary to reply. It was bad enough having to spend Thanksgiving with a man who didn't like me, let alone a girl I wasn't sure had ever gotten over my boyfriend.

Connor let me stew, and I appreciated the silence. Sometimes, you need to sit with your feelings. Let them marinate before you moved on.

By the time we pulled into his parents' driveway, I felt a little better. Connor was my boyfriend, and Sara was engaged now. I could survive two days with her and Mr. Morgan.

I climbed out of the truck while Connor fetched our bags.

"Oh, Connor," Mrs. Morgan appeared on the porch. "And Ella, it's so lovely to see you again."

"Helena, thanks for inviting me."

"Don't be ridiculous, love," she said, pulling me in for a hug. "You are always welcome."

"Mom, it's good to see you," Connor said, coming over to us. She let go of me and wrapped her son into her arms.

"Oh, sweetheart. What does Coach Tucker have you eating up there in Lakeshore. I'm sure you've grown bigger since the last time I saw you."

His eyes collided with mine, amusement playing on his lips. "Just working hard, Mom. Where's Dad?"

"Where do you think he is? In your room, making sure it's perfect."

"I'll go on in and see him." Connor glanced at me again, and I nodded.

"I'll keep Ella company. She can help me make the cookies for tomorrow."

"Sounds good, Helena."

"I'll take our bags up."

Connor disappeared into the house.

"Gosh, it's good to have him home. We miss him so much. Is he eating enough? Getting enough sleep? Are you making sure he looks after himself? I know that hockey is intense, but he can't perform to the best of his ability if he's not—"

"Connor does all the right things," I reassured her.

"And you, Ella? How are classes?"

"Everything's great, thank you."

"Well, come on. Let's get inside and get to work." She patted my arm. "We have Sara and her fiancé joining us tomorrow, so we want everything to be perfect."

She might as well have kicked me in the stomach, but I plastered on a smile and nodded.

"Of course you do," I said. "I'll do whatever I can to help."

Connor was gone for a good thirty minutes. It wasn't uncommon, though. Mr. Morgan liked to dominate his son's time whenever we visited. But Helena kept me distracted, telling me all about their latest trip to Lake Huron.

They were both retired and enjoyed traveling. Mr. Morgan was a big fishing enthusiast, and Helena was all too happy to follow her husband in his endeavors.

"There are my girls," Connor entered the kitchen and strolled right up to me, nuzzling my shoulder from behind.

"Where's your—"

"Ella," Mr. Morgan's cool greeting made my stomach drop.

Connor turned us slightly so I could see his father, and I forced a small smile.

"It's nice to see you again, Ted."

He gave me a curt nod, and that was that.

"Have you heard from Sara?" he asked Connor, and I twisted to look at my boyfriend, wondering what his answer might be.

"No, Dad. You know it's not like that with me and Sara anymore. We've both got our own lives."

"I know, but you shouldn't forget about your friends, Son. Sara has always been there for you."

So much for things being different.

Slipping out of Connor's arms, I tucked my hair behind my ear and busied myself with the stack of dirty pots and pans.

"Babe, you don't need to do those," he said.

"It's fine. I don't mind."

"Let's sit, Son. Have a drink with your old man. Helena, fetch the good whisky."

"Dad, come on..."

"One won't hurt. I want to hear all about the season so far. It's senior year, Connor. After the disappointment at the tournament last season, I hope Coach Tucker has a solid plan to take you all the way."

"The plan is simple. Play hard and win," he chuckled. "We're going to do it this year, old man. Don't you worry about that."

"That's the spirit, Son. One last championship before you graduate. And then it's onto the pros." His unforgiving gaze landed on me as I dried my hands on a towel.

"It's going to be a different level of commitment, you know, Connor. Playing for the Flyers."

"I know, Dad."

"Long days. Lots of travel. You will be thrust into a world of fame, fortune, and opportunities."

"And the bunnies," Helena scoffed. "Don't forget about the bunnies."

"Mom," Connor said with a strained smile.

My stomach turned over.

"Oh gosh, Ella, I didn't mean—"

"It's fine," I said. "We both know it's going to be different for a while."

"Do you, though?" Mr. Morgan said. "You have plans of your own, surely, Ella? A bright young girl like you doesn't want to be following her boyfriend halfway across the country."

"Dad, come on, you promised."

"I just think we should talk about this, Son. Ella is—"

"Excuse me," I blurted. "I need to use the bathroom." I hurried out of there, unwilling to stick around and hear Mr. Morgan list all the ways in which I wasn't suitable for his son.

An hour.

I'd been here less than an hour, and the atmosphere was already unbearable.

After calming down in the Morgans' bathroom, I went upstairs to Connor's room. We stayed in here each time we visited, but it still never failed to surprise me.

It was a living museum of Connor's childhood—his success and accomplishments. Hockey trophies and framed newspaper cuttings littered the shelves. His old high school jerseys had been framed and hung on the wall.

I knew the second Connor slipped into the room. I always knew when he was close by.

"I'm sorry."

"It's fine," I said, running my fingers over one of the trophies.

"It's not. But he's..."

"Your dad. I know."

Connor looped his arms around my waist and dropped his chin to my shoulder. "It was a shitty thing to say. He's just worried."

"That I'm a distraction from your shot at NHL stardom?" I arched a brow. "Because I feel like if anyone should worry here, it's me."

"What the fuck is that supposed to mean?" He turned me in his arms.

"You're going to do great things, Con. Fulfill all your dreams with the Flyers. You've got this whole big adventure ahead of you, and—"

"Whoa, slow down, kitten. We, *we've* got this whole big adventure ahead of us."

"Connor..."

"No, El. Tell me you know that. It's you and me against the world, baby." He picked me up and spun me around.

"Put me down, you big goofball."

"Sorry, I can't hear you." He kept spinning me. "I'm too busy thinking about how fucking great our lives are going to be after graduation."

"You're crazy," I shrieked, a little dizzy.

Finally, he stopped, letting me slide down his big body. "Crazy, you say?"

His expression was intense, turning everything inside me molten.

"Kitten, I'm fucking gone for you. Heart. Body. Soul." He leaned in, practically whispering the words onto my lips. "You own me, Ella Henshaw. Own. Me."

CHAPTER 9

CONNOR

It was a bad idea to bring Ella home with me for Thanksgiving. I thought my old man would be over it by now.

Ella and I were stronger than ever, and I knew Mom filled him in on our lives in Lakeshore. But from his lukewarm reception earlier, I'd clearly miscalculated.

Fuck.

The devastation on her face as she fled from the kitchen, had me questioning if it was the right time to broach my plans with them. Mom would be supportive. I knew that. But it wouldn't be enough.

I watched Ella sleep, the gentle rise and fall of her chest as she dreamed.

I couldn't sleep.

I was too wired. She had put on a brave face when

we'd joined my parents for dinner. Conversation was strained to say the least, but Ella was nothing but gracious.

She didn't speak much after that, and I didn't really blame her. We'd come up to bed an hour ago, and she'd pretty much gone straight to sleep.

My cell vibrated, and I reached over to grab it off the nightstand.

> Noah: How's it going?

> Connor: It's a fucking disaster...

> Noah: Your old man interfering?

> Connor: You could say that.

> Noah: You don't have to stay. I'm sure Mase's mom will find two extra seats at the table for you.

> Connor: Thanks, man. I really appreciate it. But my mom would never forgive me if I left now.

> Noah: And Ella? What does she want to do?

I glanced at the sleeping girl beside me. She wouldn't let us leave, even if I asked her. Because my El wasn't a quitter. She was selfless and kind and good.

> Connor: We're staying. Tomorrow should be fun. My ex is coming for dinner.

> Noah: Jesus, Con. Ella deserves a medal for putting up with your bullshit. You know that, right?

I winced. It wasn't like I'd personally invited Sara. She was a family friend, and I knew my parents stayed in touch with her still. But it wasn't like that between us, not anymore. We sent the odd text here and there on birthdays and holidays. And I saw her sometimes when I came home, but that was the extent of it.

Still, Ella's jealousy was cute. And I didn't blame her. I'd be the same if an old boyfriend came sniffing around. But she had nothing to be worried about.

Not a damn thing.

> Connor: I wanted to talk to my dad about everything...

> Noah: Shit. But you know, you don't need his approval or blessing, Con. You're a grown ass man now.

He had a point. And I got it. But at the same time, it was my dad. The man who had been there at every peewee game. In the stands at every high school game. He'd taken me to practice and driven me all across the state to attend games and training camps.

He'd been there every step of the way. He was my

biggest supporter and the person I'd always been able to count on. So part of me—the little kid who had always basked in his father's approval—wanted his blessing.

> Connor: Yeah, I know.

> Noah: Anyway, I wanted to ask… have you thought about who's going to be your best man yet?

> Connor: I think I just heard my mom call. Catch you later.

I grinned like a fool, imagining him muttering to himself.

I hadn't really let myself get that far ahead yet. I needed to speak to my parents, buy the ring, and then ask Ella before I started making those kinds of decisions.

> Noah: Asshole!

With a chuckle, I dropped my phone back on the nightstand and snuggled closer to my girl.

"Hmm," she started to rouse. "What time is it?"

"Early." I kissed the end of her nose.

"Why are you awake?"

"Old habits die hard, kitten."

Ella stretched, sliding her silky-smooth legs between mine. God, I loved her like this.

"Happy Thanksgiving," she murmured.

"Here's to many more."

"We've got to survive dinner with your parents and ex first." She finally opened her eyes, pinning me with an Ella Henshaw death stare special.

"El, babe. You have nothing to worry about."

"Hmm, we'll see."

"It's one day," I pouted, shifting down a little to put me face-to-face with her.

"You owe me," she said.

"I think that can be arranged. In fact, why don't I start making it up to you now." Nudging Ella onto her back, I hovered over her. "Hi."

"Hi yourself." She raked her fingers through my hair.

"I like you like this," I said. "All sleepy and sexy." My hand slipped over her waist and down to cup her ass.

"Con," she breathed as I pulled her closer, letting her feel just how much I liked her like this.

"Think you can be quiet?"

Ella nodded, her eyelashes fluttering a little. I hooked her leg over my waist and ran my fingers between her ass, dipping lower.

"Mmm," she purred as I slowly worked two inside her.

"You gotta be quiet for me, baby, okay?" I swallowed her moans as I worked her, rolling my thumb over her clit in little circles.

"Ah," she cried.

"Shh." I gently collared Ella's throat, plunging my tongue into her mouth and licking.

She rocked against my hand, desperate and needy.

What I really wanted was to replace my fingers with my dick, but I couldn't trust myself not to lose control. I was so fucking hard.

"Connor," Ella whimpered, her legs trembling as she raced toward the edge.

"Let go for me, kitten." I curled my fingers, rubbing deeper, and it set her off.

Burying her face in my shoulder, Ella's entire body went tense, her pussy locking around my fingers. "Yes... yes... just like that, oh God. Connor, it's—"

A loud knock on the door had me freezing. Ella stared at me wide-eyed.

"Rise and shine, lovebirds," Mom sang from the other side of the door. "Sara and Émile will be here earlier than expected."

Fuck my life.

Ella shoved my hand away and pulled the sheet up over her body. I went to say something, but she pinned me with an irritated look.

Another knock had me almost jumping out of my skin.

"We've only just woken up," I snapped, pissed that I'd been cockblocked by my own mother.

Even more pissed that Ella was acting like it was somehow my fault.

"Oh, sorry, sweetheart. I thought... I'll see you

downstairs when you're ready."

"El, come back here. We can finish—"

"You heard your mom. Sara and Émile will be here early." She threw back the sheets and climbed out of bed. "We wouldn't want to keep them waiting."

Double fuck.

I dropped back against the pillows and ran a brisk hand over my face.

Happy Thanksgiving, indeed.

"Connor!" Sara gave me no warning as she flew across the kitchen and into my arms.

"Uh, hey, Squat." I gently eased her back, holding her at arm's length. "You're looking good," I said.

"Oh, Con, it's so good to see you," she beamed, her eyes glittering.

Someone cleared their throat, and I turned to find a tall, brooding guy watching us. "I'm Émile. Sara's fiancé."

"Shit, man. I'm sorry." I leaned over, holding out my hand. "Connor. It's good to finally meet you."

"Sara's told me a lot about you," he said in a thick French accent. "Forgot to mention how handsome you are, apparently."

"I... okay, then. This is Ella. My girlfriend."

Ella stepped forward, smiling in that effortless way

of hers, but I saw the tightness around her eyes. "Hello, it's nice to meet you."

"Ella," Sara said curtly. "I didn't realize you'd be here."

"Connor invited me."

The fact she made it sound like I'd taken pity on her or something rubbed me the wrong way.

Didn't she know how much I wanted her here— how much I *needed* her?

My eyes slid to hers in question, but she dropped her gaze.

"Well, now that everyone is here, why don't we get settled in the living room, and I'll make breakfast," Mom said, cutting the icy tension with her sunshine smile.

"I'll help if you'd like," Ella said.

"Oh, that would be lovely, Ella. I'm sure Connor and Sara have lots to catch up on."

"Maybe I should help too," Émile chuckled, but Sara pressed herself to his side and whispered something to him.

He nodded, following her out of the room. Dad went after them, leaving me with Ella and Mom.

"Right, well, I'll make a start." Mom went into the pantry, giving us some privacy.

"Hey, you good?" I asked Ella.

"Fine."

"I know this isn't ideal. But it's one day." Banding my arm around her waist, I pulled her closer. "Then we can go home and forget all about this shit show," I muttered.

Ella studied me, her eyes softening a little. "Sorry for being a jealous bitch. But she practically threw herself at you. And did you catch Émile's sarcasm?"

I had. But I didn't tell her that. I didn't want to feed her insecurities about Sara. We could survive one day and then go on with our lives.

Maybe, if I was lucky, I could grab my old man for half an hour and make it clear that I planned on making Ella mine in a more permanent way.

Noah was right. I was a grown-ass man. I didn't need anyone's approval.

"Ella, let me make one thing perfectly clear," I said. "The only woman I've had eyes for since freshman year is you."

"Now I know you're lying." Her mouth twitched.

"It's true, babe. Did I mess around after I ghosted you? Yeah. I've never claimed to be a saint. But it was only because I was scared of what I felt that night. I knew you were special, and I wasn't ready for that."

"And now?" Her brow arched.

"I'm in, El." I crushed her to my chest. "I'm all fucking in."

"Con—"

I stole her words—my name on her lips—with a kiss. It wasn't soft or tender. It was hard and bruising. Filled with desperation and yearning.

I hadn't pursued Ella last Halloween for something

fleeting. I'd gone after her with a single thought in mind.

She was mine.

And I intended on proving that to her every second of every day.

"I love you, Ella Henshaw." *I love you so fucking much.*

"Connor, I—"

"Oh, I'm sorry."

With a groan, I dropped my face to the crook of Ella's neck. Soft laughter bubbled in her chest, doing something to reassure me that we were okay.

"It's okay, Helena. Your son gets a little needy sometimes."

"Oh, I remember those days." Mom's eyes lit up. "He was like my little limpet until he was six. Always clinging to me like a damn spider monkey. Don't tell his father, but he was a total mommy's boy."

"Mom," I groaned.

Her smile grew. "Go catch up with Sara and Émile. Such a nice young man. Ella is in good hands with me."

"Okay, okay, I can see where I'm not wanted." I gazed down at Ella, looking for reassurance that she was okay with this.

"Go," she said. "I'll be fine."

"You sure?"

"Go." This time, she pressed her hands into my chest, giving me a little shove.

"Okay. Have fun." With a little wink, I walked out of

there and headed into the living room.

"There you are, Son. I was about to send a search party."

"Is everything okay?" Sara asked.

"Yeah, it's all good. So... engaged," I said. "Congratulations."

"Oh, Connor. It was so romantic." Sara looked at Émile with a dreamy expression, and I relaxed a little.

Ella had nothing to worry about. Sara loved him. It was written all over her face as she gazed over at him.

"Yes, well"—Dad cleared his throat—"you can tell him all about that later. I want to hear all about your promotion, Sara."

"I'm so excited. My boss said that if I worked hard and proved my worth, I might be able to cover some games. How amazing will that be?"

She looked at me, a flicker of sadness there. I shifted uncomfortably in my seat.

"That's amazing, Squat. You deserve it."

"It'll be just like we always dreamed."

Émile's brows crinkled. "What is this dream you talk of?"

"Just silly childhood stuff," I said, brushing it off.

"Oh, I don't know about that, Son," Dad interjected. "They were as thick as thieves growing up. Connor always wanted to turn pro, and Sara always wanted to be a sports reporter."

"Dad, come on. We were like twelve."

"Some dreams never die, Son. Don't forget that."

I didn't like the sadness in his voice, as if I'd somehow lost sight of my dreams all because I'd fallen in love with Ella.

It wasn't like that at all.

She was my biggest supporter.

"You're having second thoughts about going pro?" Sara asked, visibly surprised.

"What? No! I'm heading to the Flyers after graduation."

"Oh, it sounded like—"

"Why don't we change the subject," I suggested, not liking how heavy the conversation had gotten. "Émile, Dad said you work in marketing."

"That's right. I'm working on a project in the Cleveland branch."

"Oh, you're not staying?"

"No, I'll return to Quebec in the summer with my wife-to-be." He smiled, pulling Sara into his side, but she didn't look so convinced.

"Quebec, huh?" I said. "That's quite the move. What about your promotion?"

"We haven't worked out all the details yet," she said a little hastily. "There's time."

"Of course." Émile dropped a kiss on her head.

Something was off.

Something I didn't want to look too closely into.

Sara's life was just that—her life.

We weren't the same people we were back when we were kids. Did I consider her a friend still? Sure. But was she the kind of friend I confided in and shared my life with? No.

"What about you and Ella, Connor? Any plans to, how do you say, pop the question?"

Dad's brittle laughter filled the room, and Sara let out a small laugh of her own.

"What's so funny?" I asked as irritation rolled through me.

"Propose?" Dad made a derisive sound in the back of his throat. "Of course, he isn't going to propose. He's about to embark on the biggest adventure of his life. The last thing he should be thinking about is settling down with some girl he met in college."

"Dad—"

"I was just bringing you all some coffee."

Ella stood in the door looking crestfallen.

She'd heard him.

She'd heard every misconceived word out of his mouth.

Fuck.

"Babe, let me get that." I jumped up, taking the tray from her hands.

"Thanks," she said. "I need to help your mom plate everything up." Ella hurried out of there without a backward glance.

"Nice, Dad. Real nice," I snapped.

"I didn't know she was standing there." He at least had the sense to look guilty. But it didn't matter.

The damage was done.

CHAPTER 10

ELLA

"I'm sorry," Connor said for the third time since we abruptly left his parents' house.

I'd told him we could stay. That I'd endure his father and Sara and all their opinions.

But he wouldn't have it.

We'd left before Helena had a chance to finish plating up breakfast.

"It's not your fault." I shrugged, staring out of the window.

It was going to be a long ride. The tension between Connor and I was suffocating. But I'd heard every word his dad had said, and Connor knew it.

Everyone knew it.

The last thing he should be thinking about is settling down with some girl he met in college.

I had to wonder if he'd feel the same if it was Sara that Connor was in a relationship with.

Don't. Don't do that to yourself.

I curled a fist against my thigh.

"El, don't shut me out. It's Thanksgiving."

"It's just not a nice feeling knowing that your father will never approve of me. I'm a good person, Connor. I've given him no reason to think I won't stand by you."

"I know, babe. Shit, I know. It isn't..." He let out a heavy sigh, taking his foot off the gas a little.

"We should have just stayed in Lakeshore or gone to Pittsburgh with Mase and Harper."

"There's still time," he suggested. "If we divert—"

"Honestly, I just want to go home."

"We could do something, just the two of us."

"Connor." I rolled my eyes at his attempts to brighten a pretty shitty situation.

"Come on, kitten. Have an adventure with me."

"What do you have in mind?"

"I don't know. We could go skinny dipping in the lake or break into the old fairground and ride the Ferris Wheel."

"You're crazy," I chuckled, feeling lighter than I had all morning.

"Crazy about you. But we have all day. Let's not waste it."

"Fine," I said with a playful huff. "I'll go on an adventure with you."

He reached over and grabbed my hand, grinning at me. "Right answer, babe. Right fucking answer."

Our adventure turned out to be some two-bit House of Wonders attraction full of bizarre and outlandish exhibitions.

"This place is kind of freaky," I said as Connor led me through the maze.

"Oh, I don't know. One day it might come in handy to know the flying fox can have a wingspan of up to one point five meters."

I looked at him, really looked at him, and my heart fluttered.

"What?" he asked, brows pinched.

"I love you," I said. "No matter what your dad thinks of me, or the fact I'm pretty sure Sara is still in love with you—"

"She's not—"

I pressed a finger to his lips, shaking my head a little. "I love you, Connor Morgan, and I want you to know that."

"Come here." His hands shaped my waist, pulling me closer. We were in a quiet part of the attraction, not that there were many people here today.

"It's you, El. Always will be."

Leaning down, he fit his mouth over mine, flicking

his tongue out to taste me. A small whimper escaped me as I fisted his hoodie, anchoring us together.

It didn't matter that we were in some freaky Houses of Wonders or that his father had said some spiteful and hurtful things. This right here was all I needed.

Because when Connor kissed me, when he wrapped me in his arms, I knew that he was it for me. Even though the future scared me, even though I knew it wouldn't always be easy loving him, I did.

And nothing would change that.

"God, the things I want to do to you." He backed me up against the wall, nestled in between a replica statue of Tutankhamun and what looked to be some kind of taxidermy bear.

"Uh, Connor, I don't think we can do that here," I chuckled.

"Yeah, you're probably right. I don't think Coach Tucker would appreciate having to ask Emerson to bury a story about one of his D-men getting caught balls deep inside his girlfriend in public."

"You did not just say that."

"Oh, I did." He grinned down at me, eyes twinkling with mischief.

"I know that look. It's time to go," I said.

"It's another two hours until we get back to Lakeshore U. I can't wait that long."

"Consider it foreplay." I tapped his cheek, stealing a chaste kiss. "Now, can we please get out of here? This place gives me the creeps."

"Come on." Connor took my hand, and we made our way out of the House of Wonders.

"Hungry?" he asked, pointing to the diner across the street.

"I could eat."

"Diner Thanksgiving it is."

The diner was a quintessential roadside café, complete with checkerboard linoleum and red leather booths.

"Grab a table, and I'll be with y'all," the server called.

Connor chose the booth furthest away as if the privacy would somehow negate the drab surroundings. "Well, this is cozy," he said with a bemused smile.

"It's... almost as bad as the House of Wonders."

"Oh, I don't know. Looks can be deceiving. Come on." Patting the space beside him, he waited for me to shuffle in before winding his arm around my waist. "Not what we had planned, I know."

"It's okay. I never liked Thanksgiving much, anyway. I'm not a huge fan of turkey."

"When we have our own place, we'll make our own traditions. You don't want turkey, fine." He shrugged. "We'll have whatever you want."

"Whatever..." I arched a brow.

"What. Ever. You. Want. Thanksgiving sushi, we'll have sushi. You want Thanksgiving tacos, bring on the tacos. We get to build our life together, El. We get to make decisions that work for us."

His words sent emotion streaking through me. "You really mean that, don't you?"

"Fuck yes. I can't wait to start our lives together. In fact, I've been thinking we should take a trip to Philly soon to get a feel for the place. Maybe after Christmas? You could visit some publishing houses. We could check out some apartments."

"Connor..."

We'd talked about it. Of course, we had. The year was whizzing by, and before we knew it, the New Year would be here. But every time the conversation got too serious, I choked.

He was giving me time, letting me process everything. But we couldn't put it off forever.

And I didn't want to.

I didn't.

But the future terrified me.

A life with Connor, the NHL star, terrified me.

He ran his hand along the curve of my jaw, tipping my face up to meet his unwavering gaze. "Look me in the eye and tell me you don't want this. A future with me?"

"You know I do."

"So why do you shut down every time I broach the subject."

"Because..." I inhaled a shuddering breath. "I'm scared, okay?"

"And you don't think I am? You don't think I worry

every single day that today might be the day you realize you don't want to put up with me?"

"Con, that's not—"

"Babe, I get it. It's not easy loving a Laker. Let alone a Flyer. But I can't do this without you, El. I can't—"

"Hey." I moved closer, leaning in to touch my head to his. "You don't need to do it without me. I'm not going anywhere."

"You promise?" His eyes searched mine.

"I promise. I love you, Connor Morgan. Even in a Flyer jersey."

The tension melted out of his expression, a smile tipping the corner of his mouth. "Fucking love you, kitten. So much."

"I love you too, Connor."

Just don't break my heart.

"Connor! It's number twenty-three, Connor Morgan," Mason's little brother Scottie flapped his hands excitedly.

"Hey, little bro." Connor crouched down but didn't get too close. "How's it going?"

"Mom caught Mason and Harper having the sex."

"Scottie, buddy, we talked about this. We were not having sex."

"Mom said you were naked."

"Well, yeah. But we weren't doing *that*."

"Were you touching Harper's tit—"

"Okay, bud." Mason grimaced. "That's enough of that. Go see Harper and Rory over there."

"Caught by your mom, huh?" Connor said with a grin once Scottie was out of earshot.

"It wasn't like that." Mason turned fire-truck red, glancing over at his brother, who had Harper and Rory hanging off his every word.

"We were in bed, yeah. But there was nothing happening."

"If you say so."

"Don't be a dick. And don't bring it up again around Scottie."

"You have my word." The smirk on Connor's mouth wasn't convincing at all. "Did you have a good Thanksgiving?"

"Yeah, it was good. Scottie loved having Harper and Rory around. And it was nice for Mom to have some female company. What about you guys?"

Connor ran a hand down the back of his neck and murmured, "Long story."

"Well, you're here now."

We hadn't gone back to Lakeshore, after all. Instead, we'd pulled into a motel and gotten some sleep before detouring to Pittsburgh to Mason's house.

The guys needed to be on campus first thing tomorrow for their game against the Wildcats. So we planned to spend the day together before heading back.

Noah spotted us and jogged over. "Didn't expect to see you here," he said, holding his fist out to Connor. But Connor being Connor, pulled him in for a manly hug.

"Missed you too, hotshot."

"I think Mase has stolen that title."

"Oh, fu—" He cleared his throat, looking over to his brother again.

"Heard that," Scottie called.

"Didn't say it," Mason replied.

"Cut him some slack, buddy." Harper smiled at the brothers, her love for both of them shining in her eyes.

God, I loved this. All my boyfriend's friends finding their own happily ever afters. Aiden and Dayna had their own place now. Noah and Rory practically lived together. Harper was completely smitten with the Steele boys. And despite the disastrous trip to his parents, Connor and I would figure it out.

"Connor. Connor Morgan," Scottie called over.

"Yeah, bud?"

He beckoned Connor over, and of course, he went willingly, unable to deny the kid. He had most of the team wrapped around his finger. But then, he was the Lakers' number-one superfan.

"He's such a sweetheart," I said.

"Oh yeah, butter wouldn't melt," Mason grumbled.

"But fuck, I love that kid. And watching Harper with him..."

"Damn, you've got it bad." Noah clapped him on the shoulder. "I'm happy for you, Mase. Both of you."

"You good?" Mason asked, surprising me.

"I... yeah."

"You know whatever Connor's old man thinks about your relationship is his problem."

"Mase is right," Noah added. "Connor won't let anything come between you."

"I know."

"Good because you're the OG couple. The rest of us look to Con about this shit."

"Speak for yourself," Mason muttered.

"Okay, this is getting weird. I'm going to—" I thumbed toward Connor and the girls.

"Ah, come on, El. We're bonding," Noah chuckled, and I found myself smiling back.

These guys were more than just a team. More than friends bonded over their love of hockey. They were family. And to be a part of that was something special, especially when your own family didn't always make things easy.

"There you are," Rory said when I reached them. "Everything okay?"

My eyes flicked past her to Connor, who was deep in conversation with Scottie, and I smiled. "Yeah," I said. "Everything is great."

"Fuck, I needed this." Mason took a long pull on his beer, hugging Harper closer to his side.

She gazed up at him, completely lovestruck. "He had so much fun today. You did a good thing letting him tag along."

We'd planned to go bowling, but when Scottie found out, he'd wanted to come with us.

Mrs. Steele had done everything to persuade him to let us have some grown-up time, but in the end, we decided to take him with us.

She'd picked him up an hour ago, and we'd headed to the nearest bar.

"He's a good kid," Connor said, his fingers tracing little circles along my spine.

"Yeah, he's the best. But he's cockblocked me like three times in two days."

"Mase," Harper shrieked, jabbing him in the chest.

"What? It's true."

"Yeah"—she blushed—"but you don't need to tell everyone."

"Get used to it, Dixie," Connor said. "Nothing stays a secret for long between friends." He winked at her, and Rory laughed.

"He's right. It took a little getting used to, but it's better to just roll with it."

"Maybe I should stay in the guest bedroom next time," she said.

"Yeah, not happening. So get that idea out of your head." Mason hooked his arm around her shoulder and nuzzled her neck, making her shriek again.

"Oh, to be young and in love," Connor teased. "Remember those days, babe?" He practically smoldered at me.

"Con," I whispered, my breath hitching at the intensity in his eyes.

"Only three more weekends before winter break."

"And we have two tough teams," Noah said.

"The Hawks will be a challenge; everyone's talking about their attack this year. But the Bears should be a shoo-in."

"Nothing is guaranteed," Connor said. "We've just got to keep a level head, keep our eye on the prize, and not get too complacent."

"I'll drink to that." Noah lifted his beer in the air, and Mason and Connor joined him.

"To winning," Connor said.

"To going all the way." Noah grinned.

"Does anyone else feel like we're imposing on their moment?" Harper fought a smile.

"It did get pretty intense," I said.

"Oh, it's like that, huh?" Connor reached for me, pulling me into his chest.

"If you're looking for a group of girls to blow smoke

up your ass, maybe you should have called the bunnies."

"Ooh, burn," Noah chuckled.

"Come on, babe, we all know come game day, you'll be in the stands wearing my number."

Okay. He had me there.

Still, I poked my tongue out at him, and everyone laughed.

"So, who do you think will be next?" Noah asked.

"Next?" Mason frowned.

"Yeah. Next over to the dark side."

"Fucking idiot."

"What? It's a valid question."

"My money is on Austin." Connor gave Rory a little nod.

"Con..." She warned.

"Big brother needs someone who will put him first."

"Fallon is more than willing," Noah pointed out.

"Yeah. But she's never going to stand up to him. Give him something to fight for."

"You've given this a lot of thought," Rory said.

He shrugged, shoving a handful of tortillas into his mouth. "Don't want to see him go down a dark path, is all."

"You'd never let that happen."

"Damn straight, little Hart. Damn fucking straight."

CHAPTER 11

CONNOR

December arrived, bringing with it twinkle lights, Christmas trees, and the smell of spiced apples everywhere I turned.

It had been ten days since Thanksgiving, and Christmas had well and truly arrived in Lakeshore. Even the media room had a fully decorated tree that Coach vehemently denied he was responsible for.

I fucking loved Christmas. The food, the music, the tradition. But this year felt bittersweet. Because this year I was going to get down on one knee and propose to the girl of my dreams... without my old man's blessing.

He'd called me a couple of days after the shit show that was Thanksgiving and apologized. But while he was sorry he'd upset Ella and me, he stood firm in his opinion that she was a distraction my hockey career didn't need.

I could still hear his words now.

She's a nice girl, Son. But do you really want to start your career in the pros with that kind of baggage?

He'd called her baggage.

My Ella.

The girl who held my heart in the palm of her hand.

It hurt. Cut fucking deep to know he couldn't see what I saw. But still, I knew that, in his own way, he was only looking out for my future.

My cell vibrated, and I read the incoming text.

> Ella: It's so cold out today. Just got to the library. Mrs. Cadger is in a mood.

> Connor: Send her my love.

> Ella: Asshole.

> Connor: But you love me.

> Ella: Yeah, I do. Have fun with the guys.

A little pang of guilt went through me. She didn't know the truth behind my bonding time with Austin and Noah today. And I had zero plans on telling her.

"Yo, asshole, you ready?" Austin bellowed from somewhere in the house.

"Coming," Noah replied, his footsteps heavy on the stairs.

"What took so long?" I heard Austin ask.

"It takes time to look this good, you know." My lips twitched as I texted Ella back and double-checked the route on my phone. Holden might have been in deep with Rory, but he was still a vain motherfucker.

"I still don't know what she sees in you," Austin grumbled.

"You need to get over it, Aus. It's been almost three months. I'm not going anywhere. Besides, secretly I think you're pleased I'm dating Aurora."

"What the fuck would make you think that?"

"Because one day, we might be more than just friends."

"The fuck are you talking about?"

I smothered my laughter. Noah really knew how to push his buttons.

"We might be brothers-in-law."

"Take that back, Holden. I swear to God, take it back right fucking now. Connor," he yelled. "He's doing it again."

That was my cue. Standing, I pocketed my cell and headed for the kitchen. "You called?" I stuck my head around the door.

"He's talking about marrying her again," Austin grumbled.

"Could be worse." I shrugged. "Rory could be dating Adams or Cutler."

Abel Adams might have been a Laker, but he wasn't a friend. Not by a long shot.

"Not helping."

"Seriously, man, you need to let this shit go," I said. "Noah is a changed man. Maybe if you hadn't screwed things up with Fallon, you would feel differently about—"

"I didn't screw things up. I ended it. There's a difference."

He'd dropped that bomb a few days ago. Not that any of us were surprised. Austin was in a bad place.

"Sure, keep telling yourself that. Know what I think? I think you caught feelings, got scared, and ran like a pussy."

"You don't know what the fuck you're talking about," Austin scoffed.

"He has a point," Noah added.

"Oh, fuck off, both of you. I happen to like being single. It's too much drama having a girlfriend."

"I thought she wasn't your girlfriend."

"She wasn't."

Noah and I glanced at each other. Austin was full of shit. Things had started to get serious with Fallon, and he had bailed.

"Whatever," he muttered, grabbing his car keys. "We doing this or what?"

"Hells yeah," I grinned, my stomach doing an excited little flip. "Let's go pick my girl a ring."

"What do you think?" I asked the guys as the store assistant stepped away to let me get a better look at the ring I'd picked out.

"It's... a ring."

"No shit, asshole."

Noah snickered as I gave Austin an irritated look.

I got it. He was in a 'he wasn't happy, so he didn't want anyone to be happy' phase, but he was still one of my best friends.

I valued his opinion.

"I like it. It's not too flashy, but it looks expensive."

"Because it is expensive," Austin grumbled.

"Ella's worth it. Can I pick it up?" I asked the assistant, and she nodded.

Carefully, I plucked the princess-cut diamond ring off its pillow and brought it closer to my face. "I can see her wearing this."

"I feel like a proud Dad, watching his son say ker-ching to the ring."

"The fuck?" Austin balked.

"You know, like that show. Say yes to the dress. Connor's saying ker-ching to the—"

"Yeah, yeah. I get it. I just don't know how we're still friends."

"What?" Noah shrugged. "I thought it was cute."

"He thought it was cute," Austin murmured.

"Guys," I hissed. "You're ruining the moment."

"I need some fresh air." Austin stalked out of the store, and the server suppressed a smile.

"Ignore him. Austin is just—"

"The guy needs to remove the stick from up his ass."

"Holden!"

"What? It's true. Anyway, I say go with that one. I like it."

My lips twisted with amusement. "I'm glad it gets your seal of approval."

"It's a very pretty ring," the assistant said with a dreamy expression.

"Okay, I think I'll take it."

She took the ring back. "I'll just grab a tablet so we can get your order processed."

"Holy shit," Noah breathed. "You're really doing it."

"Well, yeah. I didn't bring you here for shits and giggles."

"I know, I know." He ran a hand through his hair. "I just thought... Fuck. You're going to propose."

"Feeling the pressure?" I grinned.

"I love Aurora. But let's give it time, yeah." His laughter was laced with nervous energy.

"Tell me you don't see it one day, though. Little Hart in a white dress, walking down the aisle toward you."

"Oh, I see it." He swallowed thickly. "But I also know it's too fucking soon. So let's keep today about you and Ella." Noah nudged me with his shoulder and added, "I'm happy for you, man. And just remember who stuck by you when you need to choose your best man."

"Maybe we'll elope," I teased.

It would avoid having to make the tough decisions, like which one of these assholes to have standing beside me at the altar.

"You wouldn't do that to us."

"We'll see." I shrugged. "My old man isn't going to be happy."

"I mean no disrespect to your dad, but fuck what he thinks. You and Ella are made for each other, Con. Don't let anyone else tell you otherwise." Noah squeezed my shoulder, and I gave him a small appreciative nod.

"I knew there was a reason I liked you."

"I'm going to check on Austin," he said. "See you out there?"

"Yeah, I'll be out soon."

Noah left, and I waited for the sales assistant to return.

"Okay, so I'll just need a few details," she said, sliding the tablet toward me. "I take it you know your girlfriend's ring size?"

"I do." Thanks to a little help from Aurora and Dayna.

"Great, so if you can just fill in all the sections, I can process your order. Do you have something romantic planned for the proposal?"

"I'm working on it," I said, not feeling entirely comfortable talking to a stranger about it.

"Well, it's a stunning ring. She's a lucky girl."

"Nah, I'm the lucky one. Here you go." I handed her back the tablet.

"Perfect. I'll just get that arranged. We require a deposit today and then full payment upon collection.

"That's fine." I dug out my wallet and gave her my credit card.

But she was gawking at the tablet. Slowly, her eyes lifted to mine, surprise there. "Connor Morgan. Lakeshore U Lakers Connor Morgan?"

"That's me."

Shit.

"Oh my God, my boyfriend is a huge fan."

"He's obviously got good taste," I joked, hoping she wouldn't have some kind of freak out.

"Okay, wow. I... Okay."

"Hey, Jessie, is it?" She nodded, and I offered her one of my trademark smiles. "I'm going to need you to keep this to yourself, okay?"

"Oh, of course. We pride ourselves on discretion here. Your secret is safe with me."

"Not even your boyfriend."

"Not even him."

"Thanks, I appreciate it."

Because the last thing I needed was some fan

leaking it on social media that they'd spotted me buying an engagement ring.

I wanted everything to be perfect, and that meant keeping it under wraps.

Jessie went to walk off but hesitated at the last minute. "I don't suppose I could ask you for an autograph? It really would mean a lot to my boyfriend."

"Yeah, I think I can arrange that."

It was the least I could do.

She'd helped me pick the perfect engagement ring for Ella.

If that didn't deserve an autograph, I don't know what did.

"So what happened with Fallon?" Noah asked Austin as we tucked into our sliders.

"Got bored. Ended it."

"You know we're not buying that bullshit, right? You two were—"

"Fucking. We were fucking."

"Aus, come on, man. It's us. You don't have to pretend to be such a hard ass all the time. You liked her."

"I liked fucking her."

"I'm not buying it," I said. "Did she give you an ultimatum or something?"

"You know I only came today because you asked. I didn't sign up to be interrogated."

"Stop being such an asshole and talk to us. Did she fuck around on you? Get bored of the fuck-buddies situation you two had going on?"

"I'm not doing this."

"But it's so much fun." Noah smirked, and Austin flipped him off.

"You think we'll beat the Hawks this weekend?"

"Don't change the subject."

"Stop asking questions I don't want to answer, then."

"We're only pushing because we care," I said.

"You're pushing because you're nosey bastards, more interested in gossiping than hockey—"

"Now, that's not fair. Happy teammates make for a happy team."

"You're a fucking idiot." Austin blew out an exasperated breath, but his grumpy mood didn't deter me.

I was flying on cloud fucking nine.

I'd found the ring.

Now all I needed was to wait until Christmas Day to pop the question.

"He's in love," Noah chuckled. "Don't knock it until you've tried it, bro."

"Quit calling me bro, *bro*."

"You do know you're only a ring away from—"

"Don't even say it, Morgan. I swear to fucking God."

"Jesus, you're wound tight," I said. "I'd tell you to get laid, but I guess that won't be so easy if you've called things off with Fallon."

"Plenty more bunnies where that came from," he murmured.

But I still wasn't buying it.

Austin was a tough nut to crack, but he'd stuck with Fallon for a reason.

"You know what I really need?" he said. "Some new friends."

"Cheap shot, asshole."

"Nah, you'd be lost without us."

"Keep telling yourself that." Austin glowered. "If I have to see Holden mack on my sister one more time..."

"I do a whole lot more than just mack on— Oof." Noah clutched his side, face contorted in pain from where Austin had punched him. "You saw that," he said. "If I can't play this weekend, it's his fault."

"Quit it with that shit, then. Rory is my sister, my *little* sister."

"She's nineteen—"

"Not the point."

"Get used to it because I'm not going anywhere."

"Lucky me." Austin drained the rest of his soda.

Noah's cell phone vibrated, and he picked it up, checking his messages.

"Let me guess. It's Rory."

"Yep. If we're all done here, I'm going to take off."

"Sure, and thanks for coming today. I really appreciate it."

"Any time." Noah held out his hand, and I shook it. "Tell little Hart I said hi."

"Tell my sister that I'd appreciate it if she could not walk around the house in just your jersey. I'm scarred for life after that."

"We barely stay at the house," Noah said as he got up. "I'll see you both later."

I gave him a small salute.

"You know, things might go a lot easier if you just gave them your blessing."

"Blessing? He crossed a line going after her."

"He makes Rory happy. Doesn't that count for something?"

"Yeah, I just... fuck, I don't know. Everything is messed up."

"What really happened with Fallon, Aus?"

"It doesn't matter now. It's done, and honestly, I think it's for the best." He glanced down at the table.

"Maybe you should talk to someone."

"To someone... you mean a shrink?"

"It might help."

"Fuck that. I'm fine."

"It's okay if you're not. You know that, right?"

"I love you, Morgan. But you've got to stop doing this."

"Doing what?" My brows crinkled.

"Acting like you can fix everything. Some people get dealt a good hand in life, and some people don't."

"Yeah, but don't forget it could always be worse."

A shadow passed over his expression, and I wondered what secrets he was hiding.

CHAPTER 12

ELLA

"What did I miss?" I squeezed into my seat, anticipation heavy in the air.

"Nothing yet," Dayna said. "They're just warming up."

Unwinding my scarf, I tucked it into my bag and shoved it under my seat.

I'd had to cover a late shift at the library, and then Mrs. Cadger's car wouldn't start, so I offered to wait with her.

Thankfully the tow truck arrived in time for me to dash here and make the start of the Lakers' second game against the Hawks.

After a draw last weekend, the team had been relieved to get the win last night, but they wanted the double.

Connor had talked about nothing else all week. It was the last weekend of games before winter break, and they wanted to go out on a high.

Christmas had well and truly arrived in Lakeshore, but I wasn't really in the holiday spirit. We'd planned to get together with both of our families, but Connor had nixed that idea after the disastrous trip to his parents. So the plan was to spend Christmas Day with my mom, Margo and Jonah. I figured it couldn't be any worse than spending it with the Morgans. At least my family liked Connor.

The team's fight song blasted into the arena, jolting me from my thoughts, and I chuckled at Dayna's rather loud rendition of *Saturday Night's Alright for Fighting*.

I glanced at Rory, and she shook her head a little. "No Harper tonight?" I asked.

"She's in Pittsburgh with Scottie and Mrs. Steele."

"She is?"

"Yeah." Concern washed over her. "Something happened with Scottie, and Mason couldn't get there, obviously, so she went."

"I hope everything's okay."

"Just friend drama, I think. But she said he was pretty worked up."

"God, I love it when they do that," Dayna blurted.

Rory and I looked out to the ice to find the guys laid out on it, stretching their legs.

"I've never understood why they need to do that"—Rory blushed—"it's so… suggestive."

"Just giving the fans what they want." Dayna grinned, not caring one bit that she was practically drooling, watching Aiden dry hump the ice with vigor.

My gaze scanned the ice, landing on number twenty-three. Okay, Dayna had a point. And suddenly, Connor wasn't using the ice to stretch his glutes and hamstrings; he was above me, pressing into me with slow, measured strokes.

"Okay, you have a point," I breathed, growing hot all over.

Dayna burst into laughter, nudging me with her elbow. "You should see your face."

"Oh, hush. Like you weren't thinking exactly the same thing."

"Damn straight I was. I feel silly saying this, but I'm so freaking jealous of that ice right now."

"Seriously?" Rory gawked at us. "You're both turned on by that?"

"You're not?"

"Not really." Her nose crinkled. "I guess I've never really thought about it."

"Little word of advice," Dayna said. "Tonight, ask Noah to use those moves on you. You can thank me tomorrow." She winked, and I smothered my laughter at Rory's stunned expression.

"You mean you've—"

"Hell. Yes. I let Aiden do a little stretching on me— Oh, they're almost ready."

Our focus returned to the ice, the starting lines

already skating into position. Connor glanced over and thumped his heart.

"Swoon," Dayna said.

I almost rolled my eyes at her, but I didn't. Because she was right; it was pretty sweet.

"Get it, Lakers," she roared, cheering along with the crowd as the referee skated out to meet the two captains.

"Come on," I whispered. I knew what it meant for the team to win, for Connor to win.

They were halfway into the season. They couldn't afford to start losing games if they wanted to win their conference and get the automatic bid to the playoffs.

Aiden won the face-off, flicking the puck down the left wing to Mason, who took off toward the goal. But a Hawks player checked him, winning the puck and zipping behind the net. Two of them filed in behind him, the three of them flying toward Austin in our goal.

The rumble of the crowd was deafening as Connor slammed into one of their players, missing his chance to intercept the puck by a mere fraction.

"Shit," I cursed as the Hawks forward pulled back his stick and took the shot, the puck hurtling through the air and right past Austin.

The buzzer sounded, the visiting crowd going wild, while our section lost its voice.

"It's okay." Dayna clapped. "They'll get it back. Come on, Lakers. Let's go."

Connor and Aiden traded words as the lines changed.

"He's pissed," I said, watching Connor grab a water bottle and slump against the board. His eyes flashed to mine across the rink, and I mouthed, "You've got this."

Lost in his intense expression, I missed Abel's breakout and goal.

The buzzer sounded, and the crowd went wild, Dayna and Rory on their feet, cheering.

Connor leapt up, hauling himself back over the boards, Coach Tucker bellowing instructions at his team.

It went like that for the whole period. They scored. We scored one back. It was fast-paced and intense, and I was on the edge of my seat more than once, watching Connor and the guys get slammed into the boards by Hawks players.

By the time the whistle blew, signaling the end of the period, the team looked tired.

"The Hawks aren't playing around." Dayna sank back in her chair with a little huff. "The guys need this win."

"They'll do it," Rory said confidently, and we both looked at her. "What?" She shrugged. "I think they will."

"We just have to hope the first and second lines don't tire and that Aiden can find the back of the net." She grimaced.

It was true; his aim had been a little off tonight. But it sometimes happened, especially against a powerhouse team like the Hawks.

"Last game before winter break," she added. "A loss will sit with them. They'll stew on it."

"There are still two periods left," I pointed out. "Plenty of time to turn it around."

"Connor's looking good out there."

"He's been like a bear with a sore head since we visited his parents."

"I get that. It can't be nice being pulled in two directions. Shit, El, I didn't mean—"

"Relax, I know what you mean." My heart sank.

She was only speaking the truth. Connor did feel pulled in two. Even if he didn't want to. And I got it. It was his dad—the man who had always been there for him.

We hadn't really talked about it again. It was easier that way. But it didn't stop me from thinking about it.

"I heard Mason is hung... like a freaking donkey. I would so take that for a ride." Some girls behind us snickered, and I whipped around, glaring at them.

"Problem?" The blonde sneered, flicking her hair off her shoulder.

"Oh shit, Ginnie," her friend said. "I think that's Ella Henshaw."

"So, who's that?"

"Connor Morgan's girlfriend." She at least had the decency to look apologetic.

"You're Connor's girlfriend."

"Sorry, am I supposed to know who you are?"

Dayna and Rory watched the entire exchange.

"Ginnie doesn't go to LU. She knows some of the guys from Sirens."

"The strip club?" Rory blurted.

"Don't sound so scandalized," the blonde scoffed. "All the guys hang out there." She pinned me with a smug look.

"I call bullshit," Dayna finally spoke, and I was relieved I didn't have to formulate a reply because I had nothing nice to say.

"A) most of the guys are under twenty-one, and Coach would have their asses if they ever got caught partying at a strip club," Dayna said without missing a beat. "And B) at least four guys on the team are spoken for."

"Most of the guys who come around the club are wearing a wedding ring. Doesn't mean shit." Her smile turned wicked.

"Ignore her," I said to Dayna, who looked ready to leap across the back of the chairs and throw down.

Thankfully, the game got back underway, and I could focus on Connor and the guys and not the little seed of doubt she'd planted.

Less than one minute in, Noah took control of the puck and hit a slap shot that sent the place into a frenzy. Rory was on her feet, screaming his name right along with the five-and-a-half thousand fans.

The game moved quickly. But the Lakers looked in control, shutting down two breakouts to take back control and score. And by the end of the second period, they were three points ahead.

"I need to pee," I said.

"The line will be halfway around the arena," Dayna said.

"If I don't go now, there's a good chance I'll end up sitting in a puddle of my own making."

"Okay, just hurry. The intermission will go fast."

"Rory?" I asked.

"I'm good. I'm going to stay here."

"I'll be quick."

But when I made it to the restrooms, it was apparent that I would not be quick.

I joined the line and checked my cell.

> Mom: What day are you arriving? Margo is planning to take me to the spa so I want to make sure it doesn't clash.

> Ella: I'm not sure yet. I'll call you tomorrow.

> Mom: We're looking forward to spending some time together since you didn't bother to come home for Thanksgiving.

My lips pursed. Of course, I was in the doghouse about that. I hadn't even bothered telling her what had happened with Connor's dad. There was no point. She'd have nothing supportive to say.

The line took time to move, and I got a message from Dayna saying they were about to reset the third period.

"Come on," I muttered as I finally reached the front.

There was no way I could go back to the stands without peeing first. So I quickly did my thing and washed my hands.

An almighty roar echoed through the building, and I smiled to myself. Someone had just scored, and it was the Lakers.

Sure enough, Dayna texted again to say that Mason got the goal.

Making my way back to the stands, I paused in the aisle, a strange trickle of awareness going through me.

Connor battled a Hawk player for the puck, the two of them unwilling to relent. He looked a little bit scary when he was like this. Nothing but sheer power and aggression.

He came off victorious, though, moving down the ice until a clear path opened up to send the puck flying toward one of our forwards. But the pass never came.

A Hawk player bodychecked him, sending him careening into the boards. The air sucked out of my lungs as I watched Connor go down at a funny angle.

"Oh, shit," I breathed, clutching my throat.

I'd seen Connor get the wind knocked out of him

more times than I could count. Every time, it felt like my heart stopped for those few seconds he was down.

But this time, he didn't get up.

He didn't jump up on his skates and shake it off.

He lay there, hand reaching for his leg.

"Get up, babe. Get up," I murmured.

I didn't even realize I'd moved to the edge of the boards until my hand touched the cool plexiglass.

Because something was wrong.

Something was very wrong.

People swarmed around Connor, as my entire world narrowed at the sight of him lying there.

This couldn't be happening.

It couldn't—

"Ella, thank God." Slender arms wrapped around me, and I blinked up at Dayna.

"I... I need to go to him," I said, casting an eye back to the rink, where they were moving Connor off the ice on a stretcher. "I need to go—" A sob caught in my throat.

"Come on," she said softly. "Let's go check on your guy."

I paced back and forth outside the team's locker room. They wouldn't let me in yet, which I both understood and hated.

"Babe, you need to—"

"Miss Henshaw." A man in a Lakers jacket appeared. "He's asking for you."

"Thank God."

I glanced back at Dayna, and she smiled. "Go. I'll be here when you need me."

Just like that. No question. Because she got it. She knew what was going through my mind.

"Thank you."

She gave me a small nod, and I followed the man inside the locker room.

I'd been in here a few times when Connor had given me the behind-the-scenes tour. But it was different seeing it on game night; bags and clothes and extra kit strewn everywhere.

The man led me across the vast room to another door that opened into a small hall. "He's down here, in the medical room."

"How is he?"

"Pissed."

"Yeah." My lips twisted. If Connor was injured, and he couldn't play the rest of the season—

No, I didn't want to think about that.

"Found her," the man said as he pushed open a door and motioned for me to go inside.

"Connor," I cried, the sight of him prone on the bed, hand thrown over his eyes like a punch to the stomach.

"Con?" I approached the bed, my heart racing in my chest. He didn't acknowledge me at first. Gently prying his hand away, I threaded our fingers together and squeezed. "Babe?"

He looked at me, his expression stricken, pain etched into every corner of his face.

"It's bad, El." Defeat laced his words. "It's really fucking bad."

CHAPTER 13

CONNOR

So close... and yet so far.

That's all I could think as the EMTs got me strapped to the stretcher and wheeled me out to the ambulance.

It wasn't part of my plan to end up at the hospital on the last game before winter break. But here I was, in fucking agony, my entire future on the line, while my teammates played on without me.

Fuck.

I'd known the second I went down that something wasn't right. My knee had twisted all wrong as I hit the ice, a popping sensation going through me as pain lanced down my muscles like red-hot pokers.

I was used to the odd injury: sprains, strains, and bruising.

But this had been different.

When you trained as hard as I did and played a contact sport like hockey, you learned to read your body. You learned pretty early on to differentiate between 'I can play on' and 'I think I need to sit this one out.'

But a torn MCL? That could put me out for the rest of the season.

My final season with the team.

I shut down *those* thoughts. Even if it was my MCL, as the team doctor predicted, there was still every chance I'd only sprained or partially torn it.

With treatment and physical therapy, I could still make the end of the season. It would be hard fucking work, but I'd do it.

Because if I couldn't...

Nope.

Not going there.

"How's the pain?" One of the EMTs asked me.

"Bearable," I said.

They'd given me a dose of pain meds back at the arena.

"You're a senior, right?"

"Yep," I grimaced.

"Unlucky."

My lips twisted, frustration and anger flaring inside me.

Four years.

I had almost four years playing college hockey and never sustained more than a sprain or a little concussion. And only months before the Frozen Four, I had a potentially season-ending injury.

No one tried to fill the awkward silence after that. I didn't want to talk, didn't want to pretend everything was going to be alright. Because chances were, they weren't.

So I closed my eyes, shut off my mind, and prayed to a God I'd never believed in to give me a lucky fucking break.

I was half asleep when Ella burst into the room.

"I'm sorry. Parking was a nightmare. I didn't—"

"It's fine. You're here now." I patted the bed beside me, and she came over.

"Oh, babe. I'm so sorry." She leaned down, brushing the hair out of my eyes. "How's the pain?"

"It's fine. I'm fine."

"Connor, don't do that. Not with me."

"What do you want me to say? That I'm in agony? That I'm fucking terrified it will put me out for the rest of the season? Thinking like that won't get me anywhere. It won't..." I inhaled a ragged breath.

I was pissed.

I'd been in the hospital for over an hour, and nothing had happened yet. But an emergency had come in, and all non-urgent patients had been pushed to the back of the line.

At least the nurse had hooked me up with some intravenous pain relief because it was hurting like a motherfucker; now my body's own adrenaline had worn off.

"We don't know how bad it is yet. It might not be—"

"It's bad, babe."

"How do you know?"

"I just do." I glanced away from her, my body vibrating with a potent mix of irritation and disappointment.

On the ride over, I'd tried to stay positive. Tried to shut out the negative thoughts. The little voice whispering what my head already knew and what my heart didn't want to believe.

The pop I'd felt when I went down wasn't normal. And it wasn't a small injury I was just going to get over.

"Well, we don't know anything yet." She kissed my brow. "I'll stay positive for the both of us."

I didn't argue.

There was no point.

All the positive thinking in the world wasn't going to change the fact my MCL was torn.

"Did they win?" I asked her.

"Yeah, nine, six."

"Well, at least that's something."

"They're coming straight here, obviously."

"No," I rushed out. "Tell them not to do that."

"Connor..."

"You can keep them informed, and I'll text them later. But I... I can't see them, not yet."

Not until I knew what the fuck I was going to say.

"Okay." She let out a resigned sigh. "Did you text your parents, or do I need to call them?"

"I texted my dad. They're driving down first thing."

Her expression tightened. "They're coming here?"

"Well, yeah. Dad wants to be here—"

"Of course." She pulled away, the distance telling.

"El, come on."

"It's fine. Of course, they want to come and see you. I get it."

"Hey." I reached for her hand, entwining our fingers. "I'll still need you the most." The smile didn't reach my eyes, but it was all I could manage, given the circumstances.

A twinge of pain shot through me, and I winced. "Fuck, that hurt."

"Should I get a nurse?"

"No, they said it might come and go. The sooner they can do the scan, the better. I want to know what I'm dealing with."

"What we're dealing with," she said, concern clouding her eyes. "We might have to settle for a quiet Christmas," she said with a soft chuckle.

"I can think of worse ways to spend it."

I swallowed over the lump in my throat. Because I

had plans. Big fucking plans that hung in the balance now.

How the fuck could I propose if I couldn't get down on one knee? If I couldn't fuck my fiancée the minute after I slid the ring onto her finger.

My mood plummeted, right along with my heart.

"I love you, Connor. No matter what happens, nothing will ever change that." Ella gazed down at me as if her love and her unwavering support would fix everything.

And I wished it was that simple. I wished I didn't feel like my entire future was unraveling before me.

I managed to force out, "Love you too," as I reached for her, threading my fingers into the back of her hair.

Our foreheads touched, and I breathed her in, letting her familiar scent ground me.

The fact she was here was everything. But it wasn't enough to fix me.

No amount of love was.

And although I didn't voice the words, they swirled around us, making the air thick and heavy.

"Connor, I—"

The door opened, and a doctor came inside. "You must be Connor."

I nodded, letting go of Ella so she could step aside.

"I hear you had a nasty fall on the ice." He flicked through my notes.

"That's right."

"Well, let's get you down to MRI and see what we're dealing with, shall we?"

"Sounds good."

"Pain level?"

"Bearable."

"Okay, but don't be a martyr. If things get too much, ask for something else."

"I will."

"And you are?" he asked Ella.

"Connor's girlfriend."

"I'm afraid visiting is limited to family only after nine."

"Ella is family, doc."

"We might be able to give you an extra hour, but she'll need to leave for the night and come back in the morning."

"I'd prefer—"

"Connor." Ella shook her head. "It's fine."

"Okay. I'm going to send the nurses up to get you, and we'll take a look at what we're dealing with and go from there. How does that sound?"

"Fine."

He scribbled something down on my notes and dropped the clipboard in the holster at the end of my bed. "I'll speak to you once we have that MRI."

"Thanks, doc."

The second he was gone, I released a weary sigh. "He could work on his bedside manner a little."

"He's only doing his job." Ella smiled.

"I don't want you to leave."

"I don't want to leave either, but I don't want to get you into trouble. I'll come back as soon as I can in the morning."

I nodded, emotion getting the better of me.

"I'll wait until you get back from the scan," she said.

"Okay."

The nurses arrived then.

"Connor." They smiled. "We're here to take you down."

"Good luck." Ella leaned over and kissed me. "I'll be right here."

I gave her a small nod. It was all I could do without breaking.

Without letting her see just how scared I was.

By the time I got back to my room, I was tired, cranky, and in a shit ton of pain. But the second the nurses wheeled me into my room, I had a whole other headache to deal with.

"Here he is." Noah grinned.

"What the fuck are you doing here?"

"Nice to see you too, bro."

My eyes flitted to Ella, and she shrugged. "I told them not to come."

Austin held up his hands. "It was Holden's idea."

"We're a team. Which means we don't leave one of our guys in the hospital without checking in," Noah said.

"It's late. I'm tired. You couldn't have come tomorrow?"

The nurses got my bed secured and left us to it, but not before reminding us that visiting hours were officially over.

At least I wouldn't have to put up with them for long.

A bolt of guilt went through me. They were here because they cared, because our bond was beyond that of teammates. These guys were my family, and if our roles were reversed, I'm not sure I would have stayed away, either.

"You look like shit," Austin said.

"So would you if you'd have been carried off the ice on a stretcher, asshole."

"Do you want me to give you guys some space?" Ella asked.

"No." I reached for her, and she came over, dropping into the chair beside the bed.

"So we won?"

"Beat their asses for putting you out of the game, didn't we?" Noah's mouth twitched.

"Oh, yeah, you sure let them have it, with all that falling on your ass you were doing." Austin rolled his eyes, but I saw the humor there. He just liked to give Noah shit.

"Their D-men were huge."

"So what's the verdict?" he asked.

"Won't know until the doctor takes a look at my MRI."

"But it's just a sprain, right? You'll be able to play again before the season's out."

An awkward silence descended over us.

"We'll know more later," I said.

"Even if it is a tear, you can do the PT, then get it braced," Noah said. "Players do it all the time."

"Yeah, maybe." I squeezed Ella's hand, hoping like fuck she'd pick up on my signals.

I needed them gone.

I loved my friends like brothers, but I couldn't do this right now. Not while I was so fucking on edge.

Her eyes slid to mine in question, and I yawned.

"We should probably go," she said. "It's getting late, and we're already here past visiting hours."

"Yeah, okay. But we'll be back tomorrow. Mase and Aiden wanted to come too, but Mase had to get back to Pittsburgh, and Aiden and Dayna were visiting her parents."

"It's fine. I'm not exactly good company right now."

"Just make sure they keep giving you the drugs." Noah smirked, moving to the side of the bed. "You seem far too lucid right now."

He held out his fist, and I bumped it with my own. "I'll let you know what the doctor says."

He nodded. "It's going to all work out, Con. We've

got a championship to win, and we don't plan on doing it without you."

"Holden's right," Austin grumbled. "Rest. Take the drugs. And see what the doctor says."

"Will do."

"Bye." Ella got up and hugged them both. "Thanks for coming."

"You're not leaving with us?"

"I will in a minute. I want to say goodbye."

"You mean you want to fool around in the hospital bed. Gotcha." Noah grinned like an idiot.

"Get out of here." I pinned him with a hard look, and they both chuckled as they skipped out of the room.

"I'm so sorry," Ella said. "I had no idea they would just show up."

"It's fine. They're gone now."

"You know, they only wanted to be here to support you."

"I know. But I... I can't. Not yet. Not until I know exactly what we were dealing with."

I couldn't explain it. All I knew was I felt like I was one second away from losing it.

"Do you need anything before I go?" Ella asked.

"No. I'm fine."

Fine.

I fucking hated that word.

Because I most definitely was not fine.

"Connor..."

"Babe." I forced a smile. Putting on the face of the strong, confident guy she knew and loved. "I promise I'm fine."

"I can stay—"

"No, you should go home and get some rest." I curved my hand around the back of Ella's neck and pulled her closer. "I love you." I brushed my mouth over hers.

"I love you too, so much. And we'll get through this, I promise. Whatever the doctor says, we'll figure it out."

"I know."

I kissed her, pouring everything I would never say into every stroke of my tongue.

Ella clung to me; her fingers twisted into the hospital gown the nurses had me change into for the MRI.

"I'll be back first thing tomorrow, okay." Tears dripped down her cheeks, and I brushed them away with the pads of my thumbs.

"Don't cry, kitten." *Because it fucking guts me.*

"I'm sorry. I just know what this season means to you."

"Nothing's set in stone until the doctor gives me his verdict."

"You're right." Ella sniffled, giving me a sad smile. "There's still hope."

There wasn't.

But I couldn't make myself say the words.

Not tonight.

Not to her.

"Go home and get some rest." I kissed her brow. "I'll see you tomorrow."

"I love you, Connor Morgan. Don't you forget that." Ella inhaled a shuddering breath as she moved away from me. "I'll see you tomorrow."

I gave her a sharp nod, watching as she left me.

I shouldn't have felt relief at her absence. She was my rock. My partner in crime. But I didn't want her to see me like this.

I didn't want her to see me cry.

CHAPTER 14

ELLA

I was almost out of the door when my cell phone started ringing.

"Hello?" I rushed out, desperate to get to the hospital.

"Ella, darling, it's Mom."

No shit.

I bit my tongue.

"Now isn't a good time, Mom. Connor is in the hospital—"

"Oh my God. Is he okay?"

"He went down pretty hard last night and hurt his knee. He's waiting for the results of the MRI."

The doctor had gotten called to another emergency last night before he could speak to Connor. So they'd given him more pain meds, made him comfortable, and left him to sleep.

I was partly relieved because I wanted to be there when he got the news.

"Oh, sweetheart, send him our love. I'll tell your sister. I wanted to discuss plans for Christmas dinner, but it can wait."

"Thanks, Mom. I'll text you when I know anything." I hung up, shoving my cell in my purse, and headed out.

I'd barely slept, too worried about Connor. He'd been a little off last night. Putting on a brave face, no doubt.

The cold air smarted my lungs as I cut across the lawn to the small parking lot behind my building. About to climb in my car, I paused, frowning when I spotted Austin leaving the next building... in the same clothes I'd seen him in last night.

Dirty dog.

"Austin," I called, unwilling to give up the chance to embarrass him a little.

"El?" He paled.

"What are you doing here?"

"I... fuck." He ran a hand down the back of his neck, looking anywhere but at me.

Sensing his discomfort, I backtracked a little. "I'm heading in to see Connor."

"How is he?"

"I wish I knew. His replies this morning have been

mostly one or two words. The doctor should be round soon with his results."

"He'll be okay," he said.

"Yeah. Well, I should probably go." I motioned to my car. "See you soon."

"Tell Morgan..." He hesitated. "Just tell him I said hi."

I nodded, giving him a little wave as he walked off.

Slipping into my car, I dug out my cell and opened my message thread with Connor.

> Ella: Just saw Austin leaving the building next to mine.

> Connor: Check out Hart getting back on the horse. Good for him.

> Ella: I guess things with Fallon must really be over.

> Connor: Don't even try to get in his head...

> Ella: I'm just leaving, I'll be there soon.

> Connor: I told you there's no rush.

His dismissal rankled me. But I ignored it because I refused to let him shut me out, no matter what happened.

> Ella: See you soon xo

"Can I help you?" A nurse stopped me as I made my way to Connor's room.

"Oh, I'm here to see my boyfriend. Connor Morgan. He's in room twenty-one."

"The hockey player. Such a shame."

A sinking feeling went through me. "What—"

"And his final season, no less," she went on. "But at least he should be fighting fit, ready for the new season."

What?

"You go on through, dear. I'm sure seeing you will brighten up his day."

With a tight smile, I left her and headed down the hall. Connor was sitting up in his bed when I entered. "Hi," I said quietly, still reeling from the nurse's revelation.

"Hey."

He looked tired. Dark rings circled his eyes.

"How are you feeling?"

"I'm okay."

"Did the doctor come by?" I asked.

"Not yet."

My heart sank as I sat down. "So you still don't know the results—"

"No."

The lie hung between us. Maybe Connor didn't know that I knew, but I did. And I couldn't keep that to myself.

"Connor," I swallowed over the lump in my throat, "I know."

"Know what?" His brows crinkled, and for a second, I thought maybe the nurse had gotten it wrong. That perhaps she was getting ahead of herself.

"The nurse..."

"Fuck."

That one word spoke volumes.

"Why would you lie to me?" I asked, trying to keep my voice soft.

"Because I'm done, El. I'm out for the rest of the season. It's a grade three tear."

"Con, I'm—"

"Don't." His eyes shuttered. "Just... don't."

I sat rigid, my heart breaking for the man I loved. Hockey was everything to him. The Lakers were his family. His life.

To have that ripped away from him halfway through his final season—I didn't know what to say.

So I kicked off my sneakers and climbed on the bed next to him, careful not to get too close to his leg. To my relief, Connor lifted his arm and tucked me into his side.

"I'm so sorry, babe." I laid my hand on his chest, wishing I could fix this.

Wishing I could ease his pain.

"It was my season, El. My final—" The words got stuck, and he cleared his throat, trying to stifle the emotion.

"It's okay." I snuggled closer.

Heavy silence pressed in around us as we lay there.

"Nothing about this is okay, El. Not a damn thing." He fisted his hand on my shoulder.

"Maybe you should get a second opinion. We could—"

"Son." Mr. Morgan burst through the door. "It's okay, we're— Oh, sorry. I didn't realize you had company."

Company.

Like I was nobody.

"Hey, Dad."

"Shit, Con. I'm sorry, Son. I'm so damn sorry."

I slipped off the bed, trying to ignore the pinch to my heart as he let me go.

The door opened again, and Helena came inside. "Oh, sweetheart." She rushed to his bedside and grabbed his hand.

"I'm okay, Mom," Connor grimaced.

"What the hell happened?" his dad demanded.

"It was an accident, Dad. A player checked me, and I went down pretty hard, twisting my knee badly."

"What has the doctor said?"

"It's a full tear."

"Fuck."

"Ted," Helena gasped, her eyes flicking to mine. "Sorry, Ella, but Ted has been worried sick."

"It's okay," I said. "Maybe I should go and get us all something to drink."

"Babe, you don't have—"

"I'll take a coffee. Extra shot, no cream," Mr. Morgan didn't bother looking at me as he barked his order.

"Why don't I come with you?" Helena suggested.

"It's okay. You stay here, and I'll go." I gave her a weak smile.

"I wouldn't mind a coffee. Thank you."

"Connor?" I asked.

He gave a little shake of his head, apology glittering in his eyes.

I made for the door. "I'll be back soon."

But nobody replied because the Morgans were holding onto their son like he might disappear at any moment.

And Connor was hugging them back just as tightly.

Twenty minutes later, with a tray of coffee in my hands, I returned to Connor's room only to find the doctor there too.

"Come in, sweetheart," Helena whispered as if I was interrupting something.

Mr. Morgan had taken up residence on one side of the bed, Helena in the chair on the other. Leaving me nowhere to sit.

I placed the tray down on the table and hovered near the window.

"Explain it to me again," Mr. Morgan said.

"It would be my recommendation that we operate. Research has shown that in the case of professional athletes, especially hockey players, surgery leads to better outcomes given the amount of stress the knee will be under once the patient returns to the ice."

"But if I don't have the surgery, recovery time will be reduced," Connor said.

"Possibly."

"I can do the physical therapy, wear the brace, and work on getting back on the ice."

"Son, please." Mr. Morgan shut him down. "What are we looking at here, doctor?"

"Without the surgery, Connor's right. If the tear heals nicely, he could be back at practice in six weeks. With the surgery, that number could increase significantly.

"We can leave it to heal without the surgery, but the reality is, given the nature of the tear, the ligament will be weak. Even with the brace, you might find it hard to skate with the same speed and range you're used to."

"But if I have the surgery, I'll be out for the rest of the season, and my speed and range might still be affected."

"I know you're disappointed, Son," Ted said. "But it's not just this season you have to think about; it's your future."

"Look, I need to be in a meeting in fifteen minutes," the doctor said. "I know this isn't an easy decision, and it isn't the news you hoped for. But the sooner we move on this, the sooner you can start rehabilitation."

"Thanks, doctor." Ted held out his hand.

"If you need anything or have any questions, one of the nurses will be able to help you."

He left, taking the air with him.

"We'll get a second opinion, Son. Whatever it takes, we'll figure this out. We need to talk to Coach Tucker and the coaches up at Philly. In fact, I'm going to call Joe now."

"Dad, I can—"

"Let your father handle it, sweetheart." Helena patted Connor's hand.

I felt like an uninvited guest. It wasn't about me. I knew that. But Connor and I had a life together here. I was his person.

At least, I was supposed to be.

Ted walked out of the room with his cell phone pressed to his ear.

"I think you should have the surgery, sweetheart. You don't want to risk further injury if you don't do it."

"I think your mom is right," I said, joining them at the bed.

"It'll put me out of action for too long. If I opt for no surgery, there's a chance I can play in the playoffs."

"Connor, I'm not sure—"

The door swung open, and Ted marched back inside. "Joe wants to talk to you." He held the phone out for his son.

Connor took it, his expression going through the full range of emotions as he listened to whatever Coach Tucker had to say.

Ted came to stand beside me. "Helena and I talked on the ride over, and we think Connor should come home with us to recoup. You have class and commitments. The last thing you need to add to your plate is nursemaid."

Unbelievable.

I inhaled a sharp breath. "I think Connor will want to stay in Lakeshore U. I can help out, and the guys will—"

"The guys will be busy. Besides, it's the holidays. People will be enjoying winter break."

"What are you two whispering about?" Connor asked, his brows pinched with concern.

"Just discussing arrangements for when you get out of here."

"Bit premature. Don't you think?"

"I think we need a plan, Son. It will be easier for you to come home with us."

"Whoa, Dad. I haven't thought that far ahead yet."

His gaze flicked to mine, but I couldn't get a good read on where his head was at.

If his parents weren't here, I would have asked him, giving him time to decide. As it was, his dad had bulldozed his way in and taken over.

"It makes sense, Con," Helena added. "I can look after you and take you to PT appointments. Ella has class and work to manage."

"Oh, it's not a problem. I am more than happy—"

"We can talk about it when I've made a decision." He cut me off.

Connor cut me off, and it was like he'd slammed the door on me.

On us.

God, I hated this. I hated that I was an outsider to their family discussion. That my opinion clearly didn't warrant consideration.

But I couldn't say anything because this was Connor's decision—his tragedy to deal with.

And I'd be damned if I was another pothole he had to deal with while his life was flipped upside down.

Loving someone was loving them through the good times, the bad times, and the times when everything felt impossible.

Connor loved me. I didn't for a second doubt that. But he was hurt and angry and scared, and he wasn't thinking straight.

My cell phone vibrated, and I dug it out of my pocket, reading Rory's text.

> Rory: How is he?

> Ella: His parents are here...

> Rory: Oh. Do you need backup?

My lips twitched at that.

> Ella: I can handle it. But I don't know how to help him, Rory. How to fix it.

> Rory: Just be there for him. Connor will get through this. We're all rooting for him. Noah is chomping at the bit to come and see him again, but maybe they should hold off if his parents are there.

"Con?" He looked over, and I went on. "It's Rory. She's asking if Noah can visit today?"

His expression dropped a little. "Not today," he said. "Tell her I'll text him later."

> Ella: He's pretty beat. But he'll text the guys later.

> Rory: Got it. I'll make sure Noah doesn't do anything stupid.

> Ella: Thank you xo

"What did she say?" Connor asked.

I moved to the end of the bed, desperately wanting

to go to him. But his parents obviously didn't plan on moving anytime soon.

"She'll handle it."

Relief washed over him.

"You know, Son—"

"Leave it, Dad. Please."

Something passed between them, but Mr. Morgan relented, giving his son an imperceptible nod.

"Why don't we give Connor and Ella some space," Helena suggested. "We need to find the hotel and—"

"We should stay," he said. "In case the doctor—"

"Ted, we can get checked in and then come back. Connor needs to rest."

"Thanks, Mom."

She patted his hand. "Can we get you anything on our travels?"

"A new MCL?" She blanched, and Connor chuckled. "Too soon?"

"What are we going to do with you?" She leaned in, kissing his cheek. "We'll be back later."

"Son." Mr. Morgan gripped Connor's shoulder. "We'll figure this out, I promise."

"I know." Connor looked broken, and it broke something inside me.

He'd walk again. Play hockey again. But he would never get his final season with the Lakers back. And to somebody who had waited his entire life for this, it was devastating.

But it could be worse. I shoved down the thought.

Nobody wanted to hear that in their moment of devastation.

Maybe in a few days or a week or a month when he could see the light at the end of the tunnel. But to say it now would be inconsiderate.

"We'll be back soon," Mr. Morgan said, barely acknowledging me as they walked out.

Connor reached for me, and I went to him, taking his hand in mine and lifting it to my mouth. "What do you need?"

"I... fuck, El. I'm so fucking lost here."

"I know, baby." I leaned down to hug him. "I know. We'll get through this, though. I'll be right here, every step of the way."

"Maybe they're right."

Everything inside me went still. I pulled back slightly to look him in the eye. "What do you mean?"

"Maybe I should go stay with them. At least until things settle down."

"You want..."

It's not about you.

It's not about you.

I inhaled a sharp breath and forced my lips into a smile. "Of course. Whatever you want."

"Yeah? You wouldn't mind?"

"It's not about me, Connor. It's about whatever you need."

"You, I need you, Ella. But I'm not sure staying here, being around the team—"

"Shh," I said. I couldn't bear to hear the pain in his voice. The sheer hopelessness.

"Whatever you want," I said.

"Get up here, kitten. I want to feel my girl."

"Connor..."

"You said whatever I want. And I want this."

"Fine." I gave him a playful roll of my eyes as I gingerly climbed up beside him, careful not to jar his leg.

"Love you, El," he whispered, so weary and defeated.

"Love you, Con," I replied, resting my head on his chest. "It'll be okay," I added, unable to find any better words.

"I really fucking hope so because I don't know who I am without hockey, kitten."

You're Connor, I wanted to say. *The man I love. The man I want a life with. A future. The man I want to marry one day.*

But instead, I swallowed the words and held him tight.

CHAPTER 15

CONNOR

"This is ridiculous," Dad barked. "He needs to make a decision, Helena. The doctor said—"

"Will you stop," I sighed. "This isn't helping."

It was my third day in the hospital, and I was no closer to making a decision.

The doctor wanted to operate imminently, but they couldn't do it without my permission. And I still didn't know what to do.

My knee hurt. It hurt like a bitch. But with the right treatment—intense physical therapy and rehabilitation—there was every chance I could play again before the season was out.

Having the surgery meant that it would be unlikely I would ever see NCAA game time again, not to mention the whole other issue that after surgery, some players were never the same again.

Either way, my odds were pretty crap. But it was my final season with the Lakers—the culmination of four years of blood, sweat, and tears. Choosing the surgery felt like abandoning them.

Stupid and irrational but real, nonetheless.

The reality was no matter which option I chose, the consequences could be dire.

"Connor, be reasonable. If the doctor says—"

"I want a second opinion," I said. "Doctor Bowens is good, but he isn't a specialist."

"Fine." Dad blew out a frustrated breath. "I'll go talk to him again." He stormed out.

"Oh, sweetheart," Mom said, taking my hand in hers. "He means well."

"I know that, but I can't make the wrong decision here, Mom."

"Has it occurred to you that there isn't a right or wrong decision, Connor?"

"I want a second opinion," I said, trying to buy myself some time.

A couple of days wouldn't matter when the outcome could be the difference between six weeks and six months.

Training camp was in the late summer. I needed to be there. Not being there could jeopardize my shot at playing for the Flyers.

But I needed to be there and be the Connor Morgan

their scouts had noticed—the Connor Morgan who had made the right impression during the development camp last summer. I needed to be *that* guy.

I didn't need to be a guy who could barely skate straight, thanks to his busted knee.

"No Ella today?" Mom asked, changing the subject.

"She has a shift at the library. I told her not to miss it."

"She's a good girl, Connor."

"Why do I sense a but coming?"

"I know she wants to look after—"

"Actually, she agrees that I should come home."

"She does?"

"Don't look so surprised." I grimaced. "She wants the best for me, too."

"Of course."

"Besides, it's the holidays. She can come and stay with us for a little while."

"Oh, I see."

"You can't honestly expect me to stay at home and not see my girlfriend?"

"That's not... let's not get stressed out about it now. I'm sure we can discuss it ahead of time and work out a solution that is best for everyone."

"What is his problem with Ella, Mom?" I asked. "I don't get it. Ella is one of the best people I know."

"Oh, sweetheart." She squeezed my hand. "It's nothing personal. You know how stuck in his ways he gets. And he always thought you and Sara—"

"Seriously, Mom." I could hardly believe her with this crap. "We were fifteen. You've both got to let that idea go."

I'd always known they loved Sara because she was safe. In a way, she was already like family. When her parents died, my parents took her under their wing. It had made things a little bit awkward for a while, but we were in high school. Most relationships were only fleeting back then.

It wasn't like we'd planned a life together—a future.

"Connor, I know that ship has sailed, but your father... he loves Sara like his own. We don't know Ella, not really."

I let out a bitter laugh. "And why is that, Mom? He hasn't exactly made it easy to bring her around. I love her, Mom. I love her so fucking much. She's it for me. She's—"

"Shh, Con. It won't do you any good getting all worked up like this. I'll talk to him."

"Good because she's not going anywhere, Mom. She's not—"

The door opened, and Ella poked her head inside. "Bad time?"

"What? No." I beckoned for her to come inside.

"Hi." She rounded the bed and came closer, stroking the hair off my brow. "How are you feeling?"

"I'm okay."

Mom raised a brow at that but didn't say anything. "Can I get you anything from the café?" she asked us.

"No, thank you." Ella flashed her a small smile.

"I'll give the two of you some space and go hunt down your father."

Mom slipped out of the room, taking some of the tension with her.

"What was all that about?"

"Nothing." I reached for Ella, curving my hand around the back of her neck to draw her down for a kiss. "Missed you."

"Mmm, I missed you too." She brushed her lips over mine, deepening the kiss.

"I fucking hate not being able to touch you properly."

"You have hands." Her soft laughter was like a balm to my broken heart.

"Not sure I want everyone hearing you cry my name, kitten." Our breaths mingled as we stayed close. Wrapped in our own little bubble.

"Any update from the doctor?"

"He wants me to make a decision," I said. "I want a second opinion."

"Okay. How do we make that happen?"

"My dad is talking to them now."

"I know how important this season is to you, but you have to think about your future too, Con."

"I am. Trust me, kitten, I am." I kissed the top of her head. Wishing like fuck circumstances were different. "Whatever I decide, I'm going to be out of action for a little while."

Ella's eyelashes fluttered as she caught the suggestion in my voice. "I'm sure we can get creative." She gently scraped her nails across my jaw.

"Oh yeah, what do you have in mind? I'd love to—"

Someone knocked and came into the room.

"Dad," I muttered under my breath.

"Sorry, Son. Ella," he said curtly. "But I spoke to the doctor, and there's a specialist who might be able to come to take a look."

"Good. That's good." I squeezed Ella's shoulder, but she nudged me away to slip off the bed.

"You know, Dad. I've been thinking, you and Mom don't have to stay—"

"Don't be ridiculous, Connor. We're staying until you're ready to leave the hospital. Did the two of you talk about you coming home with us for a little bit?"

"We did," Ella said, surprising me. "I agree. I think Connor should stay with you and Helena."

"Good, I think it's the right decision."

"But," I added, bracing myself for the inevitable fallout, "I want Ella to stay too. At least over the holidays."

"Connor…"

"No, babe. I need you with me through this, okay?"

She gazed at me, tears pooling in her eyes. "Okay."

It was unfair to put her on the spot like that. But I couldn't risk that she would say no.

"Connor, we need to talk about—"

"No, Dad," I said, not taking my eyes off Ella. "You want me to come home? That's my condition."

"Fine." He gave me a curt nod, but I saw his displeasure.

It didn't matter, though. My entire senior year had gone to shit. I had no intention of letting my relationship suffer too.

"Connor," the nurse said as she poked her head inside the room. "Dr. Kirshner is here to see you."

I gave her a small nod, rubbing my eyes. Lying around doing nothing for hours on end was hard fucking work. When Ella and my parents left earlier, I'd closed my eyes just for a little while.

But the clock on the wall said that two hours had gone by.

"Ah, and you must be Mr. Morgan." The doctor came inside. "Sorry to disturb you."

"It's fine. I was just resting. Not much else to do around here."

"No, I imagine not." He let out a throaty chuckle. "I hear you got yourself quite the injury."

"Oh, I don't know. I think a little R and R, and I'll be back on the ice in no time."

"I wish I could tell you that will be the case. But I've

taken a look at your MRI, and my recommendation is—"

"To do the surgery."

"I know it's not what you wanted to hear."

"Honestly, I don't know what I wanted to hear. But I won't lie. The thought of surgery doesn't fill me with joy."

"If you want to have a long and successful career in the NHL, trust me when I say you need the reconstruction surgery."

"That simple, huh?" I pressed my lips together.

"It's that simple."

"Best case scenario for getting back on the ice?" I asked, despite the fact any hope I felt had withered inside me.

"It would be remiss of me to speculate. These things take time, and everyone's capacity for healing and physical therapy varies. But you're young, fit, and healthy. It could be a lot quicker than you think."

"What if I can't skate the same?"

"Any injury like this carries some risk and long-term implications. Maybe you don't come out the other side skating quite the same. But maybe that gives you an edge over the skater you were before."

"Can you do it?"

"Me?" His brows pinched.

"Yeah. If I agree to the surgery. I want you to do it." There was something about him that, despite his brutal honesty, put me at ease.

"That's something we'll need to discuss with Doctor Bowens."

"And my dad. He'll want to be in the loop."

"I'll speak to Doctor Bowens, and we'll move on this as quickly as possible. Who knows"—he smiled—"we might have you home in time for Christmas."

A bolt of anguish went through me. For as much as I wanted out of the hospital, the last thing I wanted was to be at home Christmas Day knowing that I'd planned to propose to Ella.

"Do you have any other questions?"

"I don't think so. I appreciate you taking the time to come and see me, doctor."

He gave me a small nod. "We'll get you back on skates in no time."

"Good to know," I said, my words at odds with the doubt inside me.

Athletes tore their MCL and ACL all the time. I would recover, and I would go on to play hockey again. But the road ahead of me was paved with uncertainty, and if there was one thing I didn't like, it was having things out of my control.

Especially during such a pivotal time in my life.

The second Doctor Kirshner was out the door, I exhaled a weary breath. It wasn't the news I'd hoped for, but it was the news I'd suspected.

I needed the surgery.

Which meant I needed to say goodbye to my final season as a Laker.

"You're vibrating," Ella said as we lay watching the TV.

After the confirmation from Doctor Kirshner that I needed the surgery, Ella turned up with a bag of pick-me-up snacks.

We'd rented a movie from the hospital's pay-per-view channel and eaten our body weight in junk food. But it was the reprieve I'd needed.

I didn't want to talk about the surgery or the recovery process or any of that stuff. I only wanted to hold my girl, binge on Twizzlers and Swedish Fish, and lose myself in a far-fetched action movie.

"Ignore them," I said, tugging her closer.

She leaned up and checked my cell. "It's Noah."

"Ignore—"

"Con," she sighed. "They only care."

"Yeah, and I'm busy." I palmed her ass.

"Hands off the goods, remember?" Ella slipped off the bed and dropped my cell on my chest. "Answer it."

"Fine, woman. But you owe me."

She poked her tongue out at me as she disappeared into the adjoining bathroom.

Fuck, what I wouldn't pay to follow her in there and kiss her senseless.

Maybe a little more than that too. But I could barely

move my leg without red-hot agony slicing through my knee.

"Hello," I said gruffly.

"Let me guess. You weren't going to answer, but Ella made you."

"Fuck off," I murmured. "What do you want?"

"Nice to speak to you, too," Noah chuckled.

"Sorry, I'm tired."

"Any news from the doctor?"

"I..." Fuck, I could lie. Or I could rip off the Band-Air and give him the truth. "I need the surgery."

"Shit."

"Yeah, shit."

"Fuck, Con. I'm sorry. I know you were hoping—"

"Doesn't matter. It's done. My season is over."

"Hey, come on now. We don't know that for sure. Medical miracles happen all the time. And it's still fifteen weeks until the tournament.

"You could still make it."

"I think we both know that's not going to happen."

"I'm sorry, Con. Really fucking sorry."

"Yeah, me too."

"Have you talked to Coach yet?"

"No. He knew I was getting a second opinion. I'll call him later."

Or tomorrow.

Or whenever I was ready.

"We're going to miss you, man. I... shit."

"Yeah."

"So what's the plan?"

"The doctor said they want to move quickly. He mentioned being home in time for Christmas."

"Home?"

"My parents want me at their place."

"What does Ella say about that?"

I glanced at the bathroom door. "She's cool with it."

"You sure about that?"

"She said she is."

"Yeah, but come on, you know she didn't—"

"Yeah, okay," I blurted as Ella came out of the bathroom. "I'll let you know the plan when I speak to the doctor."

"Con? What the—"

"Thanks for calling. Tell the guys I'll send a group text soon or something."

"Don't you dare hang up on—"

I ended the call, hardly surprised when it pinged with a text message.

> Noah: Not cool, asshole. Not. Cool.

> Connor: Ella's here you idiot.

> Noah: How the fuck was I supposed to know. Tell her I said hi

> Connor: Tell her yourself.

A second later, Ella's phone chimed, and she frowned. "Let me guess, Noah?"

"He's an idiot."

She read her text and chuckled. "He's a good friend."

"Yeah," I murmured.

Because for as much as I wanted him to stay out of it, I couldn't deny he was the kind of guy you wanted in your corner.

CHAPTER 16

ELLA

"They should have called by now."

I checked my phone for the third time.

"I'm sure they will as soon as he's out of surgery," Rory said, laying her hand on my arm.

She'd offered to spend the morning with me while Connor was in surgery. I could have stayed with his parents at the hospital, but I needed some distance from Ted.

The passive-aggressive comments were slowly eating away at me.

It was obvious he didn't want me to stay with them over the holidays, but Connor had insisted. And there wasn't much I wouldn't do for the man I loved. Especially when his final year with the Lakers had been ruined.

So I would go to the Morgans' and play the doting, dutiful girlfriend. But this morning... Well, this morning, I really needed my friend.

"I hate this," I said. "I feel so powerless and useless."

"Don't say that, El. Connor needs you. The next few weeks are going to be tough on him, especially if the team makes the playoffs."

Because he'd have to watch the team he'd devoted three and a half years of his life to playing without him. Potentially win without him.

I couldn't even imagine how he felt.

"Yeah, I know. I just don't know what I'm supposed to do here. His dad swooped in and took over everything."

"El, come on. It's his dad. He only cares."

"I know, I know. But you should see how he acts around me, Rory. Like I'm a temporary fixture in Connor's life. It hurts."

"Well, then you just need to show him that you're not going anywhere."

"Easier said than done," I grumbled into my latte. "Anyway, how are you and Noah?"

"We're good. Looking forward to spending some time together over the holidays."

"Will you visit your mom?" I asked.

"Maybe. I'm not going to put pressure on myself to go home. But if Austin wants to see her, I might too. I'm content staying in Lakeshore U, though. We can visit with Mason, Harper, Aiden, and Dayna, and there's plenty going on around town."

"Yeah, Lakeshore sure does love the holidays." I glanced around the hospital coffee shop, noting all the fairy lights and expertly hung wreaths.

It all seemed like such a waste now. There would be no Christmas tree shopping with Rory and Noah. No parties. No skating in Market Square. No Christmas movie specials at the local movie theater.

"I know it sucks," Rory said. "But the important thing is he's okay. And he will get through this, El."

I stared at nothing, trying to contain the emotion that had bubbled inside me ever since I saw Connor carried off the ice.

My head told me Rory was right—that he would get through it. But my heart knew that missing the end of his final season would be detrimental to Connor. And I knew without a doubt there would be some dark days ahead.

My cell phone vibrated, startling me, and I snatched it up. "It's Helena," I said.

My heart crashed wildly in my chest, blood roaring between my ears as my finger hovered over the screen.

Be okay, please, God, let him be okay.

"Hello?" I answered.

"Ella?" she said.

"Hi, Helena." I waited.

"He's out of surgery, sweetheart. Connor's out."

Connor's hooded eyes tracked me as I entered the room.

"Hey," I said quietly. "How are you feeling?"

"Like they gave me some really good drugs." He managed a goofy smile, but it didn't reach his eyes even in his post-sedation haze.

I moved to the side of his bed, taking his hand in mine. "I'm so happy you're awake."

"Love you, kitten," he murmured.

"Love you too. The nurse said the surgery went well."

"Feels great." Strangled laughter rumbled in his chest.

"Shh, babe. You don't have to do that. You don't have to pretend with me."

"Not gonna lie, El. It fucking sucks. I thought if I didn't need..." Connor inhaled a shuddering breath.

"Shh. I'm here." I pushed the hair from his face and leaned in to kiss his forehead. "I'm right here."

Connor didn't cry. He rarely did. But I felt the anguish radiating from him in thick waves.

"It's done now. You can focus on getting better."

He didn't answer. Instead, he closed his eyes and turned his face away from mine.

It hurt.

But I didn't resent him.

Connor needed to process things in his own time.

"You know I'm going to be miserable fucker through this, El."

"Not possible," I chuckled, laying my head on his chest, listening to the steady beat of his heart.

Connor was one of the strongest, most steadfast guys I knew. His humor and heart were two of the reasons that made loving him so easy. So to see him so broken and unsure of himself... well, it broke something inside of me.

"I'm going to apologize now and ask you to promise me that you'll stick by me."

"Connor, don't be—"

"No, El," he said, desperation bleeding from his voice. "I need you. I need you so fucking much." His arm came around my shoulder, practically crushing me to his chest.

"Oh, Connor," I breathed. "It's going to be okay, babe. Everything will be—"

"Sorry, are we interrupting?" Helena and Ted stood in the doorway. She wore a soft smile, but Ted's eyes were filled with irritation.

Lovely.

"You beat us to it," he said.

"I didn't realize it was a competition."

He scoffed. Thankfully, Connor was too out of it to notice the tension crackling between us.

"How are you feeling, Son?" They came closer, and I sat up, keeping hold of his hand.

"I've felt better, Dad."

"It's done now, and the doctor said it went great. I've already talked to him."

Because, of course, checking in with the doctor before you checked in with your son was normal.

I refrained from rolling my eyes. Connor's hockey career meant everything to Connor and his dad, but I loved him beyond his game stats and future prospects. Being a hockey player was a part of him, not his sum total.

But I swallowed down the urge to give Ted a piece of my mind because all that mattered was that Connor got the help and support he needed to make a full recovery.

Everything else was secondary.

"The good news is, you can come home soon," he added. "Then the hard work will really start."

Ted's laughter grated on me. If Connor noticed, he didn't let on, his expression tired and weary.

"Something to look forward to," he managed to choke out.

"Don't worry, Son. Your mom and I will be on hand to help where we can."

"I draw the line at showering you, though," Helena chuckled.

"Don't worry, Mom. I have Ella for that." Connor

gave them a half-grin, and I gawked at him, wondering what the hell he was thinking.

But I supposed he wasn't thinking. Too strung out on the drugs still lingering in his system.

"Yes, well," Ted cleared his throat, a heavy awkwardness descending over the room. "Ella, why don't you help Helena fetch us some drinks."

Code for: I want to speak to my son alone.

"Fine." I pasted on a fake smile. "I'll be right back." Dusting my fingers across Connor's cheek, I leaned down and kissed him.

"Don't be too long," he murmured.

"I won't."

"Any special requests?" Helena asked.

"Just return my girl in one piece," he said.

She managed a small smile, but Ted looked less than impressed.

"Just my usual," he said.

"Connor?"

"Whatever, Mom." Agony rippled across his features.

"Are you okay?"

"Sore. The good drugs must be wearing off." A pained smile tugged at the corner of his mouth.

"I'll speak to someone," I said.

Before Ted could tell me that he or Helena could handle it, I walked out of the room and went in search of a nurse.

Two days later, Connor was discharged.

His parents insisted on driving him back to Dayton, so I'd opted to travel up in my own car.

I didn't want to spend four hours cooped up with Ted, and besides, Connor needed a lot of space to keep his leg rested.

Before I left, I stopped by the guys' house to grab some of his favorite things.

"Hey," I said to Austin as I let myself in.

"How is he?"

"I'm sure he's fine."

"Are you okay?"

"I'll be fine."

"That's a whole lot of fine going on there." He arched his brow.

"Mr. Morgan is a very difficult man."

"Are you sure it's a good idea for you to go stay with them?"

"Connor wants me there." I shrugged, too weary to really get into it.

"And I get it. I do, El. But it doesn't seem very fair to you."

I blinked at Austin. I think this was the most we'd ever talked, and he was being so... so reasonable.

It was a little disconcerting.

"You're in an awfully good mood," I commented, studying him.

He looked the same, yet there was something different.

"What? I can't ask how you're doing now?"

"No, that's not... sorry, I'm just tired and cranky."

"Yeah, I'm fucking exhausted."

"Someone, keep you up all night?" I teased. Except he didn't laugh. In fact, his whole demeanor shifted.

"Nah, I couldn't sleep. Bad dreams." His expression darkened, but I got the sense he wasn't being wholly honest with me.

"Well, I'm just going to grab a few things of Connor's to take with me." I headed for the staircase, but Austin stopped me in my tracks.

"I know I've been a miserable ass the last few months, but Connor is a good friend. If you need anything..."

He let the unspoken offer of help hang between us.

"Thanks, Aus. I appreciate it."

Up in Connor's room, I grabbed a few of his favorite t-shirts, hockey jerseys, and sweats. I also packed some of his college books, assignments, and his laptop. Studying would probably be the last thing on his mind, but he would need to get back to it eventually.

A trickle of sadness went through me when I pulled the door shut behind me. It wasn't supposed to be like this. It was our last Christmas together before we graduated—one last winter break to be college kids and spend time with our friends, laughing and loving and living without the pressure and responsibility of adult life.

Forcing down the ball of emotion in my throat, I shook my head and fixed my expression before heading downstairs.

"Got everything?" Austin asked, and I nodded. "Come on. I'll carry those out to your car." He grabbed the bags off me and made for the front door.

In some ways, I'd considered this house my home for the last year because Connor lived here, and he was my home.

It was the reason I'd said yes to staying with his parents.

I followed Austin out of the house only to find Noah and Rory, and Aiden and Dayna standing there.

"What is this?" I said, emotion surging inside of me. They were supposed to be off doing their own thing, visiting family, and enjoying the festivities.

"We wanted to come and say bye."

"Guys, we're not leaving forever."

"We know. But this whole thing is shit," Noah said. "And we wanted you to know that we're here for you, El. Always." He pulled me into a hug, and the comfort of his embrace had silent tears rolling down my cheeks.

"I'm really going to miss you guys," I said.

"As soon as he feels up to it, just say the word, and we'll be there."

"His dad will love that," I mumbled.

"Fuck his dad. Connor needs us. He needs you, El." Noah squeezed my arm before releasing me.

"Thank you." I dried my eyes with the back of my hands. "Whew. I didn't realize this would be so hard."

"You can do this, babe." Dayna pulled me in for a hug next. "I'll text you every day."

"You don't need to do that."

"Hush. You're important, too, El." She kissed my cheek, gently shoving me into Rory's arms.

"Dayna's right. We're all here for you."

I nodded, pulling away, trying desperately to compose myself.

This was silly.

Connor wasn't gone forever. We would both come back to Lakeshore after the holidays. Once he was a bit more mobile, and classes started up again.

"Okay, I'm going." I inhaled a shuddering breath. "I'll text when I get there."

"You'd better, Henshaw," Noah chuckled. "Or else."

"Drive safe," Austin said, and I gave him a small smile.

The girls walked me to my car, and Dayna opened the driver's door. "We're only a phone call away."

"I know." I climbed inside, trying to hold it together while they were still here.

But it was impossible.

I didn't want to leave.

I didn't want to go to Dayton and stay with the Morgans.

I wanted to be here, in Lakeshore, with Connor and our friends.

He needed me, though, and I wasn't going to be forced out by Ted and his idea of where his son's focus should be.

But as I backed out of the driveway and pulled the car onto the street, giving our friends one last wave, a deep sense of loneliness hit me. These people were my support system, my rock. If I didn't have them around, who was going to hold me up when things got too hard?

Because I had a feeling they were going to be anything but easy.

CHAPTER 17

CONNOR

"How does that feel, sweetheart?" Mom asked as she fluffed and fussed with the pillows behind me.

"Seriously, Mom. It was fine the first two times."

"Sorry, I just want everything to be perfect."

"Mom, come on. You don't have to do all this. I had knee surgery. It's not the end of the world."

Even if it felt like it.

"Ella should be here soon," I said, rechecking my cell.

She'd left Lakeshore hours ago. I didn't particularly like the idea of her driving here by herself, but it made sense. She would need to go back to Lakeshore at some point, with or without me. And it wasn't like I would be driving anytime soon.

I'd left Noah my keys so that he could use my truck.

"I've got the guest room all set up."

"Mom, we already talked about—"

"It's only until you heal a little bit. The doctor told your father you need to minimize movement for the first few days."

"Seriously?" I gawked at her. "They're going to ship me off to physical therapy before the week is out. I think I can share a bed with my girlfriend."

"Well, your father and I would prefer it if you didn't." She gave me the 'mom look.' The one that told me the only way I was going to win this argument was to upset her and piss Dad off.

"Fine. Two nights max."

"Thank you." The corners of her mouth tipped. "You know, you're a good boy, Connor. Always had your head screwed on, a clear goal in mind—"

"If this is the part where you side with Dad, Mom. Save it. I'm not interested. Ella is—"

"A wonderful young woman, she is. And if she's what you truly want, then I will never stand in the way of that, love." She took my hand in hers. "But you're destined for greatness, Connor. The NHL. If she's not the one, if you can't see yourself having a long and happy future with her, maybe it would be better to cut your losses now than put her through that."

"Jesus, Mom," I choked out, feeling very uncomfortable with where she'd taken the conversation.

"I'm just saying it's okay if she's not the one."

"She is."

"Oh, sweetheart, you say that now, but when you're in the city with the team, life will be different. You might realize—"

"Okay, Mom. Good talk, but I am not discussing this any further. Ella is my girlfriend. The woman I love. The woman I see myself having a future with."

"I see." The smile she gave me didn't reach her eyes. "Well, you're capable of making your own decisions, Connor."

"I am, so let's drop it, okay? Ella will be here soon, and I would really appreciate it if you and Dad could at least try and make her feel welcome."

"Of course we will." She had the audacity to look offended.

Mom wasn't a bad person. She was just an extension of my father sometimes, unable to think for herself and desperate to keep the peace.

I loved them both dearly, but this shit with Ella had to stop. Especially, if we were going to all be staying under the same roof. And over Christmas, no less.

"Okay, sweetheart. I'll be downstairs if you need me."

She left me alone, and I checked my cell again. Ella would be here any time now. I couldn't wait to see her. To hold her and kiss her. I knew she didn't want to stay here, but I couldn't bear the thought of being apart from her.

My cell phone vibrated, but disappointment welled

in my chest when I saw it was the group chat and not my girl.

> Noah: How is it being back at mommy and daddy's house?

> Connor: Asshole.

> Austin: He has a point, Con. Is your mom going to give you a sponge bath and comb your hair?

> Connor: I hate you both.

> Noah: Did Austin hit a nerve?

> Rory: Don't be mean to him...

> Connor: Thanks, Rory, baby.

I smiled, relieved that they weren't treating me differently.

Yet.

I silenced that little voice of doubt.

It was too soon to be worrying about the what-ifs and maybes.

> Rory: Is Ella there yet?

> Connor: Not yet but she shouldn't be long.

Rory: Promise me you'll look out for each other. I know this is really hard on you, but it's going to be hard on El too.

Noah: Yeah, don't do anything to screw it up!

Connor: I'm leaving this chat now.

Austin: Don't be a pussy.

Connor: At least I have regular pussy.

Rory: Connor Morgan! Take that back. Take that back right now.

Noah: Relax, shortcake. It's just a little five lettered word. P U S S Y

Rory: You'll be getting NO PUSSY if you carry on.

Austin: Sister, remember. SISTER.

Noah: Oh, fuck off, Austin. If you haven't already accepted that I'm regularly petting Rory's pussy, then that's on you.

Rory: Oh my God. You're all pigs.

Austin: And you're the one who fell for Noah's bullshit.

I heard a commotion downstairs and figured Ella had arrived.

> Connor: I think Ella is here. I'll catch you assholes later.

> Noah: Stay strong, Con. And don't let your parents cockblock you. It's not good for your recovery.

> Connor: Not sure it's my parents I need to worry about.

I was out of action for the foreseeable future. I could hardly flex my leg without pain flaring through me. For as much as it pained me, sex was off the table for a while.

But it didn't matter when Ella knocked on my door and then stuck her head inside. Because the second I saw her smile, the knot in my stomach unraveled, and I felt lighter than I had all morning.

This woman was my world. My everything.

She was the future Mrs. Morgan.

"Hey," she said, closing the door behind her and coming to the side of my bed. "How are you feeling?"

"Better." I looped my arm around her waist and tugged her down beside me. "Better now you're here."

"Connor!" she shrieked.

"Missed you, El." I nuzzled her neck, breathing her in. My body stirred to life at her proximity. "Fuck, I want you." A frustrated sigh escaped me, pain throbbing in my leg.

"I'm here, babe. I'm right here." She smiled at me again, her eyes twinkling with love.

"I can't fuck you the way I want, but I'd settle for a PG-13 kiss."

"How can I resist?" she chuckled, sliding her hands on either side of my face.

Ella leaned in, brushing her lips over mine, teasing the seam with the tip of her tongue. "Love you, Connor," she whispered.

"Love you, too, kitten. Now put your mouth on me and kiss me better."

"Okay, we've got chicken burgers, fries, and green salad." Mom wandered in with a tray of food. "Where do you want it?"

"On the desk is fine, Helena, thank you," Ella said, climbing off the bed to help her.

We'd spent the day watching movies and making out like teenagers. At least I knew my dick was working —it had been hard from the second Ella got on the bed and kissed me, despite the constant pain radiating through my knee.

But I was a grown-ass man. I could control my wants and needs.

At least for a little while.

"Do you need anything else?"

"I think we're good, Mom. Thanks for this."

"Of course, sweetheart. It's nice having you home, even if it's under less-than-ideal circumstances. Enjoy."

She left, and Ella set about giving me a tray loaded with my dinner, a drink, and some condiments.

"Do you need me to feed you?" She smirked.

"Watch it, kitten. Just because I'm out of action for a little while doesn't mean I won't punish you."

"You could try." Ella grinned, and fuck if I didn't fall a little bit more in love with her.

She was here, and it made it easier to park all the anger and disappointment.

"Mmm, I like the sound of that... being at your mercy." I waggled my brows suggestively, and her laughter filled the room.

"Stop teasing me and eat. You need to keep up your strength and energy to be ready for PT."

"Don't remind me," I grumbled.

"Hey." She cupped my face and forced me to look at her. "It'll be fine. You've got this, Morgan."

"Oh, it's Morgan now?"

"It is when you're acting like a scared little baby."

Ella pressed a kiss to my forehead, lingering for a second. I wanted to soak it in—to tell her that I was scared and felt completely out of my depth—but I didn't because a positive mental attitude went a long way.

Even if it was all fake.

"This looks so good." Ella got comfy in my desk chair and tucked into her burger.

"I'm glad at least one of us is hungry."

"You're not?"

"Not really." I shrugged. "Side effect from all the pain meds, I think."

"Well, I'm famished. So whatever you don't eat, pass my way."

We chatted about everything and nothing as we ate. Ella told me about Jordan and Noelle's holiday plans, and I told her about the latest news from the NHL. The Flyers were having a fucking awesome season and had a real shot at making the playoffs. It was surreal to think that this time next year, I could be playing for them. Gliding down the ice to the sound of twenty thousand fans cheering my name.

My chest tightened, panic surging inside me.

"Connor?" Ella noticed my grim expression.

"I'm fine," I lied. "Just a little heartburn."

"Have some water."

"Yes, *Mom*," I teased, trying to distract her from my sudden change of mood.

I'd never been the kind of guy to worry, not really. But going down on the ice that day, I saw my entire future flash before my eyes.

It was to be expected, though. To be so close and sustain a potentially career-ending injury.

"My mom and sister send their love," she changed

the subject. "They're sad we won't get to visit over the holidays."

"You can still go."

"I'm not leaving you."

"El, babe—"

"No, Connor. I want to be here with you. Now hush and eat up."

"Yes, ma'am," I chuckled, but it sounded strained.

"Have you spoken to Coach Tucker?"

"Yeah, he called this morning. Wanted to make sure I was settled in okay. Gave me the numbers of a couple of physical therapists that come highly recommended."

"That's good."

"Yeah."

Silence enveloped us as we finished our meals. When we were done, Ella collected the trays and took them downstairs.

The next three weeks were going to be torture. Being here, with her. Knowing my old man didn't want her here. Knowing she didn't really want to be here.

Not being able to love her the way I wanted. At least Sara had gone out of town with Émile for the holidays, so I didn't have to worry about her showing up and causing a scene.

Jesus. I blew out a weary breath, running a hand down my face.

I wasn't used to being out of action. Helpless and dependent on people to care for me.

It was a big adjustment.

One I wasn't sure I could handle.

"It's late. I should probably vacate to the guest room." Ella refrained from rolling her eyes, but I saw the displeasure there.

"Stay. I'm twenty-two. What's the worst they can do, ground my ass?" I cupped the back of her neck, anchoring her in place.

"Connor..."

"Stay, kitten. I really want you here." Grazing my lips over the corner of her mouth, I turned to the art of seduction.

But Ella was immune to my tactics.

"I know you do." She let out a soft sigh. "But I don't want to upset your dad the first night I'm here. Besides, it's too risky for your leg."

"Fine." I flopped onto my back, fighting the urge to go into full tantrum mode. It was nice spending the day with her in my room, cuddling and watching movies. But I wanted more.

I wanted her naked and snuggled up next to me.

"You need to get some rest, and once you take your last pain pills, you'll be out for the count." Ella laid her hand on my cheek and leaned over me. "It's only for a little while, and once you're up and mobile, we can knock the guest room situation on the head."

"Yeah."

"Connor," she chuckled. "It's one night."

"So tomorrow you'll—"

"Sleep, babe. I'll see you in the morning. Want me to get you anything before I head to my room."

"A quick blow job?"

"Horndog!"

"It's been almost a week. I'm ready to bust a nut, babe."

"Maybe if we have the house to ourselves tomorrow, I'll help you out with that."

"Tease."

"Always." She pressed a chaste kiss on my lips before standing. "If you need me, I'm only a text message away."

"I want to go on record and say I hate this."

"Take it up with your parents." Ella shrugged before grabbing her overnight bag and slipping out of my room.

Pissed and horny as fuck, I grabbed my phone and opened the group chat.

> Connor: Ella just left to go sleep… in the fucking guest room.

> Noah: I thought we talked about this. Don't let your parents cockblock you.

> Austin: Dude, he's just had surgery. That shit has got to hurt.

> Connor: Not as much as my aching dick right now.

Austin: TOO MUCH FUCKING INFORMATION.

Noah: You've got a right hand, use it.

> Connor: I can't get to the bathroom unaided yet and I don't have any tissues on hand.

Austin: Make it stop.

Noah: Quit being a baby. Con needs our help in his hour of need.

Austin: Yeah, I'm out. Assholes.

> Connor: I don't think I can do this.

Noah: Do what?

> Connor: Stay under the same roof as Ella and my parents for three weeks.

Noah: Hey, we offered to take care of you…

> Connor: Yeah, I know, just don't tell Rory about this conversation.

Rory: Too late, Con. You're in our group chat.

Fuck. I must not have checked which one I was in.

> Connor: Excuse me while I go die.

> Rory: You shouldn't say things like that.

> Connor: Sorry, little Hart. But please don't repeat any of this to Ella.

> Rory: I promise I won't, if you promise never to talk to me about your... issues again.

> Connor: You have my word.

> Rory: Hey, Con?

> Connor: Yeah?

> Rory: If it makes you feel any better, you're not the only one struggling with this.

Fuck.

Did she mean...?

Double fuck.

My eyes flicked to the door, and I groaned.

It was going to be a long three weeks.

CHAPTER 18

ELLA

> Connor: Are you awake?

I bit my lip, glancing at the door. It was both annoying as hell and a weird kind of forbidden lying in my boyfriend's parents' guest room, texting said boyfriend in the middle of the night.

> Ella: Yes, I can't sleep.

> Connor: Bet you'd be sleeping if you were here in my bed.

> Connor: Or maybe not…

A lick of heat went through me.

> Ella: Connor, it's late and you're supposed to be sleeping.

> Connor: But here's the thing, kitten. I'm wide awake and horny as fuck.

A picture followed of the very obvious, very large tent in his tight black briefs.

> Ella: You really should do something about that.

> Connor: You want me to jerk off and come all over my hand just say the word, kitten.

Damn. He was good at this. Knowing which buttons to push, what dirty words to say.

> Connor: Are you wet for me?

> Ella: I don't know…

I smiled to myself, getting comfortable under the cotton sheets.

> Connor: Touch yourself, El. Put two fingers inside your pussy.

Oh, God. It shouldn't have felt so good, slipping my hand into my pajama shorts and touching myself.

Another text came through—a photo—Connor fisting himself, his crown pointed right at the camera.

Shit. Dick pics weren't really my thing. I preferred

the real thing. But there was something so illicit, something so very hot about doing this in his parents' house, so I went along with it.

> Ella: I'm so wet.

> Connor: Curl your fingers real deep, babe…

> Ella: Are you imagining I'm there? Sucking you?

> Connor: Fuck yeah, you suck me so good, kitten. Are you playing with your clit? Rubbing it nice and fast?

I smothered a whimper, bolts of pleasure firing off around my body as I continued touching myself. Pretending it was Connor's fingers inside me. His mouth on my skin. His weight above me.

> Connor: Send me a photo…

> Ella: I can't.

Heat flooded my cheeks as I writhed beneath the sheets.

> Connor: I want to see my pussy.

Oh, God. I wasn't really going to do this, was I?

> Connor: Don't keep me waiting, babe. I want to come to a photo of you.

Without second-guessing myself, I pushed off the sheet and angled my cell phone down my body. It wouldn't show him everything, but he'd get the idea. I pressed the button and then quickly sent it to him.

> Connor: Fuck, that's hot. Wish I was there, El. Want to feel your pussy clenched around me, squeezing me tight.

> Ella: I'm so close, Connor.

My stomach coiled tight as I raced toward the edge, rolling my thumb over my clit in precise tiny circles.

> Connor: Shit, babe... I'm so fucking hard. Need you babe. Want to fill you up.

I came hard, crying into the pillow as waves of bliss crashed over me.

> Connor: Did you come?

> Ella: So hard. Are you okay?

> Connor: Came all over my hand like an eighth grader. But it was worth it.

> Ella: I love you.

> Connor: Love you more, kitten. Sweet dreams.

> Ella: xo

I quickly cleaned up and climbed back under the sheets, closing my eyes, feeling more relaxed than I had in days.

My cell phone was vibrating.

"Huh?" I cracked an eye open, looking for the source of annoyance. Digging it out of the sheets, I brought it to my ear and murmured, "Hello."

"Good morning, beautiful."

"Mmm, good morning." I rolled onto my back and rubbed my eyes. "What time is it?"

"A little after nine-thirty."

"Nine-thirty, wow. I didn't plan on sleeping so late."

"Guess you must have been tired out after—"

"Connor..."

"Yeah, babe?"

"It's too early for sex talk."

"It's never too early for—yeah, Mom. You can come in."

I smiled as he grumbled to himself about his mom's perfect timing.

"Come give me a good morning kiss?" he asked a second later.

"I'll be right over." Hanging up, I dragged my sluggish butt out of bed and went into the small en suite to wash up.

When I was done, I slipped on a hoodie and headed across the hall to Connor's room. I knocked and stuck my head inside. "Hey."

"Ella, I'm just giving Connor his morning pain pills."

He chuckled, "I think I can manage, Mom."

"Oh, don't ruin this old lady's fun. It's been ages since I had you home to take care of. Would you like me to bring you a coffee up, Ella?"

"I'm okay at the minute, thanks."

"We'll ring the bell if we need anything," Connor added with a grin.

He seemed in good spirits, which was good.

"Your father and I need to pop to the store later. If you need anything, you can add it to the list."

"Will do, Mom."

She left, and I carefully climbed up on the bed. "You're in a good mood this morning."

"Babe, my dick still works, and you heard my mom. They're going out later. Which means we'll have the house all to ourselves. Today is a good fucking day."

I burst into laughter. "You're crazy."

"I'm horny, kitten. So fucking horny." Connor's

expression turned serious as he stared at me. "Last night was... fuck, El. You never cease to amaze me."

"We've sexted before."

"Yeah, I know. But it was different."

"Yeah." I nodded, my cheeks flushing. "What's on the agenda today?"

"I'm thinking you can ride my face and then suck my dick. Maybe at the same time if I'm lucky."

"Oh my God," I snorted. "You did not just say that."

"You bet your sweet ass I did. Now get over here and kiss me."

Playfully rolling my eyes, I nudged closer, leaning over Connor so that our noses brushed. "Good morning."

"It is. A very good morning." He buried his fingers in my hair, angling my face down a little to sweep his lips across mine. "Missed you."

"You were sleeping most of the night."

"Still missed you." He cupped the back of my neck and kissed me deeply. When he pulled away, I was breathless and flushed.

"That was some good morning."

"Nothing but the best for my girl." He kissed the end of my nose. "How did you sleep?"

"Fine. I can't believe it's Christmas in a few days."

Something passed over his face, and my brows crinkled. "What's wrong?"

"I'm sorry I ruined all our plans."

"Con, it isn't your fault. Besides, Christmas isn't

about what you do; it's about who you do it with. I want to be here with you."

"You promise?"

"I do. Now do you need help getting to the bathroom? If you want a shower, we can try and figure it out."

"Will you be coming in with me?"

"I'm not sure that's a good idea."

"But I'll need someone to scrub my back."

"You, Connor Morgan, are an insufferable flirt."

His cell phone started ringing, so I grabbed it off his nightstand and handed it to him.

"It's Coach Tucker."

"Answer it then. I'm going to get some coffee. You want?"

"No, I'm good," he said. "Coach, what's up?"

I left Connor on the phone while I went downstairs. Voices drifted from the kitchen, but I couldn't quite hear what they were saying, which was probably for the best, given that Ted had made it more than clear that he didn't want me in his son's life.

"Good morning," I said, entering the kitchen. "I came in search of coffee."

"Just brewing a fresh pot," Helena said. "How is he?"

"He's surprisingly upbeat."

"That's the spirit. A positive mental attitude will go a long way."

Ted scoffed, "Wait until he starts physical therapy. He'll need all the help he can get then."

"Ted, try and be a little more supportive."

"Oh, I'm supportive, Helena. I just think it's going to take a bit more than a positive attitude to make sure his recovery goes smoothly."

His heavy gaze landed on me, and I forced a small smile. "Connor will give it his all," I said, feeling the need to defend him.

"We'll see," he said before grabbing his coffee mug and strolling out of the kitchen.

"Don't mind, Ted. He's just worried Connor will fall prey to the injury blues."

"I know it's a huge disappointment for him, but his career isn't over."

"We know, love. It's just Connor wants it so much. That kind of pressure..." She let out a weary sigh. "If he can't play the same—"

"He'll be fine. He'll do the physical therapy and be fine." But as I said the words, there was a little voice whispering what if he wasn't fine.

What if he couldn't play the same?

"You're right. I'm sure everything will be okay." Helena pasted on a bright smile. "Why don't you take him up one of his protein drinks and some cookies. I just pulled a fresh batch out of the oven."

"He'll still need to eat healthily," I pointed out.

"I know, but one won't hurt. I'll make sure I serve him extra vegetables with dinner." She winked and plated up a couple of cookies for me. "I won't keep checking in on you, but if you need anything…"

"Thanks, Helena. I know it isn't ideal having me here." My eyes flicked to the door.

"Connor wants you here. That's all that matters."

If her words were meant to reassure me—they didn't.

When I got back upstairs, Connor was asleep.

"Con?" I whispered, tiptoeing across the room to him, but he didn't budge.

I guess the meds and pain were going to take a few days to wear off.

I discarded the plate and drink on his desk and grabbed the television remote. It wasn't like I could go downstairs while he slept.

There was an old holiday movie on, so I settled in and tried to focus on that and not the huge knot in my stomach.

I didn't like being here, knowing that Ted thought I was nothing more than a college fling. He'd always been dismissive of me and our relationship but never outwardly rude until Thanksgiving.

Maybe that was because he had finally realized I wasn't going anywhere. But that worried me because a threatened animal usually lashed out.

Still, I was here, and I had no intention of leaving him. Connor needed me, and I needed him to know I would support him no matter what.

The vibration of my cell phone startled me, and I plucked it off the nightstand.

> Dayna: How is day one going?

> Ella: It's… going. Connor is asleep.

> Dayna: Already? It's only like ten thirty.

> Ella: I went downstairs to get a coffee and came back up and he was fast asleep.

> Dayna: It can't be easy on him.

> Ella: No, it isn't.

> Dayna: And how is his dad?

> Ella: Oh, you know, making it obvious at every opportunity that he thinks our relationship won't survive past college.

> Dayna: Shit, babe. I'm sorry.

> Ella: It is what it is. I'm not here for him, I'm here for Connor. How's Dupont Beach?

She and Aiden had gone to her parents for the holidays. Aiden's mom Laura was joining them for a few days as well as Assistant Coach Walsh. Or Carson as he was better known to Dayna and her family.

> Dayna: I love being home. Not loving all the bonding Aiden and Carson are doing though. It's hard to believe things weren't always smooth sailing between them.

> Ella: Aww, do I sense a budding bromance?

> Dayna: Yes, and it's unacceptable. Carson needs to find a girlfriend.

> Ella: Connor told me he doesn't date. Like ever.

> Dayna: Connor would be right. He's as bad as the guys on the team.

I glanced down at Connor and smiled to myself.

> Ella: Not all of them.

> Dayna: No, I guess you're right. We're heading out to the Christmas market but I'll text you later.

> Ella: Have fun xo

My heart sank a little. There would be none of that for me this year. Unless Helena and Ted invited me to take in some of Dayton while I was here, which, let's face it, was very unlikely.

No, I was destined to spend my Christmas cooped up in Connor's room.

But so long as we were together, that's all that mattered.

"Mmm, I could get used to this." Connor ran his hand along my thigh.

"You're awake."

"Sorry about that. One minute, I was saying goodbye to Coach Tucker, the next..."

I leaned over and kissed him. "You obviously needed it."

"How long was I out?"

"Like two hours."

"Shit, El, I—"

"Hey, I said it's fine."

"I hate that this is how it's going to be. Me flaking out on you."

"I know you can't help it. Besides, I watched *Miracle on Thirty-Fourth Street*."

"It'll get easier once I'm more mobile."

"I know," I said. "Are you hungry? Thirsty?"

"Babe, I don't need you to be my maid. That's not—"

"Oh, hush. I like taking care of you. Dayna texted earlier. It sounds like Aiden and Carson are striking up quite the bromance."

"I'm hardly surprised. He's Coach Walsh's favorite on the ice."

"You had some messages while you were sleeping. Want to read them?"

"Nah, they can wait." He leaned in, licking the seam of my mouth. "What time are my parents going to the store?"

"I have no idea. But they said later this afternoon."

Connor pouted, "And here I was hoping we could fool around for a little bit."

"Later." I kissed his jaw. "Are you sure I can't get you anything? You didn't have any breakfast. You must be hungry. I can go—"

"Jesus, El, stop."

"What?" I blinked at him, taken aback by his tone.

"I didn't ask you to come here to baby me."

"Connor, that's not... I just want to help."

"Yeah, I know." He blew out an exasperated breath. "But if you're going to become Mom 2.0, you're going to suffocate me."

"Sorry."

Dejection washed through me like ice as I pulled away.

"Shit, babe. That's not... that came out all wrong. I'm just tired and cranky and in a shit ton of pain. Of course, I know you're only trying to help. Just tone it down a little, maybe."

Tone it down...

My stomach dropped.

It had been one day.

One day and I was already annoying him.

I really didn't know what to say to that.

"I'm going to the bathroom," I said, climbing off the bed.

"Come on, babe. I didn't mean... fuck."

I didn't acknowledge him as I locked myself in. I hadn't even grabbed my phone, so I couldn't text the girls an SOS.

Come on, Ella. Get yourself together. He doesn't mean it, not really. He's just hurting.

But the words were out now.

He couldn't take them back.

CHAPTER 19

CONNOR

I didn't mean to snap at her.

But the second Ella had started asking me if I was hungry or thirsty, annoyance had flooded me.

I wasn't annoyed at Ella. I was annoyed at the situation. The fact was that I was lying in my childhood bed in my parents' house when I should have been planning the perfect proposal.

I wanted some alone time with her. Needed it more than air. But I couldn't exactly make a move given my incapacitated situation.

When Ella finally came out of the bathroom, the temperature between us had cooled to below freezing.

"I'm sorry."

"It's fine," she said, barely looking at me.

"Will you come lie down with me? We can watch another movie."

"Actually, I'm going to do some homework." She grabbed her laptop out of her bag and fired it up. "Do you want anything?"

"I'd like my girlfriend to stop freezing me out."

"I'm not—" I flashed her a skeptical look, and she relented. "You hurt my feelings." Her confession sucker-punched me right in the chest.

"I know, and I'm sorry. You've got to be patient with me, kitten." I dragged a hand down my face. "One minute, I think I'm fine with everything. I'm ready to get on with my recovery. And the next... Well, let's just say, I have some pretty dark thoughts."

I didn't want to admit that to her. But it was Ella. The one person I could tell anything to without fear of judgment.

"I'm scared, El."

"Oh, Connor." She perched on the edge of the bed, taking my hand in hers. "I can't imagine how devastating this is for you. But you will get through it."

"What if I don't? What if something—"

"Hey, none of that." She smiled, cupping my face with her other hand. "I love you so much, Connor. You're one of the most focused and determined guys I know. A little injury isn't going to keep you down."

Little injury.

It didn't feel very little.

The pain was constant, a dull ache that roared every

time I moved my upper body or good leg, even with the compression sleeve.

"Your faith in me might be a little misguided," I murmured. Because I knew once physical therapy started, I'd probably become a monster.

"Never." She smiled. "Now, how about we try and get you into the shower?"

"You don't have to do that. I'll ask my dad—"

"Connor, I'm here. I've seen you naked more times than I can count. Let me do this."

"I can't get my leg wet."

"I know. We'll figure it out. Come on." She stood and inhaled a sharp breath.

"Okay."

I managed to swing my good leg over the edge of the bed, and slowly pulled my injured leg around. The pain took my breath away, but I managed to grit my teeth through it.

"Okay?" Ella asked, and I nodded. "I'll get your crutches."

Once I was up on my feet, she moved ahead of me into the bathroom. It was small, and there wasn't a lot to work with, but the walk-in shower meant there was enough room to add a plastic chair for me to sit on.

"Hmm, so maybe if you stay right there. I'll strip your shorts first."

"You got it, nurse," I chuckled, but it came out a bit strangled.

Ella hooked her fingers into my shorts and pulled

them down my legs, careful not to disturb my compression sleeve and dressing. My dick bobbed between us, and she looked up at me, arching a brow.

"What? I'm a walking, talking hard-on at the minute."

"Maybe I can help with that once you're clean."

"Fuck," I hissed. She was going to be the death of me.

"So I'm thinking if you sit on the chair, I'll wrap your knee in some saran wrap and wash you with the sponge."

El stood, and I released a crutch to hook my arm around her, dragging her body closer.

"I am sorry about earlier."

"I know. It's going to take time for both of us. I feel helpless here, too, Connor."

"Baby, just you being here is more than I will ever need. I promise."

She laid her hand on my chest, gazing up at me with so much emotion I wanted to drop to my knee and propose.

But I couldn't, not like this. So I swallowed the words and gave her ass a little squeeze, turning to my old friend, humor, to get me through.

"Get naked, kitten."

"I don't need—"

"Get. Naked."

"Fine," she huffed. "But only because I love you."

Ella stepped back and slowly stripped out of her hoodie and pajama shorts, giving me quite the show.

"You're such a cocktease."

Smacking her lips together, she blew me a kiss as she grabbed the box of saran wrap off the vanity and started wrapping my knee.

"How does that feel?" she asked.

"Yeah, okay." Pain pinched my voice, but I could handle it.

I could handle a lot of fucking things if it meant I got to see my girlfriend in nothing but her black lacy panties.

When she popped back up, I reached out and grazed my thumb over her nipple.

"Connor," she gasped. "Don't start something you can't finish."

"Want to put that to the test?"

"Shower first," she said.

"You ruin all my fun."

With a little tsk, Ella slipped behind the shower glass and turned on the water. "Think you can make it to the chair in one piece?"

"Yeah, I can manage."

With a lot of deep breathing, I managed to haul my ass into the shower and drop onto the chair, keeping my leg as extended as possible. Pain fired off around my body in vicious waves, but I locked it down, focusing on my very beautiful, almost-naked girlfriend.

The water bounced off my shoulders, but I was far enough out of the jets for my leg to stay relatively dry.

Ella ran her hands over my shoulders and leaned down, pressing a kiss to my cheek. "I love you."

"Love you, too." I twisted my face to kiss her, but she pulled away. The little tease.

The sponge felt incredible against my grimy skin and tense muscles. But when she dipped it down my torso, letting her fingers brush my pubes, my entire body shuddered with need.

"Fuck, El," I hissed.

She didn't linger, though; instead, gliding the sponge back up and over my shoulders, working out the tension with her firm touch.

By the time she had thoroughly cleaned every inch of me, I was aching for her—desire heating my blood.

She came around to my front, standing before me like a goddess sent from the heavens.

"You are so fucking beautiful," I drawled, soaking up every inch of her damp skin, every curve and dip, every freckle and blemish.

It was a heady thing, knowing someone's body almost as well as you knew your own. I learned how to make her whimper, moan, and gasp. I knew exactly how to make her scream my name. And I planned on spending a lifetime doing just that.

Ella ran a hand up her stomach, her eyelashes fluttering as she played with her perfect tits.

"Babe," it was a low, throaty growl. Because I couldn't take it. I couldn't fucking—

Her knees hit the tiles in front of me. "Do you think you can spread your legs a little?"

"Babe, I would cut my leg off right now if it meant getting your mouth on me."

Her laughter rose over the water spray.

She brought a hand to my shaft, circling it with her fingers. I hissed, the contact so familiar and so fucking good that I almost came right then.

It was a tight fit, given my saran-wrapped knee, but Ella made it work—half leaning between my thighs to lower her mouth to my crown. Her tongue sneaked out, licking the precum from the tip.

"Fuuuck," I choked out.

I'd died and gone to heaven. That was the only explanation for the out-of-body sensations streaking through me as she took me into her mouth, swallowing me down her throat like a goddamn pro.

"Shit, El. That feels... fuck."

She pulled off me with a pop. "You good?"

"Babe, I swear to fucking God, if you stop, I'll die." I leaned back against the chair, the water spray catching the back of my head.

But I didn't care.

I didn't care one bit as my girl took me to blow-job heaven with her hands and teeth and magical fucking mouth.

"I love your dick," she preened, swirling her tongue

around the tip before licking the vein along the underside of my shaft.

"I fucking love you," I groaned as she swallowed me down again, root to tip. "Gonna come, kitten. I'm gonna — fuck."

Pleasure barreled down my spine as I shot down her throat. Ella licked me through it, swallowing every last drop.

"Better?" She gazed up at me, all lust drunk and flushed.

"Mmm, much." I ran a thumb over her pouty lips. "Want me to repay the favor?"

She stood up, and I slid my hands around the backs of her thighs to cup her ass.

"I wouldn't say no to—"

"Sweetheart, are you okay in there?" Mom started rapping on the bathroom door.

"Jesus." My jaw clenched as Ella stepped away from me.

"Connor, sweet—"

"Yeah, Mom, I'm good. Just getting a shower."

"It's like she knows," Ella mumbled, throwing me a dirty look.

"Do you need any help?" Mom called.

"I said I'm good, Mom. Ella is quite capable of helping me."

"Oh... *oh*. Well, I'll just... I'll go."

"Fuck." I ran a hand down my face, sitting there like

a fucking idiot because I couldn't get up without my crutches, and Ella needed to hand me those.

She grabbed a towel and wrapped it around her body before passing me them. "It's slippery."

"I've got it."

Still, she waited until I'd got my balance. "Okay?"

"Yeah. At least they'll be out later."

"Yep." Her lips pursed.

Shit. I was in the doghouse again.

And to be honest, I couldn't really blame her.

I didn't try my luck once my parents left. Ella had given me the cold shoulder most of the day, and the truth was, I was fucking tired.

Post-surgery exhaustion was no joke.

So we settled in for another movie, the distance between us icy cold. But I didn't push, and she didn't extend an olive branch.

It was shit, but that was the theme of my life right now.

A big, old bag of shit.

"You know, you don't have to stay for the entire holiday," I said out of nowhere.

It wasn't that I didn't want her to stay. I did. But things were already tense. I didn't know if we'd survive another three weeks of this.

"Shut up. I'm staying."

"Just... hear me out," I said. "You could go to your mom's for a few days. Celebrate Christmas with your family—"

"You're my family." She cut me with a scathing look.

"Babe, come on. I don't know what I'm supposed to do here. It's been a couple of days, and I already feel like I'm crawling out of my goddamn skin."

She blanched, and I muttered under my breath. "Didn't mean you, El. I just mean the situation. Living under my parents' roof. It's like I'm a teenager all over again."

"Because your parents are overbearing."

"That's not fair. They only care."

"Every time we get close, your mom pops up like a fucking Jack-in-the-box, Connor. Are you sure they don't have cameras in here?"

My strangled laughter barely cracked the ice between us. "Maybe I shouldn't have asked you to come."

Hurt flashed in her eyes. "Maybe you should have considered staying in Lakeshore."

"I can't..." A deep painful sigh rolled through me. "I can't be around them right now."

"But they're your best friends. If anyone understands—"

"That's just it, El. They don't understand; they can't."

My friends hadn't had their life's dream snatched away from them in an instant.

I had.

And I didn't want to end up resenting them because I got unlucky. That wasn't fair to me, and it wasn't fair to them.

I needed to stay away until I was in a better headspace. Until I could at least see some light at the end of the tunnel.

"Do you want me to leave?"

"No, fuck... no." I palmed her cheek, wishing she could see into my head. Wishing I didn't have to try and find a way to verbalize everything running through my mind.

"You know I want you here more than anything. But I can't help but think maybe it would be easier on you—"

"Stop trying to put words in my mouth." She swatted my hand away. "I came because that's what you do when you love somebody."

"You love me, Ella Henshaw?"

"You know I do, you big idiot." A small smile cracked her dejected expression. "I know how hard this is for you. How out of control you feel. But I'm begging you, don't push me away. I'm sorry I got annoyed earlier, but it's not easy on me either."

"So let me make it up to you." I leaned in, pressing a kiss to her shoulder. I was so fucking immobile that it made everything hard work, so I'd need her to work with me if I was going to touch her the way I was desperate to.

But Ella didn't budge. If anything, she pulled away slightly, putting more space between us.

"It's been a long day," she said. "Can we just chill?"

"Sure."

Something curdled in my stomach. I wasn't insecure enough to think Ella turning me down meant anything beyond the fact today had been another trying day. But her rejection still stung.

"We could cuddle?"

"Cuddle, yeah." I lifted my arm, letting her tuck herself into my side. "Maybe once I'm up and about, we can go out."

"I'd like that." She toyed with my t-shirt, winding her fingers into the soft material.

"You and me, babe," I murmured.

Always.

CHAPTER 20

ELLA

Christmas Eve was awkward as hell.

Connor managed to make it downstairs so we could have dinner with his mom and dad, but the atmosphere was less than festive.

He seemed lost in his own thoughts, barely managing a smile when I plucked a sprig of mistletoe from one of Helena's wreaths and held it above our heads.

He leaned in, grazing my cheek with his mouth.

My *cheek*.

Covering my hurt with a tight smile, I turned my attention to the excess spread laid out on the Morgans' dining room table. "Helena, this looks—"

"Too much," Ted scoffed. "I told her not to go crazy."

"Dad," Connor warned.

"It's okay, sweetheart." Helena fussed over some of the dishes. "I just wanted to make an effort since things are so disappointing for you right now."

"The boy isn't dead—"

"Dad!" Connor slammed his fist down on the table, and I startled.

"Sorry, Son. This is proving hard on everyone."

"Look, you guys, I get it. You're worried about the future, my contract with the Flyers..."

"Connor, sweetheart, that's not—"

"It's okay, Mom. I'm worried too. But Doctor Kirshner said the surgery was a success. I guess only time will tell if he's right."

"The physical therapist will be able to give you a better assessment," Ted said. "He comes highly recommended."

"Can we talk about something else? This is supposed to be a celebration dinner," Helena said. "It's Christmas Eve."

"I'd rather pretend it wasn't," Connor said grimly.

"Son, why would you say that? I know things are hard right now, but you're here, and you're safe, and Ella is—"

"Just... leave it, yeah? In fact, I'm not feeling so good." He glanced at his dad. "Can you help me back up to my room?"

"Of course, Son." Ted stood and came around to Connor's chair.

"I can help," I whispered.

"No, you stay here with Mom and eat some of this food. I'll see you in a bit."

"But—"

Connor was already half out of the chair, Ted supporting him while he reached for his crutches.

"I'll plate you something up," Helena said.

"Don't worry, Mom. I'm not hungry."

He didn't even glance at me as his dad guided him out of the room. Helena offered me a sympathetic smile but looked as disappointed as I felt.

"He didn't even try," I said, almost choking on the words.

"Maybe it was a silly idea. I just thought—"

"You did nothing wrong, Helena. Connor has been quiet all day."

Maybe he was hurt that I didn't want to fool around the other night. But I wasn't so sure.

Yesterday, he'd napped on and off all day, and when he had been awake, he'd barely wanted to talk.

Helena had warned me this might happen, but I hadn't wanted to believe it because it was Connor.

My Connor.

My upbeat, positive, happy-go-lucky guy.

I'd never seen him so... so crushed.

I didn't like it, but I knew that I had to give him time and space to process and come to terms with things at his own pace.

Still, part of me wanted to go up there and shake

him for quitting so easily. If I could manage to survive a Christmas Eve dinner with his parents, so could he.

"I don't suppose you're hungry now," Helena said, sadness coating her words.

I wasn't. But I couldn't do that to her. So I plastered on my best smile and started to load my plate.

"It looks too good to waste," I said, and a flicker of gratitude passed over her.

She gave me a small, appreciative nod and started filling her own plate.

"You know, Ella," she said with a softness I rarely heard from her. "I can see why my son loves you so much."

Connor was asleep when I finally headed up.

Ted never reappeared, and I'd felt bad leaving Helena on her own. So we'd eaten and drank, and then she'd gotten out Connor's baby albums.

We didn't talk about the serious stuff. About our plans for after graduation. Or what might happen if Connor's recovery didn't go well. But for once, I felt on the same wavelength as his mom.

Helena loved her son and only wanted the best for him. And that was something we could both agree on.

I didn't linger, closing his door quietly and heading

down to the guest room, where I got ready for bed and then texted the girls.

> Ella: Happy Christmas Eve. I hope you've all had a better time than me xo

> Rory: Oh, El. That bad?

> Ella: It wasn't good. Connor hasn't been himself the last couple of days. I'm worried about him.

> Dayna: He's under a lot of pressure, and he probably just hates the fact it won't be much of a celebration tomorrow.

> Ella: What do you mean? It's just Christmas.

> Rory: Dayna just means he'd probably planned to make it super romantic and buy you loads of gifts.

It hit me then. Unless he was super organized—which no college boyfriend ever was—or had enlisted the last-minute help of his mom, I would be waking up to zero presents tomorrow.

> Ella: I'm not worried about a pile of presents under the tree. I just wish I could make it all better for him.

> Harper: Just be there for him. When he's ready, he'll come to you.

> Rory: Harper is right. Give him time. We love you and we're all here for you xo

Tears clung to my lashes as reality set in. It was stupid. I didn't need presents or grand gestures. But I hadn't even stopped to think about how tomorrow would make him feel. There were more important things at stake.

Connor had a big heart, though, and he loved showering me with attention. Maybe the girls were right. Maybe he felt disappointed that tomorrow wouldn't be special for me.

> Ella: Thanks girls. I hope the big red man brings you something special tomorrow. I'll speak to you soon xo

I read their replies, then silenced my cell and curled up on my side.

Maybe I could think of a way to cheer Connor up tomorrow. We didn't need presents or big plans or any of that.

Not when we had each other.

I woke early, feeling a keen sense of determination. It was Christmas Day, and even though things were pretty dire for Connor, I would do everything I could to make the most of the day.

Starting with cleaning myself up.

By the time I'd showered and dressed, it was eight-thirty. He hadn't texted me yet, so I assumed he was still sleeping.

But when I went across the hall, he was awake.

And he wasn't alone.

"Ella, Merry Christmas." Helena stood and came over, pulling me into a hug. "Go easy on him," she whispered. "He isn't feeling himself."

"What's wrong?" I asked, my eyes shooting to his.

Connor shrugged. "Didn't sleep well."

"Oh."

He hadn't texted me. He hadn't even texted me this morning.

But I brushed off the dejection and pasted on my best smile. "Merry Christmas."

"I'll leave you two to it. We can talk about dinner later." Helena gave my arm a pat before leaving.

"What do you think?" I twirled. "I didn't have much to work with."

"It's nice." Connor stared right through me.

"Con, come on." Moving to the bed, I sat down on the edge. "We can still make the most of the day. I got you something."

"Shit, El. I didn't manage to get—"

"It doesn't matter. I'm not giving you this to make you feel guilty, babe. I just want to make you smile." I plucked the small box out of my ridiculous candy cane hoodie and placed it on his chest.

"The fuck is that?" he gritted out.

"What?" I gawked, a little taken aback by his outburst. "It's just a box. Open it."

He stared at it as if it was a bomb about to detonate at any given moment.

"It won't bite." Nervous laughter spilled out of me.

But he didn't laugh.

In fact, he looked positively nauseous.

"It doesn't matter." I went to take it back, realizing I'd completely misread the situation. "I just thought—"

"Shit, babe. I'm sorry." He covered my hand with his. "I just feel so fucking useless. I had all these plans for today..."

"What plans? Tell me more," I grinned, hope bubbling inside me.

"Doesn't matter now."

"Oh."

God, this was hard work. But I refused to be defeated because one of us needed to stay positive.

"Open it," I encouraged with a smile. "It's nothing expensive. But I saw it and thought of you."

It was the only thing I'd wrapped and brought with me.

Connor picked up the box and tore into the gift wrap. "It's not jewelry, right?"

"Just open it." I rolled my eyes.

He flipped the lid and peered inside. "What—"

"It's a keychain. But you have to read the inscription."

He lifted out the puck-shaped keychain, and a flicker of a smile ghosted over his face. "I pucking love you."

"There's a photo, too. See." I flipped it over to reveal the photo of us on last New Year's Eve, gazing at each other as the clock struck midnight.

"I pucking love you, too," he said.

"Yeah?"

"Yeah. And I feel like a giant shit that I didn't get you anything."

"Stop. It doesn't matter. I'm here. You're here. I have all I need."

"But still..."

"Connor, it doesn't matter."

He gave me a small nod, but I saw the hesitation in his eyes.

"Merry Christmas." I leaned in, chancing a kiss.

For a second, I thought he might not kiss me back, but then his hand curved around my neck and his mouth crashed down on mine. He plunged his tongue into my mouth, devouring me.

"Connor," I breathed, twisting my fingers into his t-shirt to try and steady myself.

"Fucking need you, El," he drawled, trying to pull me into his lap, his fingers digging into my hip.

Panic flooded me, and I pressed a hand against his chest. "Slow down. We should slow—"

"Fuck... *fuck*." He pulled away abruptly, icy frustration rolling off him.

"Hey, it's okay," I said when he dropped his gaze, building a wall between us. "Connor, please, don't shut me out. We can be intimate. Just not—"

"Did you speak to your mom?"

"Not yet," I said, frustrated that he'd changed the subject. But aware that if I pushed, he would only shut down more.

"You should call her. Tell her I said Merry Christmas."

Utterly defeated, I slipped off the bed and stood. "Do you need anything? Breakfast? Coffee?"

"Mom will bring me something." He didn't look at me, his dismissal as clear as day.

"Okay then," I said. "Perhaps when you're done acting like a child, you could let me know, and I'll come and spend some time with you."

"El, wait..." He called after me as I reached the door.

"Yes?" *Apologize. Apologize, and I'll let it go. We can salvage the day, and everything will be okay.* "Connor?" I offered him one last olive branch.

But he didn't take it.

"Thanks for the gift."

His words landed like bullets, ripping straight through my heart.

But I didn't let him see my pain as I marched out of there and left him all alone.

Later that day, Helena knocked on the door to the guest room.

"Ella?" She stuck her head inside. "Are you sure I can't interest you in some dinner? There's enough to feed a small army."

"I'm fine, but thank you."

"Oh, sweetheart. You shouldn't be in here all alone on Christmas Day. I feel just awful that Connor—"

"Honestly, Helena. I'm fine." I wasn't, but the lie sounded better than the truth. "Have you checked in on him?"

"Yes, but he isn't very good company."

"Do you think we need to be worried?"

"Physical therapy starts the day after tomorrow. That will be the real test."

"Maybe I underestimated how much this would affect him."

"Hockey is in that boy's blood, Ella. Without it, he doesn't work right."

I knew that. But I guess I didn't think he would shut me out so easily.

I'd been there right beside him over the last year. I'd supported him every step of the way. I knew the team almost as well as he did. Because it was his life, and I wanted to be a part of it. So I guess, in my head, there would never be a scenario where he wouldn't turn to me.

I loved him, with or without the jersey.

But maybe I hadn't paid close enough attention.

"I don't know what to do," I confessed, hating that she got to see me like this. Especially knowing that she could use it against me with Ted.

But we'd bonded last night over too much food and one too many glasses of wine.

"You just be there for him," she said. "Connor loves you, and if you're going to be together, this won't be the last test you endure."

I nodded, too choked up to reply.

"If you need anything or want some company, I'll be downstairs. That husband of mine isn't much fun when he's moping, either."

"Thank you."

"I know it isn't the Christmas you'd planned together, Ella. But plans change. It's what's in here"—she touched her chest, right over her heart—"that doesn't."

Helena's words stayed with me long after she'd gone.

Connor was angry. Disappointed and frustrated. And I was the person closest to him. It made sense I would bear the brunt of his mood swings.

How did the saying go? You always hurt the ones you loved the most.

It would be okay, though. Soon he would text me and apologize.

Only he didn't.

And Christmas Day passed me by without another word from my boyfriend.

The man I loved more than life itself.

CHAPTER 21

CONNOR

Physical therapy was a new kind of torture.

And that was saying something, given my girlfriend had barely spoken more than five words to me in the last forty-eight hours.

I deserved her wrath. I knew that.

I'd been awful company Christmas Day, taking my anger and frustration out on her and my parents rather than letting them try and make the most of the day.

But when Ella had handed me that small box, all my plans came crashing down around me again. It was supposed to be *me* presenting *her* with a box. Me down on one knee, asking her to marry me.

It had felt like a fucked-up kind of karma.

One I couldn't just bury or forget about.

So yeah, I didn't blame her for shutting down or

barely talking to me. And the truth was, I didn't know how to explain it to her.

I didn't know how to apologize.

"That's good, Connor," Kieron, the therapist, said. "A little more."

"Fuck," I muttered as he helped me slowly extend my leg. Even with the brace, it hurt like a bitch, but it was all part of the process.

"You might need to take some extra pain pills after we get done here," he chuckled.

As if anything about this situation was even remotely funny.

"I'll live," I said. "How long do you think it'll be before I'm back on the ice?"

"You know I don't have the answer to that question." He gave me a sobering look.

"Yeah, I know. But ballpark figure?"

"Assuming you put in the work and everything goes to plan, it could be as little as four months."

"And assuming it doesn't?"

"You could be looking at upwards of six to nine months. But that's a worst-case scenario."

"Fuck," I breathed, curling my hands over the table, focusing on the bite of pain.

Anything to replace the numb-fucking emptiness I felt in my chest.

I needed to get back on my feet, into my skates, and out on the ice as soon as possible. Anything else was not an option.

"How does it feel?"

"Sore."

"That's to be expected. Okay, I don't want to push you too hard today. You've got the sheet with the exercises on it?" I nodded, and he went on, "Follow the plan, gradually building up the intensity. Don't try and skip a step. It builds for a reason. I'll see you again on Thursday."

"Great, can't wait." Sarcasm dripped from my words, but if he noticed, Kieron didn't acknowledge it.

"I know it feels like you'll never get there," he said as I grabbed my crutches to support my weight and lowered myself off the table.

Pain ricocheted through my leg, taking my breath away, but I managed to lock it down.

"You don't need to be a martyr, Connor."

"I'm fine," I gritted out.

"Don't push too much too soon. This is a process. You need to move through all the steps."

"Got it."

"Right, get out of here. I'll see you next time."

I hobbled to the door, and Ella jumped out of her seat, rushing over to open the door for me.

"How was it?"

"Torture. But I survived."

"Do you need any help?" she asked. "I can get a wheelcha—"

"No, I've got it." I brushed past her and started toward the sliding doors.

"Do you want to go for lunch, maybe? We could—"

"Mind if we rain check?" I said. "I'm kind of beat."

"Oh, okay."

"Ella, fuck, I'm sorry. I'm just—"

"It's fine. I can make us something when we get back."

I let out a weary sigh. I didn't want to fight. All I wanted was for things to go back to how they were before I got injured and life went to shit.

But that wasn't going to happen.

This was my reality now.

"Noah called again," Ella said as we left the medical center. "They want to come and see you."

"Not yet," I said.

"So when should I tell—"

"I'll speak to him."

"Okay."

Fuck. I hated seeing Ella so defeated and upset. She put on a brave face, snapped back at me when I was acting like a giant ass, and refused to let me miss PT this morning.

But it didn't matter.

None of it mattered.

Something inside me was broken, and I didn't know how to fix it. And with every hour that passed, I felt myself get sucked deeper into the black void circling me.

When we reached my truck, Ella yanked open the passenger door and let me hoist myself inside. "Are you sure you don't want to go for some lunch? It might make you feel be—"

"Not today." I couldn't meet her eyes because I knew what I'd see there.

Coward. You're a fucking coward, Morgan.

"I might drop you back at the house and go out then. I could do with some fresh air." I felt her eyes on me, pushing me to man the fuck up, but I still couldn't meet her stare.

"Sounds good."

"Connor, please." She let out a heavy sigh, one I felt all the way down to my soul. "I know things are hard right now, but I'm trying.... Forget it. You can't even look at me."

"I'm sorry," I said. Wishing I could be different.

Wishing I could handle everything better.

But it was only a couple of days after Christmas. Ella was supposed to be wearing my ring. She was supposed to be my fiancée. Instead, she had become my caregiver and chauffeur all rolled into one.

"Yeah," Ella said quietly, her voice full of defeat and disappointment. "Me too."

"How did it go?" Mom asked the second we got into the house.

"It was fine." I made a beeline for the couch,

dropping my sticks and lowering myself down a little too hastily.

A pained groan spilled off my lips, and Mom sighed.

"Connor, you need to watch yourself," she said. "Ella, sweetheart, there's fresh coffee in the pot."

"Actually, I'm going to go out for a little while."

"You are?" Mom glanced between us, and I shrugged.

"Yeah, I need some fresh air. Do you need anything while I'm gone?"

"Nope," I said, Mom's eyes burning holes into the side of my face.

The tension was stifling. Thick and heavy, it pressed down on my chest.

It was like being stuck underwater, trapped beneath layers of ice. I could see the surface, but I didn't know how to get there.

I didn't know how to break through.

"I'll see you later," Ella said, leaving me and Mom alone.

"Is everything okay?" Mom asked.

"I think we both know it's not," I clipped out, staring at the wall.

"Connor, love, I know things aren't easy right now—"

"Understatement of the century, Mom. Do you know what the therapist said? He said the worst-case scenario is that I won't be back on the ice for six to nine months. Nine months... that'll be September."

"And best case?"

"What?"

"You said that's the worst case. What is the best-case scenario?"

"It doesn't matter." I turned away from her.

But my mom wasn't so easily deterred. Coming around to sit in front of me, she took my hand in hers and gave me a soft smile. "Connor, this isn't you. This isn't the boy who spent hours out on the lake in winter learning how to skate—the boy who begged and begged us to let him join the peewee league.

"I know the injury has ruined your senior year, sweetheart, but you will recover, and you will play hockey again. It isn't—"

"You don't get it," I said.

"So talk to me, Son. Because shutting yourself off certainly isn't helping. Ella has been nothing but supportive, and you're pushing her away. I'm worried, Connor. We both are."

"I don't know what you want me to say, Mom. I'm sorry, I can't just snap out of it. I'm sorry, I'm fucking terrified that my career might be over before it's even started."

College hockey was competitive, but the NHL was a whole other league. One wrong move, one little injury and it could all be over.

"Connor—"

"No, Mom. The odds were slim to start with. Did you know that around only half of the players drafted ever play?"

"You've never let that deter you before."

"I think I'm allowed to wallow, Mom. I wanted to go all the way with the team this year. I wanted… fuck," I muttered, blowing out an exasperated breath.

She didn't get it.

How could she?

How could anyone who had never dedicated their entire life to something?

Hockey was my end goal. There wasn't a plan B.

It was hockey… or it was nothing.

So excuse me while I licked my wounds and felt fucking sorry for myself.

The surgery was done, yeah. But the hard work was only just about to start, the hard work that could make or break my future with the Flyers.

"I know, Connor. I know." She gently squeezed my hand as I fought the surge of emotion rising inside me.

She had a point. I couldn't keep doing this. But I didn't know how to stop.

The pressure, the crushing devastation I felt every time I so much as thought about the team making it to the playoffs, was too overwhelming.

"Maybe you and your dad could go and watch a game. It might—"

"Mom." I sighed.

She was worse than Ella.

"Sorry, I'm just trying to help."

"Nobody can help me," I said. "This is something I've got to do alone."

"Con—"

"I'm tired." I leaned over, grabbed my crutches, and managed to get onto my feet. "I'm going to head up to my room."

She let me go at first, but her voice stopped me as I got to the door.

"You can't keep doing this, Connor."

But as I hobbled away, the only thing I could think was…

Watch me.

Ella was gone for three hours. I only knew because I was halfway through a second movie when she knocked and came inside my room.

"How are you?"

"Where were you?" I asked.

"I told you. I was going out for a little bit."

I gave her a dismissive nod and went back to watch the television. Not that I was really watching it. It was nothing more than moving images on the screen. Sounds blurring together. But it kept me distracted from the thoughts running around my head, the constant waves of pain.

"Do you need anything?"

"No," I clipped out—the dark void dragging me under a little more.

"Connor." The bed dipped, and her slim fingers wrapped around my wrist. "Talk to me."

Lifting my eyes to hers, I pressed my lips into a thin line.

"I'm trying my best here," she said, the defeat in her voice fisting my heart. Squeezing until I felt like I couldn't breathe.

Except, I already couldn't.

Because hockey was my purpose. My focus. My only goal since I could remember.

I felt fucking lost—*lost*—without it.

The thought of not turning my dream into a reality...

Fuck.

Fuck.

Everything inside me went tense.

"Connor." Ella squeezed my arm, but I yanked it away, frustration and anger coursing through my veins like acid.

"I think you're right." She got up, the temperature in the room dropping. "I think I should go home for a few days."

I nodded, not trusting myself to speak. I'd already done enough damage. Anything else I had to say would only drive the wedge between us deeper.

"Okay, then." Disappointment coated her voice, and I didn't miss the wobble in her words.

My girl was fucking breaking, and it was all my fault.

But I couldn't fix it.

"I'll probably leave tomorrow."

I didn't look at her. I couldn't stand to see the hurt in her eyes, the bitter resentment.

"If you need anything," she added, still trying. Still being her kind and compassionate self. "I'll be in my room."

Ella left, and before I knew what I was doing, I grabbed the television remote and launched it across the room. It hit the wall and landed on the carpet.

But I felt nothing.

I should have gone to her. I should have dropped to my knees and begged for forgiveness for being an asshole.

I didn't.

Because I couldn't. I couldn't run after her even if I wanted to.

Instead, I sat there, staring at nothing, letting the dark thoughts circle my mind, dragging me deeper.

It was better Ella left. I didn't want her to see me like this. Bitter and twisted and unable to find any light at the end of the tunnel.

She was my light; she always had been. But the injury had cast too dark of a shadow over her—over everything.

My cell vibrated, and I leaned over, snatching it off my nightstand.

> Noah: How's it going?

I stared at his message.
And stared.

> Noah: You ever need to talk, I'm here.

> Connor: I'm fine.

> Noah: I think you're a fucking liar.

Asshole. I tsked.

> Noah: How was PT?

> Connor: Could have been better.

> Noah: You've got to start somewhere. It's still early days, Con. It'll get easier.

> Connor: Yeah, I know.

At least, I fucking hoped so. But even if it did get easier, it wasn't going to change anything.

My last season with the Lakers was over.

Done.

No amount of physical therapy could give me that back.

I had to find a way to be okay with that. To accept that.

But not today.

Today, I wanted to wallow.

I wanted to hate the world and everything in it.

CHAPTER 22

ELLA

"Ella, sweetheart." Mom gathered me into a hug. "It's so good to see you."

"Thanks, Mom."

"Let me get a good look at you." She held me at arm's length. "You look a little pale. Are you eating well? Hydrating? You know you need to—"

"Mom, let me at least get through the door."

"Sorry, sweetie. We've just been worried sick ever since you told us about Connor's injury."

"He's okay," I said, my heart squeezing in my chest.

"Oh, Ella. I mean you, sweetheart. We've been worried sick about you."

"Oh, I'm okay, Mom. I'm—" Tears sprung into my eyes, and she hugged me again.

"Let it out, sweetie. Let it all out."

God, I didn't want to cry. Not here. Not on Mom. She'd only use this as ammunition against me. Against Connor.

It wasn't that she didn't like Connor; she did. But she wanted more for me than to be some hockey star's girlfriend. She wanted me to chase my dreams and put myself first.

I'd tried to tell her Connor wasn't like that, that he would never clip my wings or expect me to sit around twiddling my thumbs while he traveled the country with the team. That he would never put hockey before our relationship.

She had a point, though.

Being with any professional athlete meant that there was always a third wheel in your relationship. But it hadn't ever bothered me before because Connor and I didn't sit on arguments. We talked things through. We compromised. And we understood each other.

At least, I thought we did.

"I'm okay," I said, inhaling a shuddering breath. Silently scolding myself to get a grip.

"You don't need to put on a brave face for me," Mom said as she stepped back to give me some space. "I know. Why don't I call Margo, and she can come over—"

"No," I rushed out. "Not yet. I just want to relax for a bit."

"Of course, sweetheart. Whatever you want."

"Thanks, Mom."

"Why don't you go up to your room and get settled. I'll make you some lunch and bring it up."

I nodded, not trusting myself to speak.

With a heavy heart, I grabbed my bag and headed for the stairs.

It was strange being back here, especially without Connor. But after the disastrous day yesterday, I knew I couldn't stay there a second longer. Not without one of us saying something we might regret.

Connor needed to deal with things his way, and I needed to trust that a little time and space would help him come to terms with everything.

Besides, another second of Ted's cold attitude might have tipped me over the edge. He was probably clapping his hands with glee that I'd left.

My heart sank a little more.

It wasn't like me to quit, but Connor wasn't even prepared to meet me halfway. And I wasn't going to stay somewhere I clearly wasn't wanted.

Inside my room, I dumped my bag on the bed and dug my cell out of my pocket. It was hardly surprising to see no new messages, but it hadn't stopped me from hoping that there might be something from him.

Damn you, Connor Morgan.

Despite my anger, I still texted to let him know I'd arrived safely.

> Ella: Just got here. How are you feeling?

As I hit send and waited, I don't know what hurt worse.

That I didn't expect him to reply.

Or that he proved me right and didn't.

"So he just let you go?" Rory asked.

It was a couple hours after I'd arrived home, and the second I plucked up the courage to tell her what had happened, she called me.

"Yeah. I said I thought it was for the best, and he said... nothing."

"Oh, babe. You know he isn't in a good place."

"I know, and I get it. I do. But I honestly didn't think he'd push me away. Not like this." I hesitated, wondering whether to voice my concerns. "I think he's depressed."

"It wouldn't surprise me. Rates of depression are high among professional athletes anyway. Throw in a season-ending injury, and I'm sure that figure rises."

"Yeah, but it's Connor," I said as if that changed anything.

But Rory would get it. She and Connor had a

special bond. He'd taken her under his wing when she'd first arrived at Lakeshore U.

"He's only human, El. Give him time. He loves you so much, babe. But he isn't thinking straight right now," she said. "Some time apart will be a good thing. He'll be begging you to go back before you know it."

"I hope so." Because I hated the thought of not being there for him. But I couldn't be in his parents' house without him on my side, either.

The whole situation sucked.

"You're his forever girl, El. That will never change."

Things did change, though.

People changed.

"Did you have a nice time with Mason and Harper?" I changed the subject.

"It was so nice. Mrs. Steele is sweet and so good with Scottie."

There was a hint of melancholy in her voice.

"Rory?"

"It just made me realize I've never had that. It was nice but kind of bittersweet, you know."

"Yeah, I get it." I was lucky. Mom and Margo always made a big thing out of the holidays growing up. Even though they smothered me, they cared.

Some people didn't have that.

"And I hate that Austin spent Christmas alone, but he's too stubborn to admit he needs anyone."

"He just hasn't met the right person," I replied.

"It would take a special girl to put up with the likes

of him." Her soft laughter soothed some of the tension inside me. "You know if you want me to come visit—"

"Oh no, you don't have to do that. I'm sure everything will be fine. Connor will pull his head out of his ass, and I'll make him grovel for a few days, and we'll be back to normal."

As the words spilled out, though, they felt empty. Hollow.

They felt like a lie.

No. I shook the thoughts out of my head. Connor needed me to be strong for him. For us. He needed support and patience and understanding.

So I'd give it to him.

I'd give it to him in spades. Because that's what you did for the person you loved. You stood by their side no matter what—even when they didn't want you to.

This was a minor bump in the road. One we'd ride out... together.

"Maybe Connor would like to see the guys?" she suggested.

"I'm not sure. Not yet. But soon."

"Okay. You know, they're all here for him."

"I know."

But did Connor?

That was the real question.

"Well, I'd better go. Noah is taking me out on a date."

"Lucky you." I hoped the words sounded less bitter than they tasted.

"I'll text you tomorrow."

"Sure. Have fun."

We said goodbye and hung up.

I was happy for Rory, but I couldn't deny the sting of jealousy I felt knowing that Noah was about to whisk her away on some romantic date while my boyfriend didn't want to speak to me.

"Where is she?"

I heard my sister before I saw her. "The cavalry has arrived." Margo burst into my room, hands full of grocery bags. "I brought supplies."

"Mom, really." I glowered at her over Margo's shoulder. "I thought we agreed."

"She wanted to come." Mom shrugged.

"Of course, I did, silly. I've got enough candy to fix that heart of yours."

I groaned, flopping back against my pillows. "Margo, you shouldn't have come. I'm fine. Everything is fine."

"Not what I heard." She cast Mom a knowing look, and my chest tightened.

They were doing it already, ganging up on me. It had always been like this, the two of them versus little old me. But Henshaw women were independent to a fault. It's why Mom had never settled down after dad died before I was born.

"Now, first things first, do I need to go over there and give Connor a piece of my mind?"

"Oh my God, Margo, will you stop? I'm not a child anymore. This is my life. You can't just—"

"I don't think I've seen her cry over a boy since Robbie Fredericksburg invited Candice Keller to Homecoming."

"I did not cry."

"El Bell, you hid out in your room for the entire weekend," Margo reminded me. "I had to stage an intervention then, and I'm staging one now. Mom, we're going to need spoons, bowls, wine, and tissues. Lots and lots of tissues."

"You're crazy," I said through a strained smile.

"I'm your big sister. It's what we do. Now scooch and make room. My ass isn't as small as it used to be."

Margo unzipped her hoodie, and I was hardly surprised to find her already in her pajamas.

"I thought we could watch a movie. I'm thinking *Magic Mike* or *A Walk to Remember*. Depends on what you're in the mood for. Peens or tears."

"Oh my God, stop." Laughter bubbled in my chest.

"Made you laugh, though." She grinned, and I couldn't help but grin back.

They were a lot. Always interfering in my life and acting like they knew best. But Mom and Margo were my family, and I loved them dearly. And despite being eight years older than me, Margo was right. Sometimes you just needed a big sister hug.

She passed me the grocery bag and slipped onto the bed beside me. "So," she said. "Connor's being a stubborn ass?"

"It's not like that."

"Then what's it like? Because from where I'm sitting, it looks like he hurt my baby sister, and you know that crap doesn't fly with me."

"Margo." I sighed. "I just thought maybe some space would do us both some good."

"His mom and dad not being very welcoming?"

Margo knew bits about Ted's disapproval of our relationship. But I kept most of it to myself because, knowing Margo, she'd probably do something stupid like drive to Dayton and give him a piece of her mind.

"I know you probably don't want to hear it," she added, not bothering to wait for me to reply. "But I warned you about this."

"Please, don't start."

"You'll always be second best to hockey, El Bell. I know it's a hard thing to hear, but it's the truth. And I only want to protect you. He's injured now, and it's only college. What's going to happen when he goes pro, huh?"

"I love him, Margo."

"I know you do, and I get it. I do. Your first big relationship always hits the hardest. But are you really content with following him around while he pursues his dream? It's not an easy life, El."

"You don't get to pick and choose who you love, Margo." I peeked up at her.

"No, but you do get to choose what you are and aren't prepared to sacrifice for love."

"That isn't fair," I murmured.

"No, but life isn't fair, little sis." She nudged my arm with hers. "You don't ever have to settle."

"I love him," I said again.

"I know." She kissed my hair. "And I love you, and I want you to know if it doesn't work out, you'll survive, and they'll be other fish in the sea."

I pressed my lips together, not daring myself to speak. I didn't want to argue with her. Not now. Not when I already felt so weary.

Of course, she and Mom would assume the worst. They had probably been waiting for this moment to say, 'We told you so.'

"Did you decide on which movie you want to watch?"

"You choose," I said.

"Magic Mike sounds tempting, but it might make me horny."

"Margo!"

"What? I'm just saying all that hard, ripped muscle and pelvic thrusting gets me—"

"Okay, I get it."

I did, literally.

Magic Mike was one of my favorite films. Connor loved to tease me about it. He loved to get me off while we watched it.

Tears burned the backs of my eyes, but I didn't let them fall. This wasn't the end. It was a blip. A temporary setback.

I loved Connor.

I loved him more than anything. And I would stand by him. I would. But I needed to regroup. I needed to catch my breath and shore my defenses against the storm we'd found ourselves in.

Once he found his stride with physical therapy, he would feel better. It would give him something to work toward. An end goal.

My cell vibrated, and hope burst inside of me. It had taken him long enough, but I knew Connor would text me eventually.

Except, when I plucked my phone off the nightstand and saw Dayna's name, my heart sank.

"Connor?" Margo asked, and I nodded, hoping my expression didn't betray me.

I didn't like lying to her, but I also didn't want another lecture.

She didn't get it. How could she?

Her husband Jonah had a regular nine-to-five job. They had the weekends off together to go on dates and hang out with their friends. His only hobby was golf, something Margo was all too happy to share with him.

I knew what I was signing up for when I agreed to

give Connor another chance last year. I would never walk away just because things got too hard. Being in that house, though, under the microscope of his parents, was too much and was only going to exacerbate the situation.

But now I was here, and Connor was there, and the distance had never felt greater between us.

CHAPTER 23

CONNOR

"I CAN'T FUCKING DO IT," I grunted, throwing my crutch down in a huff.

Kieron laughed.

Asshole.

I pinned him with a scathing look. "I'm glad one of us is enjoying this."

"You're acting like a pussy."

"They pay you to talk to your clients like that?"

"Your old man does." He smirked, and I wanted to wipe it right off his pretty face.

Kieron was highly recommended, and with that came a hefty price tag. But Dad had insisted.

Right now, though, I would have happily worked with the hospital physical therapist. No way would they be torturing me with all these fucking exercises already.

"You can do it," he said.

"Saying it over and over doesn't make it any more true. I. Can't. Fucking. Do. It." I slumped against the bed, running a hand down my face.

Everything inside me hurt, and for someone used to getting bumped and bruised on the ice, that was saying something.

"You're not even trying," he said. "You know, I don't think this is a physical barrier at all. I think it's all in your head."

"Yeah, okay," I scoffed.

"Where's that pretty girl of yours? I didn't see her outside in the hall. Or at our last appointment."

"Don't." The growl that came from inside me was barely human.

Kieron only grinned wider. "You don't think I've seen this a hundred times before? An athlete on the cusp of going pro gets injured and pushes away everyone around him. I could write a book on this shit."

"Whatever, can we just get on with the session?"

I didn't want to talk about Ella.

I couldn't.

Ever since she'd left four days ago, we'd barely talked. Not even on New Year's Eve, which had come and gone in a blink. And my mood grew darker every second.

I missed her something fierce. But I couldn't bury

my fear and do the right thing—apologize. Because the truth was, I didn't want to let her down.

I didn't want to let myself down.

So I kept my text messages brief, and Ella made no attempts to hide her frustration. But she didn't push.

"Are you going to actually pull your head out of your ass and engage with the session?" His teasing words pulled me from my thoughts.

"I'm leaving," I spat, anger rippling through me like fire.

I had enough to deal with without taking shit from him too.

"Okay, leave. I'm not stopping you." He stepped back, folding his arms over his chest.

I grabbed one crutch and cussed under my breath when I realized I couldn't reach the other one. Not without toppling headfirst and doing some serious damage to myself.

Kieron chuckled as realization dawned on me. "Smug fucker," I muttered.

"Now, are you ready to continue?"

"Fine."

"That's what I like to hear. Don't worry, hotshot. We'll have you up on your feet in no time."

"You're quiet," Dad said as he drove me home.

I stared out the window, wincing every time the car coasted over a bump in the road.

"Yeah, well, PT sucks ass."

"Kieron comes highly recommended."

"I know. Doesn't change the fact it blows."

"You know, Connor, your attitude—"

"Seriously, don't start. I had enough of that from Kieron."

"I thought some time apart might do you some good," he murmured. "It's not healthy for you both to be cooped up. Her fussing over you every two minutes."

"That's not—" I ground my teeth together, trapping the words.

"You need to be at home with us," he went on, oblivious to the tension growing between us, multiplying, testing the tiny bit of control I had. "Focusing on your recovery."

Thankfully, he turned onto our street then, so I didn't have to endure any more of my old man's life advice.

He meant well, always did. But he couldn't seem to accept that Ella was it for me.

The one.

My forever girl.

Probably because you haven't told him, asshole.

"Have you heard from Sara?" he asked.

"She texted to see how I am."

"Sweet girl. Not so sure about that Émile, though. They seem so... incompatible."

"They seem happy enough to me."

"Yes, but will it last? Émile goes back to Quebec soon, and Sara's life is here, in Dayton."

"Maybe it isn't anymore," I said.

"Well, it would be a damn shame if she left. Your mother and I would miss her dearly. And I'm sure you would—"

"Help me out, yeah," I said, shouldering the door the second the car rolled to a stop.

"Give me a chance, Son. I've barely got the old girl in Park."

He climbed out and came around to help me. It was hard fucking work with the knee brace and crutches, but I managed to get upright.

"Can you manage?"

"Yeah." I started toward the house.

Being unable to bear weight was no easy task, but I made it work.

"How about we have a beer and watch some of your old game footage? I could—"

"Maybe later, Dad. I'm going to crash for a while."

I didn't want to reminisce or shoot the shit or act like everything was going to be fine when we didn't know that yet.

"You can't hide up there forever," he called after me, but his words didn't slow me down.

Navigating the step up to the house was a little trickier, but I got through the front door without too much drama.

"Sweetheart, is that you?" Mom shouted from somewhere inside the house. The sugary sweet smell in the air suggested she was in the kitchen, baking up a storm, no doubt.

"Yeah, Mom. I'm going upstairs."

It was like being a teenager again, hiding out in my room in between school and practice.

I made a beeline for the stairs, determined to drag myself up them if I had to.

But the second I grabbed the rail and attempted to pull myself up, my dad rushed over, looking every bit as disappointed as I felt.

"You shouldn't be doing this right after PT. You'll overdo it."

"I can do it."

"And risk doing more damage? Be sensible, Son."

"Fine," I huffed.

Dad slid his arm around my waist, taking most of my weight. "You know, you weren't this difficult when you were a teenager."

"I wasn't facing a potentially career-ending injury then, Dad."

"You tore your MCL, Con," he chuckled. "It could have been worse."

"Guess I should count myself lucky then."

"Connor, that's not—" He stopped himself, letting out a heavy sigh. "You need to snap out of this, Son. You will recover, and you will play hockey again. It might take longer than you want, and you might have some setbacks along the way, but you're a determined young man. You've just got to find that again.

"You should invite the guys over," he added. "I'm sure your mom would enjoy having the team around to fuss over."

"Yeah, not going to happen."

"Son, you are still very much a part of the team. You can't cut yourself off. It isn't healthy."

Did he think I didn't know that? But thoughts of being anywhere near my teammates or the ice right now made me want to puke.

It would be like dangling their poison of choice in front of an addict and telling them they couldn't have a taste.

Cruel and unnecessary.

At least, that's what it felt like.

I wished my team luck for the rest of the season. I did. But I couldn't yet figure out how I factored into that.

Right now, given the choice, I'd hole up in my room until after graduation.

"I'm worried about your mental state, Son. Too much sitting around and wallowing isn't good—"

"Save me the speech, Dad. I'm fine. I'll be fine. It's just going to take some time."

He gave me a disapproving look, probably because he saw straight through my bullshit. But it was all I could offer him.

I was dead on my feet, exhausted from my session with Kieron.

"Tomorrow, I think we should go out. Get some fresh air. Get back into the real world."

"Fine," I said, hoping to placate him.

I had no plans to go anywhere, but if it meant he would leave me the fuck alone, then so be it.

"Connor... it doesn't matter." Dad shook his head a little. "I'll check on you later."

He left me alone, and I curled my fist against the bedsheets, feeling the darkness build inside of me. I was getting used to people leaving me by now. But I welcomed the solace.

The silence.

It was better than feeling their pity. Seeing it in their eyes every time they looked at me or hearing the frustration in their voices.

Dad wasn't wrong, though; I wasn't in a good place. Mentally. Physically. Emotionally. But sometimes, it wasn't as simple as saying, 'Snap out of it.' I had to work through the feelings. Acknowledge them. Sit with them. And hope to fucking God that as my physical capabilities improved, my mood did too.

With a little meticulous maneuvering, I managed to get comfortable on my bed and grabbed my phone. I went straight to my message thread with Ella, re-reading her last text.

> Ella: Good luck at PT today. Jonah and Margo are taking me to the driving range. They've promised me the time of my life. I think me and my sister have very different ideas of a good time. Maybe we can talk later? If you feel up to it?

Guilt roiled inside me. I hadn't replied. And I didn't reply now.

I was glad she was making the most of her time with her mom and sister. But any relief I felt was tinged with bitterness and jealousy.

Instead, I opened the group chat and replied to the guys' messages.

> Connor: Just checking in. PT was a bitch, but I survived.

> Noah: Wondered when you were going to pull your head out of your ass and text us back. You're lucky Rory has your best interests at heart because I was one more day away from driving to Dayton and checking for proof of life.

> Connor: You're such a drama queen.

> Noah: And you're full of shit.

> Austin: Have you spoken to Ella?

> Connor: A few texts back and forth.

Austin: What's up with that?

Connor: Things got a little claustrophobic at my parents' house.

Noah: Is she there for the rest of winter break?

Connor: I don't know.

Part of me wanted her to come back. But the other...

Noah: I hope you know what you're doing.

Austin: Holden has a point, Con.

Connor: Since when do you give a shit about our relationship?

Austin: Dude, you were going to propose. Now she's with her mom and you're stuck in Dayton.

Fucker. I ground my teeth together, hating that he was right.

Connor: Some space will do us both good.

Noah: You don't think you'll have enough of that when she's back in Lakeshore and you're not?

Frustrated, I turned off my cell phone and closed my eyes.

It was the cowardly way out, but I didn't feel much like facing reality today.

Or ever.

"Connor, love, can I come in?" Mom poked her head around the door. "Sorry, did I wake you?"

"I must have fallen asleep. What time is it?" I murmured.

"A little after five. You've got a visitor." She grinned, and a bolt of anguish went through me.

I'd wondered how long Ella would stay away before she came back to kick my ass and tell me to get a grip.

Apparently, not very long.

"I can tell her you're not up to visitors, though, if you want me to?"

"What? No." I managed to sit up. "Don't send her away, Mom."

Her smile grew. "Your father said seeing her would cheer you up. Sara, love, you can come up. He's awake."

What. The. Fuck?

"Sara?" I hissed. "What—"

"There he is." She burst into the room, her expression softening when she saw me. "Oh, Con, I'm so sorry."

"What are you doing here?"

She hesitated a second, a flash of uncertainty in her gaze as she glanced at my mom.

"Your father... we thought it might be a nice surprise."

"Maybe this wasn't such a good idea," Sara said, obviously sensing the tension in the room.

What did she expect? They'd ambushed me.

Completely and utterly ambushed me.

"Don't be silly," Mom gave her a reassuring smile. "Connor could do with a friendly face. He's sick to the bone of Ted and me fussing over him. You two catch up, and I'll go get you both a drink."

"Mo—" But she disappeared, leaving me alone with Sara.

"Oh, Con. I've been so worried." She came and perched on the edge of my bed.

"You have?" My brows knitted together.

"Of course I have. I know what hockey means to you. The future. You must be going out of your mind."

"I appreciate the concern, Sara. I do. But what are you doing here? Aren't you supposed to be in Quebec with Émile for the holidays?"

Her whole demeanor changed as tears sprang into her eyes. And she said something I never expected to hear.

"He ended it, Con. Émile ended it."

CHAPTER 24

ELLA

I LASTED at Mom's house for a week.

I loved her and Margo dearly, but being home and having my life constantly scrutinized and picked apart by the two of them was exhausting.

So I packed my things and headed back to Dayton to surprise Connor.

Our conversations had been strained to say the least. New Year had rolled around, and nothing had changed. I needed to see him. I needed to look him in the eye and know that we were okay.

Still, by the time I turned into the Morgans' driveway, I was a nervous wreck.

Shouldering the door, I climbed out and quickly checked my appearance in the glass. I probably should have called ahead, but I figured it would only have given him a chance to put me off coming, and we needed to talk, to clear the air.

From his vague, clipped replies, I knew he was still in a bad place. But hopefully, he wouldn't be too pissed about my surprise visit.

Inhaling a steady breath, I gave myself a little pep talk and headed for the front door.

A few seconds after ringing the bell, it swung open to reveal Ted.

"Ella," he said coolly. "What are you doing here?"

"Sorry for the unannounced visit, but I thought I'd surprise Connor. How is he?"

"He's been better actually the last couple of days."

"He has?" I frowned.

That's not the impression I'd gotten from his brief messages.

"Yes, it's like we've got the old Connor back."

"That's... good." There was something in his eyes. Something that had me on edge.

"Well, in you come. He's up in his room. You can go straight up."

"Thank you." I slipped past him, nervous energy bouncing around my stomach, which was ridiculous. It was Connor.

My Connor.

I wasn't supposed to feel nervous about seeing my boyfriend.

Quietly, I ascended the stairs, playing out our reunion in my mind. I wanted him to be happy to see me, relieved even, but if he wasn't, I'd deal with it. Because I meant what I'd said. I would stand by him no matter what.

I was so wrapped up in my thoughts that I almost didn't notice the laughter drifting out of his room.

My lips curved into a smile. He was laughing. Connor was laughing, and it was such a glorious sound.

Eager to see him, I hurried to his door and knocked once.

"Yeah?"

I turned the handle and slipped inside. "Surprise," I sang, my heart fluttering in my chest the second my eyes landed on him sitting upright on his bed, a huge smile crinkling his eyes.

"El?" He blanched, the blood draining from his face as his expression crumpled. "What are—"

"Ella, this is a surprise."

I hadn't noticed her sitting there. But I saw her now, staring at me with a knowing glint in her eyes.

"Sara." Dread snaked through me, my heart tumbling in my chest as I glanced from her to Connor and back again. "What are you doing here?"

"Connor didn't tell you? I've been staying here for a few days."

"No"—my gaze slid to his, full of hurt and anger—"he didn't."

"I can explain," he said, a flash of guilt in his eyes. "It's not what you think."

"Honestly, I don't know what to think right now."

He'd been laughing because of her.

The last time I'd seen him, he had barely been able to say two words to me.

"Émile broke things off," he went on. "Sara got a flight home, and my mom and dad offered to let her stay here while she figures things out."

"I bet they did," I murmured.

So much for thinking Helena and I had finally found some common ground.

I studied Sara. She didn't seem very upset for someone nursing a broken heart and the aftermath of a called-off engagement.

"I'm sorry about Émile," I said, barely keeping the skepticism out of my voice.

"It was a shock. But I'm dealing." She flashed me a saccharine smile. "Connor's been helping keep me sane."

"Is that so?"

"El," he whispered, reaching for me, but I snatched my hand away, ice trickling in my veins.

Of all the things I'd expected to find when I got here, this was the furthest thing from my mind.

"Sara, give us a minute," he said.

"Of course. I'm sure you have a lot of catching up to do." She got up and walked over to him, and my heart stuttered in my chest.

Don't do it.

Don't you dare fucking do it.

Everything inside me went unnaturally still as she

leaned down and pressed a lingering kiss to his cheek.

Connor had the sense to pull away and put some space between them, but the damage was done.

While I'd been at home, worrying every second of the day that I'd done the wrong thing by leaving him, he'd been here. With her.

Laughing and joking... with her.

"I'll be right downstairs if you need me."

I choked out a bitter laugh. "I think we'll be fine."

She gave me a smug little smile as she walked out of the room.

"El, babe, I can explain." Connor looked nauseous.

"You mean you can explain now." Confusion washed over him, and I added, "You mean you can explain because I caught you. Not because you ever planned on telling me that she was here."

"That's not... you're right." He inhaled a nervous breath. "I didn't know how to tell you. She just showed up, and she was so upset. I didn't want to tell them to make her leave."

"Yeah, I can see just how upset she is," I seethed, my blood boiling at the fact he could sit there and lie to my face.

"It isn't like that. She's a friend, that's all."

"Oh, she's a friend now? Before Thanksgiving, you told me she wasn't anyone but an old family friend. And now she's here, in your room, making you laugh when that's my job, Connor."

The tears came thick and fast, blood roaring in my

ears. "I'm supposed to be the one you turn to, the one to make you laugh. Do you have any idea how painful it was hearing you laugh and then to find out she was the reason for it."

"I fucked up." He dragged a hand down his face.

"Yeah, you did. I thought I'd come and surprise you and show you that I'm here, Con. I'm by your side no matter what. God, I am such an idiot."

"I'm sorry."

"Are you? Because from where I'm sitting, you don't look sorry. You look guilty. You look like somebody who got caught."

"Nothing happened." He held up his hands. "I swear, we've just been helping each other."

"Helping each other?" I scoffed, barely keeping a hold of the torrent of emotions raging inside me. "Helping each other, how exactly?"

"Sara isn't involved with the team. She isn't a part of my life. It's easy to talk to her about stuff."

"Wow, okay." He might as well have ripped out my heart and trampled all over it. "I really don't know what to say to that. This was clearly a mistake. I think I should go."

"Ella, come on. Don't go. We need to talk about this. I realize it looks bad, but I... I just needed to talk to someone."

"And it had to be her?" I glared at him, frustration bleeding into my voice.

How could he do this to me?

To us?

"It's hard to explain, but I swear to you, it's not what you think."

"She wants you, Connor. You have to know that."

"Babe, come on. She just got her heart broken. Émile—"

"Stop defending her," I shrieked. "For all you know, she broke things off with Émile and came back here for you."

"That's reaching," he said with a heavy sigh.

"Is it? You don't think it's a little bit weird that she turns up when things between us are strained. I mean, your dad obviously couldn't wait for me to stumble in on the two of you."

"He sent you up here?" His expression darkened.

"How do you think I got into the house? Come on, Connor. It's obvious that they're both hoping to use this to their advantage."

"That's not it at all, El. You're just being over-emotional."

"Over-emotional, wow." I started to pace.

This couldn't be happening. It couldn't be—

"Shit, that's not... Babe, can we just start over? I missed you. I missed you so fucking much."

"Missed me so much that you couldn't pick up the phone? That you couldn't tell me the truth about Sara being here? Because from where I'm standing, it doesn't seem like you missed me very much at all."

A fresh wave of tears rolled down my cheeks as I felt

something fracture inside my chest. "I came here for you..."

"I know, babe, I know. Fuck... *fuck*." He slammed his fist down on the bed, the anger in his voice making me flinch. "Shit, El, I—"

"I'm going to go back to Lakeshore."

"What? No. We need to talk about this."

"I think we need space."

"Space? What the fuck are you saying?" Panic etched into his expression.

But it was too late.

"I love you, Connor. I love you more than anything, but I can't do this."

It would be so easy to forgive him for this, to be rational and realize that it was Ted and Sara scheming behind our backs, but I couldn't do it.

I couldn't forget the sound of his laughter. Laughter that was for her.

"You won't stick around to talk things out?" He spat. "That's some bullshit right there."

"Let me put it to you another way." My voice trembled with devastation. "If our roles had been reversed, and you'd found me laughing in my bedroom with my ex, would you have stuck around?"

His expression darkened. "That's not fair."

"Isn't it?"

"El, don't do this. I'm begging you. I need you. I need *you*, babe."

I moved to the door, my heart begging me to stay,

trying to override my head's signals to leave and get some perspective.

"Don't worry," I gave him a sad smile, wondering if he could hear the sound of my heart breaking in my chest. "I'm sure Sara will be ready and waiting to fill my shoes."

I knocked again, praying she would answer. If she didn't, there was every chance I would sink to the floor and lie there until somebody found me.

I was exhausted.

Broken and lost.

"Ella?" Rory gawked at me. "What—"

"Can I come in?"

"Of course. What happened? Ella?" She hurried after me as I moved through her apartment to the kitchenette.

"Do you have wine?"

"I... uh, maybe." Her eyes drilled holes into the back of my head as I started rifling through her cabinets. "Bottom cabinet, under the sink."

I crouched down and yanked it open, pulling out a bottle of liquor. "Vodka, even better." Grabbing a glass off the drainer, I turned it the right way up and poured myself a large glassful.

"Ella?" Rory grimaced as I knocked it back in one,

retching the second I was done.

"That was... disgusting."

"Want to tell me why we're drinking vodka at four thirty in the afternoon?"

"Because my boyfriend is a liar and cheat, and it's either drink away my sorrows or call up an ex and give him a taste of his own medicine."

"Okay, that's a lot to unpack. Shall we sit?"

"Fine." I took the vodka with me.

It was extreme, yes. But the ride back to Lakeshore U had provided me with zero distractions from the cruel, tortuous thoughts running through my head.

I'd left Connor. Again. Only this time, Sara was there to help pick up the pieces.

An ugly sob spilled from deep inside me, and Rory shifted closer, taking my hand. "Ella, you're scaring me."

"She was there."

"Who?"

"Sara. Connor's ex. The girl his dad wishes he was with."

"I'm still not following. Sara is where?"

"At his parents' house. She's been staying there."

"What? That doesn't make any sense. Noah talked to Connor just yesterday, and he never mentioned— Oh."

Oh, indeed.

"I'm sure there's a reasonable explanation," she quickly added.

"He only wanted to explain because he got caught." I drank straight from the bottle. It was easier that way and would hopefully get into my bloodstream quicker.

"I'm not sure that is a good idea." Rory took the bottle away from me.

"I think it's a great idea. I'm going to get drunk, eat my weight in cookie dough ice cream, and then fall asleep on your couch."

"You know you can stay here. Anytime. But maybe you should call Co—"

"No. Nope." I mushed her lips together. "We are not saying his name today. He doesn't deserve it."

"El, you're hurting."

"Hurting? I'm devastated, Rory. You should have heard them laughing together like old friends." *Like more than old friends.* "Then she kissed him—"

"What?"

"Well, it wasn't a kiss kiss, but she had this smug look on her face like she knew she'd hurt me. I hate her."

"She sounds horrible."

"Apparently, her fiancé broke things off, but I don't buy it for a second. She wants Connor."

"So you left him... with her?"

"I couldn't stay there, Rory."

"And I get it. But Ella, this is Connor we're talking about. He would never do anything to hurt you."

"Before. He would never do anything to hurt me *before* his injury. But it's like I don't even know who he is anymore. He completely shut me out, Rory. And if I hadn't caught him with Sara red-handed, I don't think he would have told me at all."

"Oh, babe. Come here." She leaned over to pull me into a hug. "He's hurt and scared, and it doesn't excuse his behavior, but I do think it means he probably isn't thinking straight."

"I always thought I would stand by him, no matter what." I pulled away to dry my eyes on the back of my sleeve. "But he crossed a line, Rory. He knew I wouldn't want him to spend time with Sara alone."

But he did it anyway.

And I think that's what hurt the most.

Connor lied to me—or at the very least, he omitted the truth. He had more than one opportunity to tell me Sara was staying there, and he didn't.

Our relationship had always been built on truth and honesty; he'd betrayed that.

And it wasn't something I could just get over.

CHAPTER 25

CONNOR

"Connor? Can I come in?" Sara poked her head around the door.

"I'm not really up to visitors."

"Tough luck. Your mom and dad are really worried. I said I'd come and check on you."

"I'm fine." I glared at the wall, running things over in my head again, wondering how I'd let everything get so out of control.

But all I could see was the devastation on Ella's face as she stood there, silently begging me to fix things.

I'd stalled, though. I'd completely and utterly stalled, and yeah, maybe part of it was because I knew how bad it looked. The second she walked through the door, I knew she would see things that weren't there. Connect dots that didn't exist.

Sara *was* staying at my parents' house. But only because it was the holidays, and she'd arrived upset and freaked out about things with Émile. It had nothing to do with me. They loved Sara like a daughter.

"Con, come on. This is me. We used to tell each other everything." She came over and sat down on the edge of the bed, taking my hand in hers.

"Don't." I snatched it away.

"She'll come around." She exhaled a soft sigh. "She was obviously just feeling a little jealous. You know, you probably should have told her I was here."

No fucking shit.

I pressed my lips into a tight line.

Obviously, it seemed so simple now. But at the time, I didn't want to cause any more issues. Not when she'd already left with us on bad terms.

"We're friends. You're allowed to have female friends, Con," Sara went on. "And you said it yourself. You couldn't talk to her about things the way you could with me."

Fuck. I had said that. But I didn't mean it the way she made it sound.

Sara wasn't a part of my life now. She didn't know me like she used to. Talking to her about everything was like talking to a stranger at a bus stop. There wasn't any judgment or pressure or consequences. I could offload all my worries and fears without worrying that it would change the way she saw me.

Because it didn't matter.

Except, it clearly did matter because shit had hit the fan, and Ella had left.

Again.

"Fuck," I murmured, clenching my fist.

"You're frustrated," Sara said.

"What do you think?" My eyes snapped to hers.

"If she really loves you, she'll come around. It isn't like anything happened between us."

"What the fuck is that supposed to mean?" I glared at her, not liking that glint in her eye.

I'd kept telling myself Sara needed a shoulder to cry on as much as I did. That she was just hurting from her breakup with Émile. And yeah, maybe the fact we had history made things easy between us. But it was never, not once, more than that for me.

"I'm just saying I can see why Ella might be upset. But it's fine because nothing happened."

"I think you should go," I said.

"Connor, come on, don't be like that. We've had a nice few days, haven't we? Just like old times."

Sara stared at me. No, she *gazed* at me—a look of longing in her eyes that slapped me right upside the head.

Fuck my life.

Ella was right.

All this time, she was right.

"Tell me this wasn't all some scheme to get close to me."

"W-what?" She blanched.

"Look me in the eye and tell me you're not here as some bizarre attempt to—"

"Connor, it isn't like that. Your dad thought—"

"Dad? My dad put you up to this?"

"Things with Émile were never going to work." Her expression softened. "We want different things. He wants me to move to Quebec, but Dayton is my home. I don't want to leave."

"Jesus," I hissed, rubbing a hand over my face.

How had I not seen the signs?

Because you didn't want to see them, you stupid fucking idiot.

"Sara, it isn't like that for me. I'm with Ella."

"I know that. But I just thought if we spent some time together. If we—"

"Stop, just stop," I said, firmer this time. "I'm with Ella. I *love* Ella."

"So why did she leave you? If you're such a solid couple, why am I here, and she isn't?"

"That isn't fair, and you know it."

Ella had tried, and I'd been the one to push her away.

Because I was an idiot.

Because I'd let my own fears take over.

"We could be so good together, Connor." Sara swiped the tears out of her eyes, but I only felt pity for the girl I'd once known. "If you just give me a chance—"

"I'm sorry, but it's not going to happen. You should have stayed in Quebec, Sara."

"B-but I felt it. That spark we once had."

"We were fifteen, for fuck's sake. Kids. It was a high school crush."

"Not for me." Sara gave me a sad smile. "I always hoped..." She inhaled a shuddering breath, shifting closer to me.

"What are you—"

She pressed her lips to mine, kissing me. I was so stunned, so fucking caught off guard that I didn't know what to do.

By the time the rational part of my brain caught up, she'd already pulled away.

"What the fuck was that?" I growled.

"Connor, I—"

"Get out. Get the fuck out, and don't come back."

"Wait, I didn't mean... crap, I messed up. But I just thought—"

"I'm serious, Sara. You need to leave." Anger churned inside me, making me vibrate. "You need to leave right fucking now."

"Yes, okay." She got up, worrying her bottom lip with her finger. "I... I'm sorry. It was a mistake. I just thought—"

"You thought wrong." My eyes flicked to the door, hoping she would get the message loud and clear.

"I'm so sorry, Con. I—"

"Go. Just go."

Finally, Sara left, and I released a heavy sigh, hardly able to believe it.

Because you're a fucking idiot, Morgan.

I grabbed my cell phone, desperate to text Ella to tell her what a clusterfuck things were. But when I opened our message thread, a wave of guilt hit me so hard that I dropped my phone on the bed and sagged back against the pillows.

What the fuck was I going to say to make this better? I'd fucked up on so many levels.

I needed to get my head together and figure out how to fix this. Because losing Ella terrified me more than losing hockey. More than never making it to the NHL or never skating again.

But I couldn't just tell her that.

I had to find a way to show her.

"Connor, Son," Dad jumped out of his chair as I hobbled into the kitchen. "What on earth are you doing?"

"We need to talk."

"Yes, well, Sara told us—"

"Really, Dad? How could you?"

"Now, hang on a second, Con. You've been like a different person since she got here. You've been laughing and smiling. If anything, you should be thanking—"

"I want her gone."

"Excuse me?" He gawked at me.

"You heard me, Dad. If you want me to stay here, I want her gone."

"Connor, be reasonable. Sara is—"

"Ted," Mom shook her head. "I think we should listen to him."

"This is ridiculous." He sat back in his chair. "Sara is as good as family. She cares about you. She understands—"

"Dad, you need to stop this. I'm with Ella. I *love* Ella. And look," I exhaled a long breath, "I didn't want to tell you like this, but I plan to ask Ella to marry me."

If she ever forgave me.

But I'd make sure she did. What we had wasn't temporary or fleeting. It was the foundation of a future.

A forever.

"Oh, sweetheart," Mom came over and hugged me, kissing my cheek. "I'm so sorry. Ella is a wonderful young woman."

"Helena," Dad snapped. "Don't encourage him, for Pete's sake. He has his entire future to think about. He can't get married. Connor, Son, I know you think you're ready to settle down—"

"I don't think, Dad. I know it. Ella is it for me. She is the only person I want by my side when I move to

Philadelphia. And if you actually gave her a chance, you'd realize she only wants to be there for me."

"I just think you're rushing into this, Con. It's been a year. You're in college. You're not the same person now as you will be in two or five or ten years. You can't possibly know that Ella is the one."

"Ted." Disappointment laced Mom's words. "This is Connor's decision."

"Yes, well, I think he's making the wrong one."

"And if it was Sara?" I asked, failing to keep the frustration out of my voice. "Would you think it was a bad idea then?"

He stared at me, his silence speaking a hundred words.

"I don't know what's worse," I said. "That you can't give Ella a chance or that you can't trust that I know my own heart. I'm going to ask Kieron if he can recommend a PT in Lakeshore."

"Connor, don't be ridiculous." His expression crumpled. "You can't leave now."

"Actually I can, and I will."

And that's exactly what I intended to do.

"Come on, babe. Pick up, pick up."

Ella's cell rang out a few more times, and I threw mine down in frustration.

I needed to talk to her. I needed to explain.

But she had ignored all my calls.

Opening our message thread, I typed out a text.

Connor: El, babe. Please pick up. I know I screwed up. But I need to talk to you, please.

I waited.

And waited.

But she didn't reply.

"Fuck. *Fuck.*" I fisted my thigh.

My plan to move back to Lakeshore relied on someone giving me a ride there and getting a good PT.

Pulling up Noah's name, I opened our thread.

> Connor: I need a favor.

> Noah: No can do, I'm team Ella for this one.

> Connor: What the hell is that supposed to mean?

> Noah: It means Ella is currently asleep on our couch after drinking her body weight in vodka and then puking all over herself.

Shit.

The pit in my stomach churned wider.

> Connor: She's at Rory's place?

> Noah: Our place.

> Connor: You live there now?

> Noah: We're talking about it.

> Connor: Okay, I really don't know what to say to that. Congratulations, I guess. Is Ella okay?

I didn't want to talk about Noah and his happy life, I wanted to know my girlfriend was okay.

> Noah: She got here about three hours ago. I'd say tell me it isn't true but I'm guessing from the state she's in, it is... what the fuck were you thinking?

> Connor: It's not what you think.

> Noah: It never is. I know you're having a hard time right now, but Ella is one of the best I know, Con. You fucked up.

> Connor: I'm going to fix it.

> Noah: You better be prepared to do some major groveling because something tells me you're going to have your work cut out for you.

> Connor: I need to sort out a few things but then I'm coming back to Lakeshore.

> Noah: About fucking time.

> Connor: I might need a ride...

No way my dad would take me after the bombshell I dropped earlier, and Mom didn't like driving outside of her comfort zone.

> Noah: Practice starts back up in six days.

Fuck, of course, it did.

But I had bigger things to worry about right now, like getting back in my girlfriend's good graces.

> Connor: Do me a favor and don't tell Ella you spoke to me.

> Noah: What are you up to?

> Connor: I don't know yet.

But whatever it was, it needed to be epic.

> Connor: When do Harper and Mase get back?

Apparently, they were moving into Rory's old room. I didn't blame Mason for wanting to get out of Lakers

House now he had a steady girlfriend, and Harper hated her dorm room on campus.

Besides, come summer, Austin and I would be gone. Noah too by the looks of it.

Fuck, that seemed strange to think about. Some of us were moving on. Leaving the team. Leaving Lakeshore.

I guess it had never really hit me before now that it would be the end of an era.

My phone chimed, and I read Noah's reply.

> Noah: They're not coming back until the day before practice.

So with Austin and Noah's help, I could maybe pull something off before the season resumed for the team.

Because fuck knows, I needed all the help I could get.

CHAPTER 26

ELLA

"Welcome back to the land of the living," Noah loomed over me.

"Ugh," I groaned, my stomach roiling as I tried —*and failed*—to sit up. "What time is it?"

"A little after ten. Quite the show you put on last night."

"Oh God, I am so sorry. I didn't—"

"Relax. We all need to drown our sorrows at the bottom of a vodka bottle at one point or another. Here." He handed me a glass of water and a packet of Advil. "Something tells me you're going to need this."

"Something tells me you'd be right." I snatched them from him and chugged down the water before popping two pills onto my tongue and swallowing them back with another mouthful.

"Better?" he asked.

"A little, thanks. Where's Rory?"

"She popped over to the house to check in on Austin. He invited her over for breakfast, and she didn't want to cancel on him. So you're stuck with me, unfortunately." He studied me. "Want to talk about it?"

"Nope."

"Well, I'm team Switzerland. So if you do want to talk, I'm all ears." He went to walk away, but I called after him.

"Has Connor ever talked to you about his ex?"

"I didn't even know Connor had an ex." He turned back. "As far as I knew, his relationship experience starts and ends with you, Ella."

"You're just saying that."

"I swear on Rory's life I'm not. Do I know Sara exists? Yeah, sure." He shrugged. "But Connor has only ever mentioned her once or twice in passing and never in an ex-capacity."

Of course, he was saying that. I was hungover on his and Rory's couch, and he was one of the best people I knew.

"They were fifteen."

"See." He grinned. "Doesn't even count."

"They lost their virginity to each other."

"Ah, okay." His brows pulled together. "I could see how that might be a small problem."

"She's been staying at his parents' house, and he didn't tell me."

"Shit."

"Yep."

My eyes fluttered closed as I inhaled a shaky breath. Everything inside me felt wrong but nothing more than the ache in my heart.

"You want me to leave you to sleep it off?"

"No," I sighed. "I should probably head back to my place."

"You don't have to leave yet."

"I should." I tried to sit up, but the room spun as I separately tried to grab onto thin air.

"Okay, you're going nowhere. I'll take you back to your place later. But for now, hydrate." He nodded toward the glass of water I'd placed on the table. "And I'll see what we have that might soak up some of the liquor."

Noah walked off, but I called after him. "Noah?"

"Yeah?" he asked over his shoulder.

"Thank you."

"Any time, El." His mouth quirked. "You're Connor's girl, which makes you a Lakers girl. And we look out for our own."

He winked before heading into the kitchenette. I stayed put on the couch but managed to sit up and locate my cell phone.

The battery was low, but I had enough bars to check my messages. There was one from last night.

> Connor: El, babe. Please pick up. I know I screwed up. But I need to talk to you, please.

Ugh. The last thing I wanted while I felt like this was Connor trying to talk his way out of the giant hole he'd dug for himself.

So I switched off my cell and dropped it on Rory's coffee table.

He could stew for a little bit longer. Sit with his guilt and regret.

And hopefully, realize what a big mistake he'd made.

Later that afternoon, I thanked Noah and Rory for their hospitality and went home.

Except, I didn't go to my apartment. I went to the guys' house on the edge of campus.

"This is a surprise," Austin said as the door swung open. "But I'm afraid Connor isn't here."

"Haha. Very funny." I shoved his shoulder as I slipped past him.

"Come in, why don't you? Make yourself at home," he murmured, following me down the hall to the kitchen. "Heard last night was fun."

God, they were worse than girls sometimes—forever gossiping in their little group chat.

"I was burning off some steam."

"Morgan fucked up."

"I don't want to talk about it," I said.

"He said he's been trying to text you—"

I whirled around on Austin, glowering at him. "I don't want to talk to him."

"El, come on..."

"Don't El me. I'm pissed and hungover, and I really need something to eat."

"Rory and Noah didn't feed you?"

"They offered, but I couldn't stay there. They're too happy." A heavy sigh rolled through me.

"Tell me about it," he murmured. "Come on. I'll make you something to eat."

That surprised me.

Austin wasn't the kind of guy to offer a shoulder to cry on. He definitely wasn't the kind of guy to cook for anyone. But I let him move ahead of me anyway and followed him into the kitchen.

"Sit," he ordered.

"Are you always this bossy?"

"Are you always such a pain in the ass?" A faint smirk traced his lips.

I poked my tongue out at him as I sat down and dropped my head onto my arms. I felt bad, if not worse than I did this morning.

"Very mature comeback you have there."

I flipped him off, and his deep chuckle filled the room.

"Okay, party girl, what are you in the mood for? Pancakes? Bacon? Grilled cheese?"

"Nothing too heavy," I murmured without looking up at him.

I felt like death.

But it was more than that—I was off-kilter.

Freezing Connor out wasn't natural. He was my person. My sun. My entire world centered around him, and without him, I felt like I was drifting.

Lost.

Afloat without an anchor.

I couldn't just forgive and forget, though.

Not this time.

Austin banged and slammed his way around the kitchen, but I left him to it, keeping my head rested on my forearms. Maybe coming here had been a mistake, but I didn't want to go back to my empty apartment. And although I didn't want to talk to Connor yet, I wanted to feel close to him.

"Here you go. It's the best I could do."

I lifted my head to find Austin pushing a plate of pancakes and bacon toward me.

"I'm impressed." I gave him a weak smile. "It smells good."

"Yeah, well, I'm not completely useless." He moved back to lean against the counter. "So you haven't talked to Con?"

"Nope. I'm not sure I'm ready to hear all his excuses."

"But you're not going to do anything stupid like break up with him, right?"

His words hit me right in the chest, but I masked the agony. "Would you care if I did?"

"Come on, El. I'm not heartless. Connor is one of my best friends. You're his girl. If the two of you don't make it, there's no hope for the rest of us."

Something about his words caught my attention, and I narrowed my eyes, studying him.

"What?" he barked.

"What's going on with you?"

"Nothing, why?"

"I think you're lying."

"Because I took pity on you and made you breakfast?"

"You're acting weird."

It wasn't the first time I'd gotten that vibe from him. Something was different.

Something—

"You met somebody," I said.

"No, I didn't."

"I think you did."

He had that glow—well, the male equivalent, anyway. He seemed lighter somehow. Less abrasive. Soft in a way that only the right person could soften someone as prickly as a guy like Austin Hart.

"You don't know what the fuck you're talking about. I didn't meet anyone."

"Okay, but I'd put money on you hooking up with someone new. Someone you like."

He scoffed, but I caught a slight flush to his cheeks.

Austin *had* met someone.

And if she'd smashed her way through his icy exterior, she had to be pretty damn special.

"I never kiss and tell." The corners of his mouth twitched, and I chuckled.

"Oh, you've got it bad, goalie."

"I have not."

"Whatever you say, hotshot. But you know, it's nice to see you smile."

His whole demeanor shifted, that familiar shadow falling over his expression. "Yeah, well, don't go gossiping to the girls. Especially Rory. It's just a bit of fun." He shrugged like it was nothing.

But it wasn't nothing.

"I won't breathe a word of it." I mimicked zipping my lips, and he rolled his eyes.

"Why are you here again?"

My heart sank. "I didn't want to go back to my empty apartment."

"Well, I'm headed out soon, but you're welcome to stick around. I'll be back later."

"With your 'bit of fun?'" I grinned, and he glowered back.

"Not funny."

"Oh, come on. It was pretty funny." I tucked into the pancakes, small bites at first, to test my stomach's capacity for food. But they were so good I had no problem clearing the plate.

"Good?" Austin asked.

"So good, thank you."

He gave me a small nod. "You going to be okay if I head out?"

"I'll be fine. Thanks for brunch."

He nodded again, making a beeline for the door.

"Austin," I called after him.

"Yeah?"

"You deserve to be happy, you know."

A flash of something passed over him, but it was gone in an instant, and he strolled out of the kitchen as if nothing ever happened.

I kept my phone turned off for a whole four hours and twenty minutes. But in the end, curiosity got the better of me.

Part of me expected to find hundreds of messages from Connor, or at least a few.

There was only one, though.

> Connor: I'm sorry. I fucked up. I know that. But I need you to know, I love you. I love you so fucking much, El. It's you. It's been you ever since freshman year. So don't give up on me just yet... because I'm going to fix this. I swear.

Emotion slammed into me, a garbled sob getting caught in my throat.

I hated this.

Hated that we'd ended up here. Me in Lakeshore hurt and embarrassed, and Connor in Dayton also hurt and struggling with things.

But pride prevented me from forgiving him so easily. Because maybe a part of me—the fragile, nervous part that worried about the future—needed him to make an effort. To offer an olive branch.

To show me that he wanted the future he so often painted for us.

It wasn't that I wanted to test his loyalty or even his love for me, but sometimes you needed more than words.

You needed actions.

> Ella: I love you too, Connor. That hasn't changed...

> Connor: Fuck, babe. I didn't think you would reply. I should never have let you walk away again. I'm an asshole.

Soft laughter spilled out of me.

> Ella: Yeah, you kind of are.

Connor: I deserve that. Noah said you got pretty drunk last night.

> Ella: Noah has a big mouth.

Connor: I just needed to know you're okay.

> Ella: I will be.

Connor: And I meant what I said, I'm going to fix this, El.

> Ella: Okay.

Connor: That's all you've got, kitten? That's okay, baby, I can work with that. I love you, Ella Henshaw. And I don't see a future without you in it.

My heart fluttered at his sweet words, but it didn't change the fact he'd hurt me. And if I hadn't caught the two of them together...

I didn't want to consider that.

I didn't think Connor would ever cheat on me, but I didn't trust Sara in the slightest.

And he was in a dark place. A place I hadn't been able to pull him out of, and *she* had.

God, I hated it.

Hated that I couldn't give him what he needed in his moment of despair.

It wasn't a nice feeling, but I tried really hard to remember that he was going through something huge. And sometimes, when people were hurting, they lashed out at those closest to them.

I didn't text him back.

If he meant it, he'd prove it.

At least, that's what I told myself as I clutched Connor's pillow and inhaled his familiar scent.

Wishing, more than anything, that he was here.

CHAPTER 27

CONNOR

"Good, that's good. Just a little more. Good work." Kieron held out his fist to me, and I bumped it with my own as I slumped back against the bed.

Everything waist down hurt, muscles I wasn't even aware I had aching and burning. But I was determined to make the most of my time with him before I headed back to Lakeshore in a couple of days.

Between him and Coach Tucker, I'd found a good PT there who came highly recommended. And for the first time since hitting the ice, I felt hopeful.

Ella was replying to my texts. My range of motion was better since having my knee brace unlocked, even if the flexion exercises were killer. And I was going back to Lakeshore soon.

"Feeling okay?" Kieron eased my leg into a stretch, and I nodded. "You seem different."

"Pulled my head out of my ass, didn't I?" I smirked.

"Just don't go getting ahead of yourself. You've got a long way to go yet."

"I know, but it feels good to be clearheaded."

"Good. And the girlfriend?"

"I'm working on it."

"Good for you. That could definitely be a positive motivator."

"Seriously?" I arched a brow, not liking the smug look on his face.

"Like you haven't thought about it."

Only every second of every day.

I missed Ella—the feel of her curves in my hands, the warmth of her skin. I missed her hair fanned over my chest when we cuddled in bed—the taste of her lips.

I just missed her.

But I couldn't rush this.

I needed to go back to Lakeshore one hundred and ten percent ready to fix things, which meant biding my time for a couple more days before Noah came to get me.

Dad wasn't happy about it, but I really didn't give a shit.

I needed Ella.

Even when I thought I didn't need her—*especially* then.

My relationship with her was non-negotiable as far as I was concerned. I just needed to prove that to her.

Which was turning out to be quite a headache given my current physical limitations.

But I had a plan.

"I like you a lot, Kieron," I said. "But I am not discussing my girl with you."

He held up his hands. "Point taken. She's a good influence on you, though. And as you move through rehab, you're going to need that." He tweaked something on my brace and stepped back. "Okay. I think we're done here."

Slowly, I edged off the bed and stood with the aid of my crutches. It would still be a week or so before I could bear weight. But I'd get there.

"Good luck, Connor. I don't doubt I'll see you on ESPN come fall."

"I hope so."

That overwhelming sense of dread filled my chest, but I didn't allow it to consume me. I could feel scared and hopeless, but I didn't have to let those intense feelings define me.

Because I had too much to lose.

Too much to fight for.

I was down, yeah. But I wasn't down and out. Not yet.

"Thanks for everything," I said.

"Anytime. Now go get your girl." He winked, and I barked a gruff laugh.

That was the plan.

"Noah, how nice to see you again," Mom pulled him into a hug.

"Hey, Mrs. M. Looking good."

"Still a sweet talker, I see." She smiled, holding him at arm's length. "And Aurora, how is she doing?"

"She's good, thanks."

"Little Hart didn't want to make the trip?" I asked.

"Figured we needed some guys' time," he said.

"How lovely," Mom cooed. "Can I get you anything? A drink? Something to eat? I just baked a fresh batch of cookies."

"No, thank you. It's only a flyby visit."

"Noah's right. We're going to head off as soon as the truck is loaded."

"Oh, sweetheart, I'm going to miss you." She held out her arms, and I hobbled over.

"It's okay, Mom. I'll see you again soon."

"I'm so sorry it ended like this," she whispered, hugging me tight. "I love you, Connor. We both do. Your father's pride gets the better of him sometimes."

"Yeah." A weary sigh escaped me.

He couldn't even make it home to say goodbye, but he was the one that would come to regret it, not me.

"I'll take your things out to the truck."

"Thanks," I said to Noah.

"I'm so proud of you, Connor. And Ella is such a lucky girl to have you."

"Nah, I'm the lucky one."

"Yes, well, she's quite the young woman."

"I really fucked up, Mom."

"I know, sweetheart. But something tells me it won't take much to earn her forgiveness."

"I hope not."

"Oh, Con. Come here." She hugged me again, holding on like she didn't want to let me go. "You are going to get through this, love. Both of you! If you need anything—"

"Thanks, Mom. But I need to do this."

"I know, love. I know." She kissed my cheek.

"All set?" Noah returned, hovering by the front door.

"I think so."

Fuck, this was it.

Going back to Lakeshore meant facing everything head-on.

Mom waved us off, and Noah helped me into the truck. By the time I was in, I was a sweaty, breathless mess.

"Fuck, that hurt," I murmured as he climbed into the driver's seat and buckled up.

"It's good to see your face, you know."

"I would have pulled myself out of it eventually."

"Even if Ella didn't catch you red-handed?" He gave me a skeptical look.

"Come on, Holden. I told you, nothing happened."

"My one piece of advice is to make sure you tell her the whole truth and nothing but the truth because it'll all find its way out eventually."

"Nothing happened. I set Sara straight, and she left."

I hadn't seen or spoken to her since.

Part of me felt bad for her. Unrequited lust or love or whatever the fuck she thought she felt for me wasn't a nice thing, but it had never been like that for me. And I'd never done anything to make her think otherwise.

"So what's the plan?"

"The plan?" I asked.

"Yeah, to fix your mess."

"That's for me to know and you to never find out."

"Oh, it's like that, huh?" he chuckled.

"It's exactly like that."

"How did PT go?"

"Good. I should be able to do some weight bearing exercises soon. Not one hundred percent, but it's better than hopping around."

"Any update on when he thinks you can get back on the ice?"

"It's not going to be before the season ends," I said, my chest tightening.

"If anyone can do it, it's you, Con."

"I just need to focus on getting ready for training camp."

I could live with missing out on my final season with the Lakers. It hurt like a bitch knowing I wouldn't be there with them if they went all the way to the finals. But missing out on my shot at going pro, was something I couldn't accept.

"How is she? Really, I mean."

He cast me a sideways glance as he navigated out of Dayton. "You haven't talked to her?"

"We've had a few texts back and forth, but I'm giving her some space."

"You sure that's a good idea?" His brow lifted.

"I'm coming back, aren't I?"

"About time too. I know your parents meant well, but you're not a kid anymore, Con. Ella can take care of you. We'll all pitch in."

"Thanks. How are things with Rory now you've officially moved in?"

"Fucking amazing." He grinned. "I never thought I'd be into the whole living with your girlfriend thing, but I love it. I love knowing I get to wake up with her. Fall asleep with her. Fuck her whenever I—"

"Jesus, Holden," I muttered, and he laughed.

"Have you seen my girl? I can hardly keep my hands off her."

"I'm happy for you, man. It was about time you found someone to tame your wild ways."

"I was never that bad."

"Keep telling yourself that." My mouth twitched.

"She's still worried about Austin, though."

"Austin will figure it out. Can't be easy watching all your friends settle down."

"I really thought he and Fallon would become something," Noah said.

"She obviously wasn't the right girl."

"It's going to be one hell of a final semester, that's for sure. Shit, sorry, I didn't—"

"Relax, Holden. It's all good."

He regarded me for a second, keeping his hands on the steering wheel. "You know, the team won't be the same without you."

"You still better fucking win. I'm not being the scapegoat for you fucking up your shot at the playoffs."

"You're good, Con. But I think we can handle it."

"Oh, it's like that, huh?"

"Didn't Coach ever teach you there's no I in team?"

"There is in win, though," I shot back, and he burst into laughter.

"It's good to have you back, Con."

"It's good to be back."

At least, I really fucking hoped it was.

It left a bitter taste in my mouth that there was no welcome-back party. Specifically, no Ella standing outside the house waiting to greet me with a kiss and a smile. But she didn't know I was back yet, so I couldn't really hold it against her.

Austin appeared, though, giving me a slight dip of his head as he made his way over to the truck.

He opened my door and said, "Well, well, look what the cat dragged in."

"Am I the cat in this scenario?" Noah snorted. "Because seriously, dude. That's fucking weird."

Austin ignored him, and I laughed. "I see you two are getting along well."

Austin muttered something under his breath about him being a traitor, then took my crutches as I got ready to get out of the truck.

It required a bit of maneuvering and deep breathing, but I managed, Austin taking most of my weight while I got my balance.

"You're like fucking Bambi on ice."

"Fuck you, asshole. Fuck you."

We both laughed as he walked with me up to the house.

"You owe me big time for this," he said.

"Don't worry. I'll pay you back when you find a girl to grovel to."

He punched my arm, making me stumble a little.

"Low blow, asshole," I grunted. "Low fucking blow."

We got inside the house, and something stirred inside me. I'd been away less than a month, but I'd missed this place. Every memory—good and bad—

from the last three years was woven into the fabric of this place, and I was going to miss it a lot when the time came to pack up and move out.

"Did you talk to administration about your classes?"

"Yeah, I can move most of them online."

"That's going to take the pressure off."

"Yeah." I nodded.

I didn't really care about classes. I wanted to graduate, sure. But I wanted to fix things with Ella and cement my place with the Flyers more.

I wanted the future I'd been dreaming of since the night Ella agreed to be mine.

Fuck, I wanted it so much.

Part of me couldn't believe I'd almost ruined it. But I didn't plan on getting injured. I didn't plan on sinking into a black hole that seemed impossible to crawl my way out of.

Life had a way of sneaking up on you and fucking with you. But I was in control of my destiny. I needed to remember that.

"Where you headed tonight?" I asked Austin as he pulled out a chair for me.

His eyes flicked to the door behind me, and I realized he was probably looking for Noah. "I'll figure something out."

"You sure, we can always—"

"It's no big deal. Mason and Harper are back tomorrow afternoon, though, so you might want to wrap up your little love fest before lunch."

I fought a smirk and flipped him off, ignoring the fizzing in my stomach. My plans relied on Ella giving me the time of day.

"So what time is she coming over?" he asked, pulling me from my thoughts.

"Huh?" I blinked at him.

"Ella. What time is she coming over?"

"I... I haven't spoken to her yet." I rubbed the back of my neck, feeling hella awkward.

"Good luck with that then," he clapped me on the shoulder.

"He's screwing with you," Noah came in with my bags. "Ella is chomping at the bit to see you."

"Yeah?" Hope swarmed my chest.

"She loves you, Con. Even if she's pissed, it doesn't change the fact that she's worried about you."

"Just don't do something stupid like propose," Austin snorted.

"I'm not a total idiot," I murmured.

If I proposed now, she'd think it was out of guilt. A Band-Aid for my big fuck up.

"I'm going to run these up to your room, and then I need to head out," Noah said.

"Thanks, I appreciate it."

"Anytime. And good luck tonight. Just remember, be cool and grovel until you can't grovel anymore." He winked.

"He's such an annoying asshole," Austin said, watching Noah walk out.

"You're just bitter about the fact he's moved in with your sister."

"Damn straight, I am. But..." He released a steady breath. "He makes her happy."

"And that only makes it worse?"

"Yep."

"Noah is a good guy, Aus."

"He is. Just didn't ever plan on being in a situation where the asshole could become family one day."

"You don't consider me family? I'm crushed."

Austin rolled his eyes. "I'm out of here. Hopefully, Ella gives you the time of day."

He gave me a salute and left me alone.

And I didn't know which emotion to focus on more. The seed of hope rooted in my chest...

Or the pit of terror churning in my stomach.

CHAPTER 28

ELLA

"You know, staring at it isn't going to make it ring," Rory said.

"I know. I just thought today would be the day he might call."

Connor and I had been texting back and forth for a few days now.

After his big declaration—his promise to fix things—I'd been more forthcoming in responding to his texts.

Texting felt safe somehow. It didn't require me to give up too many pieces of myself. To risk getting my heart hurt all over again.

Oh, who was I kidding? I would be devastated if he didn't make good on his word to fix things.

I missed him.

I missed him so much.

"I'm sure he will," she said, leaning over to pat my hand.

"Thanks, Rory. You've been a good friend through all of this."

"You'd do the same for me." She smiled.

"Except, I didn't. Me and Connor told Noah he should call things off with you and—"

"Ella"—she let out a soft laugh—"stop. It's fine. Everything worked out, didn't it?" I nodded, and she went on, "See. And I'm sure everything will work out with you and Connor. He made a mistake, babe. He's a guy. They do that sometimes."

"Yeah, I know. I think I'll feel better once I've seen him again. At the moment, it's like we're stuck in limbo. I know he wants to fix things. I want to fix things too. But we're both avoiding the hard conversations."

"Or maybe you're just working up to it?"

"I think this is the longest we've ever gone without sex. God, I miss it."

"El!" Rory flushed.

"Come on, babe. You're telling me it wouldn't upset you if you had to go without sex with Noah for a month?"

"Well, I guess, when you put it like that..."

"Aha, I knew it." It was my turn to smile.

"I can't believe it's already January. I'm not ready for you to graduate and leave Lakeshore."

"It's not for a little while yet," I said, that familiar

flutter of excitement laced with panic going through me.

It was different now, though—an added layer of fear compounding everything.

Rory's cell phone vibrated, and she snatched it up. "It's Austin. He wants to know if we want to go over to the house and get takeout."

"I don't know. He might be fed up with me hanging around."

"Not possible," she said, getting up. "Come on. I love my apartment, but the house has so much more space."

"Fine, I guess I could eat but nothing too heavy. Is Noah coming too?"

"I'm not sure. I'll text him."

"Okay," I shrugged, getting up and shoving my feet into my boots.

I quickly checked my cell again, silently wishing it to vibrate or ring or do something.

"Come on; it'll be a good distraction." She gave me a sympathetic smile.

One that made the knot in my stomach tighten.

Because Connor hadn't called, he hadn't texted since this morning either.

And I didn't know what that meant.

"I'd forgotten how cold it can get this time of year," I said, burrowing down into my jacket as we headed towards the guys' house.

"This wind is brutal," Rory said, wrapping her arms around her waist. "Maybe we should have called an Uber."

"It's fine. We're almost there." The house came into view, and my heart did that familiar little flip it always did whenever I came over.

Except, when I walked through the door tonight, Connor wouldn't be there.

"Ahh, don't look so glum," Rory said. "Takeout will make everything better."

I wasn't so sure about that, but I appreciated her attempt at lightening the mood.

When we reached the door, I glanced back to find her hovering. "What are you doing?"

"Noah is on his way. I'm going to wait out here for him."

"You can't wait inside?" I frowned.

"Austin said for us to go straight in. The door is open."

My eyes narrowed with suspicion. "Rory, what's going on?"

"Just go easy on him and hear him out, okay?"

Connor's truck came into view, and she skipped down the driveway. "I'll text you tomorrow."

Oh my God.

They'd ambushed me.

With shaky fingers, I gripped the handle and opened the door. My heart raced as I stepped inside, listening for any sign of life.

"Hello?" I called.

There was a shuffling sound, the soft sound of rubber against the floor, and then Connor appeared. Looking every bit as gorgeous as he always had been.

"Hi, kitten." He smiled, but it didn't quite meet his eyes.

"You're here," I said, hardly able to believe it.

"Surprise." He balanced on his crutches, his biceps straining under his black polo shirt.

"But... I don't understand. You didn't call."

"Because I wanted to surprise you, and I didn't want to give you a chance to decide you weren't ready to see me."

"Connor, I would—"

"Shh, babe. Just let me get this out." He came toward me, his movements smoother than the last time I saw him. "I'm sorry. I won't try and excuse my behavior, and I won't try and blame anyone else. I fucked up. I knew it the second you walked out of my room. But I'm here to make it right. There will never be anyone else for me, Ella. It's you. Today. Tomorrow. Forever."

Tears sprang into my eyes.

He was here.

Connor was here, and he was saying all the right things.

"You look good," I said.

"I'm feeling better. Stronger. I'll be able to bear weight soon."

"That's great."

"Things aren't moving as quickly as I'd like them to be, but I'll get there."

He was different.

More present, with a look of determination etched into his expression that hadn't been there before.

"Can I kiss you?" he blurted out, dipping his head with embarrassment when he realized the words had spilled out. "Shit, El, I didn't—"

"We should probably talk first."

"Yeah, you're right, we should." He nodded, but I didn't miss the slight tic in his jaw. "Go ahead," he said, motioning for me to move ahead of him.

I walked down the hall and into the living room. "Oh my God," I breathed, a rush of emotion coursing through me as my eyes landed on the scene in front of me.

The guys had arranged the sectional to make a bed, complete with Connor's pillows and cover from his room.

Candles flickered on the coffee table and bookshelf, casting a romantic glow around the room.

I glanced back at him, failing to find words.

"I know it isn't much, and I'm not assuming anything will happen." He ran a hand through his hair and down the back of his neck. "But I wanted to do something nice for you. I've ordered your favorite takeout and thought we could hang, maybe watch a movie. No pressure."

"Connor," I choked out, so many emotions warring inside of me.

It was sweet—the sweetest. But it also came loaded with an immense amount of pressure.

"If you're worried I might try to seduce you, I'm still pretty much out of action." He gave me a small uncertain smile.

"Come on, let's sit." I kicked off my boots and climbed up on the couch bed. "This is a nice little setup."

"It's not exactly a sexy look dragging my ass up the stairs."

"I thought you weren't trying to seduce me."

"Doesn't mean I'm not hedging my bets." He smirked, and my heart flip-flopped in my chest.

It took Connor a little maneuvering to join me on the bed, but he managed, leaving a respectable amount of space between us.

I was both relieved and disappointed. I wanted everything to go back to how it was before, but we needed to talk.

To clear the air.

"How have you been since you got back?" he asked.

"Okay, I guess. Rory, Noah, and Austin have kept me company."

"Austin, huh? Do I need to be worried?" My

expression fell, and he cussed under his breath. "Sorry, I'm just nervous."

"I know, it's a little bit weird."

"You feel it too?" I nodded, and he grimaced. "That's all on me. I fucked up. I let you think—"

He stopped himself, dragging a hand down his face. Tension radiated off him, making the air thick and heavy around us.

But I felt just as tense—something I wasn't used to feeling around Connor.

"I want to know what happened," I said, inhaling a sharp breath. "With Sara, I mean."

"Okay."

"I don't want to know the ins and outs of every conversation. It was hard enough hearing you laugh with her. But I need to know if anything else happened, if she tried—"

"She kissed me."

Jealousy surged through me as I swallowed down the rush of tears. "She... kissed you?"

Connor nodded. "After you left."

"Did you—"

"No. Fuck, no, El. I would never. But it caught me off guard. I didn't shove her away as quickly as I should have. But I need you to know there was nothing from my side. Nothing." His eyes pleaded with me. "And I made sure she knew that."

"You did?"

"I told her to get out and never come back. She packed up and left that day."

"Okay."

"Okay?"

"No, Connor," my voice cracked. "It's not okay. She kissed you. After I told you she wanted you, and you reassured me it wasn't like that between you."

"I'm an idiot."

"I can't disagree there." I inclined my head.

"I should have seen the signs. But I didn't. Because honestly, El, you walk into a room, and I only see you."

"Cute but a tad cheesy," I snorted, trying to disguise the ache in my heart.

"You're really going to make me work for this, huh?"

"You hurt me, Connor."

"Shit, babe, I know. I've been in such a bad place, and I didn't know how to let you in. Because I think deep down, I was terrified that if I lost hockey, I'd lose you too."

"Connor." I sighed, my heart crashing wildly in my chest. "I don't love you because you play hockey, or you're headed to the NHL. I love you despite all those things."

"Yeah, I realize that now. Watching you walk away from... it was like suddenly everything fell into place."

"You couldn't have said all this before?"

Before I left Dayton a second time and came back to Lakeshore with my heart in tatters.

"I didn't want it to sound insincere. I knew I'd

fucked up. I knew I needed to work on myself before I came to you with a half-assed apology.

"In an ideal world, I'd be back on two feet, able to get down on my knees and beg for forgiveness. But I couldn't wait that long."

"I'm glad you didn't."

Because that would have been torture.

"I love you, Ella Henshaw. I love you so fucking much. These last few weeks have been some of the shittiest of my life. And I'm sorry. I'm so fucking sorry I pushed you away. But I promise it won't happen again. I need you, El. I need you by my side and in my bed. I need to hear your voice first thing in the morning and feel your body pressed up against mine last thing at night.

"I just need you, babe. Always."

I was crying. Big fat tears rolled down my cheeks and dripped onto my sweater.

"Fuck, babe, don't cry. I can't stand it." He reached over, catching the tears with his thumb. "I love you," he whispered, his words sinking into me and fisting my heart.

"I love you too, so much." Curling my legs beneath me, I went up on my knees to move closer to him. "Don't ever do that to me again." I twisted my fingers in his t-shirt.

He gazed up at me, regret swirling in his dark eyes. "I promise."

Dropping my head to his, I breathed him in. Letting

the familiar scent of his cologne soothe the jagged edges inside me.

I hated that she'd kissed him, that she'd dared to put her hands on my boyfriend. But this moment wasn't about Sara. It was about me and Connor and what we were to one another.

He gently grabbed the back of my neck, inhaling a shuddering breath. "Can I kiss you now?"

Too overwhelmed to reply, I nodded, angling my face right to his, offering myself to him.

The man who owned my heart.

And always would.

CHAPTER 29

CONNOR

Fuck, I loved this girl.

I loved her smile. Her laughter. I loved the way her fingers gripped my t-shirt as I shaped her mouth with my own.

I loved every single thing about her.

"Fuck, baby," I drawled, kissing her deeper. Sliding my tongue against hers, tasting and teasing her.

"Connor," she whimpered.

"I wish I could show you just how sorry I am, kitten." I breathed the words. "Lay you out and fill you up. Spend hours worshiping your body until nothing but my name is left on your lips."

"We should slow down," she said, a little breathless.

I didn't want to slow down. I wanted to speed up. I

wanted to skip to the part where we were both naked, and she was riding me toward ecstasy.

It was all I wanted, and yet—

"Fuck, yeah, okay." I dropped my head to her shoulder, forcing myself to calm the fuck down. "The food will be here soon."

"Sorry, I didn't mean to get you all worked up." Her lust-drunk eyes dropped to the obvious tent in my sweats. "Maybe later, when you've groveled a little more, I can help you out with that."

Fuck. My. Life.

She was perfect. And I hadn't even gotten a proper taste yet.

"I wouldn't say no to that," I admitted. "But I meant what I said earlier. I'll be happy just to be here with you. No pressure."

"We'll see how it goes." A faint smile traced her mouth.

A mouth I could imagine doing all kinds of dirty things to. Because I was only human, and my girlfriend was the most beautiful woman I'd ever laid eyes on. And I hadn't had sex in almost a month.

But I could see the hesitation in her eyes, the uncertainty.

I'd hurt her in a way I hadn't truly comprehended until this moment, and it fucking gutted me.

"We're good, though, right?" I asked, bracing myself for her answer.

"I want us to be. But I won't deny I'm scared."

"Babe—"

"Listen to me, please." Her voice trembled. "I was there for you, Connor. At the hospital. I came to Dayton, but you pushed me away. And I get it. I really do. You went to a dark place. A place I was more than prepared to walk with you. Because that's what we do, that's the kind of couple we are.

"At least, I thought we were."

Silent tears rolled down her cheeks, but I didn't dare touch her again. The brutal honesty in her words was so much worse than I imagined, slicing me open like shards of jagged glass.

"I'm sorry."

"I know, and I appreciate everything you've said. I do. But I can't stop hearing it."

"Hearing what?" My brows knitted.

"Your laugh."

Fuck.

"El, it wasn't—"

"I know. I know. But it doesn't change the fact you did turn to her. You gave her something that's supposed to be for me and only me. I don't think I can just forget that."

"Okay, so what can I do? Tell me what you need from me?"

"Honestly, I don't know."

Awkward silence descended over us. But it was nothing I didn't deserve.

"Do you want to leave?" I asked, scared of her answer. "I can call Noah and—"

"No, I don't want to leave," she said quietly.

Well, that was something.

"Do you want—"

The doorbell rang, and I breathed a sigh of relief. "That'll be the food."

"I'll get it." She hopped up.

And I sat there like a damn fool. Because I was still incapacitated, which meant she could escape me.

She could leave, and I wouldn't even be able to chase her.

"I am so stuffed," Ella placed her container on the coffee table and stretched out on the sectional.

We'd put a lighthearted action movie on while we ate. But I barely tasted my noodles, too fixated on watching her eat. Every now and again, she gave me a small smile.

I figured that was a win.

She was here.

She was smiling.

The rest would follow. Maybe it would take a couple of days or a week or a few months. But I had time.

I had all the time in the world.

"Still your favorite?" I asked, and she looked over at me all dreamy and doe-eyed.

"Yep."

"Good to know."

"Have you talked to Austin much?"

"We've had a few texts back and forth," I said. "Why?"

"I think he's met someone."

"Austin? Our grumpy loveable goalie? That Austin?"

"He's different."

"Just how much time have you two been spending together?"

"Careful, Morgan. You sound awfully jealous."

Oh, I was Morgan now.

It probably shouldn't have turned me on half as much as it did.

Reaching over, I grabbed Ella's ankles and yanked her legs onto my lap. Pulling off her socks, I slowly started massaging her feet.

"God, that feels good," she groaned as I worked my fingers into the arch of her foot.

"Back to Austin," I said.

"I stayed here a couple of nights."

"You stayed here... with Austin?"

"Not *with* Austin. I stayed in your room." She pinned me with a dark look. "Turns out loving someone and hating them is a very fine line."

"You missed me."

"You know I did."

"I missed you too."

"I'm sure you did with Sara so eager to keep you company."

"El..."

"I'm sorry, that was unnecessary. She just makes me so mad."

"She isn't important, babe."

I needed her to know that.

"I'm not only angry at her for making a move on you. I'm angry that she clearly took advantage of you."

"Sara is gone. She knows the deal. She knows I love you. That I want a life and a future with you."

Ella gave me a small nod. "No more Sara talk."

"I think that's a good idea. I know I broke your trust, but it won't ever happen again. I'm ready to face this head-on. I know it's going to be tough. I know things might not work out the way I'd hoped. But I'm ready."

"You'll do it," she said. "I know you will. Shall we watch another movie? I have no idea what's happening right now." Ella flicked her head to the television.

"Sure, you pick something." I offered her the remote, and she scooched closer, cuddling up beside me.

I wrapped an arm around her shoulder and enjoyed the feel of her pressed up against me. "I love you," I whispered as she scrolled through the options.

For a second, I thought that maybe she hadn't heard me.

But then she settled on a movie, hit play, and whispered back, "I love you too."

I woke up with a stiff neck and a dead arm. But it didn't matter.

Ella was curled up beside me, her soft lines fitted to the awkward curve of my body.

We must have fallen asleep, but I couldn't complain. She hadn't left. She hadn't run the second the movie ended.

No, she'd simply handed me the remote and told me to choose another one.

We didn't talk about Sara again or the deep sense of betrayal she felt. But that was okay. I was a patient man. I would wait for her to come around.

"Connor," she murmured.

"It's the middle of the night; go back to sleep."

"Why are you awake?"

"I need to go to the bathroom."

"Can you manage?" She turned over and stared directly at me.

Fuck, she was beautiful, even in the dead of night.

"I should be okay."

But it quickly became apparent I wasn't okay. "Shit," I hissed as I caught my foot on something, agony racing through my leg.

"Okay, let me help."

Ella got up and turned on the lamp. "That's better," she said. "Okay, crutches." She handed me both and stood by while I got to my feet. Well, foot.

"Okay?"

"Yeah."

I tamped down the urge to tell her I'd got it. Because the truth was, I wasn't sure I did. I was tired, a little sluggish from all the Chinese food, and the house was a lot smaller than my parents' place, so everything was a fucking hazard. But with a little help, I managed to get into the small downstairs bathroom.

"Need a helping hand?" Ella asked with a hint of amusement.

"I'm glad you find this funny."

She fought a smile as I slipped into the bathroom and made quick work of it. Unwilling to prolong the event.

Eager to get back to all the cuddling, I came out of the bathroom, misjudged the gap, and clipped my crutch on the door jamb.

"Shit," I muttered, almost falling flat on my face.

"Are you okay?"

"So much for not ruining my sex appeal," I muttered, steadying myself.

"Oh, I don't know." She batted her lashes at me. "You still look pretty hot from where I'm standing."

"Oh yeah?"

"Come on, horndog, let's get you back to bed."

I let her help me partly because I was exhausted and partly because I liked the feel of her hands on me. Liked knowing that she still cared enough to want to help me.

When we got back into the living room, Ella gave me some space to lower myself onto the side of the couch bed.

"You good?" She gazed down at me. The light bounced off her face, making her eyes twinkle.

"Fuck, you're beautiful," I said.

"Connor..."

I hooked my arm around her waist and dragged her between my legs.

"Your knee," she cried.

"Is fine."

It wasn't. It still hurt like a bitch. But the pain was nothing compared to the distance between us.

Ella hung her arms over my shoulders, her eyes searching mine. She pressed her lips together, then flicked her tongue over them.

"Tease," I murmured.

"Sorry, I'm nervous."

"Nervous?" My brow arched. "You don't ever have to be nervous with me."

"It feels different," she admitted.

"Yeah." I ran my hands up and down her lower spine, bringing her closer. "Let me make you feel good, kitten."

"I don't—"

I pushed her sweater up a little and pressed a lingering kiss to her hip bone. Ella's breath caught, a full-body shiver going through her.

She gently raked her fingers through my hair. "God, I missed you."

"Let me make it up to you," I said.

I wanted her.

I wanted her so fucking much, and it pained me that I couldn't take control the way I wanted. But there were other ways.

My hands started to roam, mapping her curves, the swell of her hips. My dick strained against my sweats, desperate to sink inside of her. To feel her warm, wet heat clenched around me.

"Can you scooch against the back of the couch?" Ella whispered.

"I... yeah."

She stepped back and began stripping out of her clothes. Her sweater went first, then her thick leggings. I didn't know where to look.

"Fuck," I choked out as she unclasped her bra and let it fall to the floor.

A million thoughts ran through my head. What had the doctor said about post-surgery sex?

Oh, fuck it. It didn't matter because Ella stood there looking like all my dreams had come true.

"Lie back, Connor," she said softly.

"Yeah, fuck, okay." My heart raced in my chest as I pulled off my t-shirt and worked my sweats off, adding them to her pile of clothes.

I managed to drag myself backward, sitting upright against the back of the couch, my legs stretched out before me.

"How does it feel?" she asked.

"It's okay."

Grabbing one of my pillows, she gently tucked it under my injured leg. "Better?"

I nodded, too fixated on her almost-naked body.

"This will probably be over before it gets started," I admitted as she carefully straddled me.

"I'll go slow." She flicked her hair over one shoulder, letting it cascade down her chest.

I wound my fingers into the back of it, using it to guide her face down to mine. "I love you, Ella."

"I love you too."

This kiss was different from earlier. For one, Ella didn't pull away. She kissed me with slow, teasing strokes of her tongue, her hands smoothing over my chest and down my abs.

Her touch set my body on fire, her hands painting a trail of heat across my skin.

She broke away first, gazing down at me. "You said something about making it up to me."

Holy fuck.

I liked her like this. Demanding and in control.

Curving my hand around the small of her waist, I dipped my head and flicked my tongue over her nipple. Ella's body bowed into me as I massaged her tits, alternating between my hand and my mouth. Licking and biting, shaping and squeezing.

"Connor," she cried, tightening her fingers in my hair.

I didn't know if she was pulling me closer or trying to push me away, but I didn't let up. Reacquainting myself with her body, taking my time to drive her wild.

She writhed above me, gently rocking her hips.

"Can you feel what you do to me?" I asked. "How hard you get me."

"Yes... yes."

She grabbed my face and smashed her lips down on mine, kissing me hard. I felt her desperation in every stroke of her tongue.

Rising on her knees a little, she managed to work my boxers down my hips just enough to free my dick. She didn't ask, didn't stop to give me time to catch up. She hooked her panties to one side and sank down on me in one smooth motion.

"Fuck, El. Fuuuck," I hissed.

"Oh God," she whimpered, taking me to the hilt.

"You good?" I asked, aware of how still she'd gone.

Panic started to rise inside me. What if she regretted this? What if she realized that—

"You're mine," she breathed.

"I am." I nodded my heart damn near bursting out of my chest. "And you're mine."

"I am." A tear slipped down her cheek.

"So show me, kitten. Take what you need. I've got you, baby." I leaned in and brushed my lips over hers in a gentle caress. "I've got you."

CHAPTER 30

ELLA

I was crying.

Riding my boyfriend, his mouth on mine, tears were streaking down my cheeks.

But I hadn't realized just how much I needed this until this very moment.

Him. Me. Us.

"Shh, babe, don't cry," he whispered, his voice a shaky staccato as I slowly rolled my hips.

I didn't want to go too hard or fast, not with it so soon after his surgery, but God, I needed more of him.

His hands gripped my hips, but he didn't try to wrest control, happy to let me set the pace. "You feel amazing," he groaned.

"Connor," I panted, grinding down on him, creating the most delicious friction between us.

"Fuck, baby. Fuck. I'm not going to last."

"It doesn't matter. You feel too good. So, so good."

"But I want you to come first. I need you to come, El." He nuzzled my neck, licking and sucking the skin there.

I grabbed his hand and pushed it between our bodies. "Touch me," I ordered.

"With pleasure." Laughter rumbled through him, the vibrations rushing over my breasts.

He caressed my clit, rubbing in just the right way to make my stomach coil tight and my breathy moans to increase. "That's it, beautiful girl, ride me 'til you come."

"Connor, God it's... ah," I cried, shattering as he started to fuck into me a little harder. A little faster.

"Fuck, El. Fuck, fuck, fuuuck." He jerked inside me, kissing me as he rode out his orgasm. "You are incredible."

"I didn't hurt you?"

"Even if you did, it would have been worth it. I love you, Ella." He gazed at me with so much intensity my heart fluttered wildly.

This was us.

Pure and honest. Nothing between us but the rapid beating of our hearts.

"We're going to be okay," I said, needing to say the words.

Needing him to hear them.

"Yeah, babe, we are." Connor flashed me a grin, melting the final pieces of resolve.

I loved this man.

I loved him without limits. And although he'd hurt me, I had to trust that he would always fix it. He would always fight for us.

For me.

"You know, Austin's going to kill us when he finds out we had sex on the couch."

"Isn't the first time," Connor smirked, kissing the corner of my mouth. "And it sure as hell won't be the last."

I woke to the sizzle and smell of bacon.

Poking my head over the back of the couch, I rubbed my eyes. "Connor?" I called.

"In here."

Throwing the sheet off my body, I scrambled around to find my clothes but settled on his polo shirt. It barely covered my thighs, but we had the house to ourselves for a little while longer.

When I entered the kitchen, I paused, leaning against the doorjamb to watch him navigate cooking bacon, shirtless with one crutch tucked under his arm.

"That looks dangerous," I said.

"I don't think I thought it through." His eyes found mine, love shining there.

"Here, let me." I went to him. "You sit, I'll cook."

"I wanted to make you breakfast in bed."

"And you'll have a lifetime of mornings to do that for me."

"A lifetime, huh?" I heard the smirk in his voice as he hobbled over to the table. "I like the sound of that."

I flipped the bacon and turned my attention to the eggs, ignoring the flutter in my chest. "Did you get any sleep?"

"Not much."

"Were you in pain?" I asked over my shoulder.

"A little, but I was too busy watching you sleep to sleep myself."

"That's a little creepy." My lips curved.

"I just... fuck, Ella." He let out a steady breath. "Last night was incredible. You were incredible."

"Yeah, it was nice."

"Nice?" He groaned. "Wait until I'm back on my feet. I'll show you nice."

A lick of heat went through me, but I didn't let him see my face, my flushed cheeks.

"Did you speak to administration about classes?" I changed the subject.

"Yeah, I can move to online classes."

"That's good. It'll take the pressure off."

"Yeah." There was a note of sadness in his voice, and I glanced back at him.

"What's wrong?"

"Everything's different."

"I know, but you'll get there."

"Yeah, I will." There was that flicker of determination again.

"Okay, breakfast is served." I grabbed two plates and divided the bacon and eggs before joining him at the table.

"Thanks." Connor wasted no time tucking in.

"Hungry?" I snickered.

"Hey, I'm a growing boy." He winked.

Things felt easy between us again as if last night had thawed some of the ice.

"What?" he asked.

"I was thinking we should probably start looking for places to live in Philadelphia."

His hand stalled, his fork hovering midair. "For real?"

"Yeah. Am I scared about what the future holds? I'd be lying if I said I wasn't. But I love you, Connor, and I can't imagine not being with you."

"I'll call some realtors tomorrow."

"There's no rush—"

"Hell yeah, there is. I don't want to give you time to have second thoughts."

"I'm not going to have second thoughts. I want this. I want a future with you."

He stared at me, the intensity in his gaze a little disarming.

Connor had always been an intense kind of guy, but this felt different. This felt like he was on the precipice of saying something important.

But it never came.

Instead, he gave me a big smile and shoved his fork into his mouth.

"I'll fix the couch soon," I said.

"Probably a good idea." He checked his cell phone. "Because everyone's coming over."

"Everyone?"

"Austin—"

"Austin lives here," I pointed out.

"Haha, funny girl." He let out a weary sigh. "Mason and Harper arrive soon, and Noah and Rory are having breakfast with Aiden and Dayna, then heading here."

"It'll be okay, you know. They're your best friends."

"I know, I just... I wish it wasn't like this."

"Connor." I went to him, gently perching on his good knee and wrapping my arms around his neck. "They love you with or without hockey."

"I'm not so sure about that, kitten."

"Well, I am." I brushed my lips over his. "You're kind and funny and loyal. You'd do anything for them, and they know that."

"I feel like I'm letting them down," he confessed.

"Oh, Con." Touching my head to his, I pressed in closer. This, this was what he was afraid of. Of letting them down and ruining their shot at the playoffs.

He wasn't only carrying the future of his career on his shoulders; he felt like he was carrying theirs too.

"Injuries happen. It's part of the game," I said.

"I know. Fuck, I know. It just sucks it had to happen now. Halfway through my final season."

"But it did. And we have to deal with that, okay?" I pulled back to look him in the eye. "You've got this, babe. And I'll be right beside you every step of the way."

He gave me an imperceptible nod. He wasn't there yet, but that was okay. I would spend every day being whatever he needed.

I would be a shoulder to cry on when things got tough or a cheerleader to support him when he needed a little push across the finish line.

I would be right there.

Always.

"It's so good to see you." Dayna pulled me into a bone-crushing hug. "As soon as we find five minutes to ourselves, I want you to tell me everything," she whispered, giving me another little squeeze.

"Hey, El. Looking good." Aiden dipped his chin in that Aiden Dumfries way of his.

"Did you enjoy the holidays?" I asked.

"It was nice, but I'm glad to be back in Lakeshore. I

won't have to share Aiden with Carson every waking minute."

"Coach Walsh and Dumfries got a little bromance going on?" Connor teased.

"We're friends." Aiden shrugged. "It's not a big deal."

"Hey," Harper and Mason joined us.

"Welcome home," I said.

"That sounds strange." Her eyes crinkled, and Mason wrapped his arm around her waist.

"Sounds pretty good to me."

"No regrets about moving out of Lakers House?"

"Fuck no."

The guys all chuckled. All except Austin.

"Hey, maybe you should move in, Aus," Noah suggested. "Take Mase's old room."

"Fuck off," he murmured, making a beeline for the refrigerator.

"Don't push him," Rory chided.

"Come on, shortcake, I was only playing."

"How does it feel to be back?" Mason asked Connor.

"Could have been under better circumstances."

"The team's surely going to miss you," Aiden added.

Connor sucked in a sharp breath, and I squeezed his hand under the table. He gave me an appreciative smile and mouthed, "I love you."

"I love you too."

The guys steered the conversation to safer topics

after that. Connor was quiet, but if anyone noticed, they didn't say anything.

"So, where'd you go last night?" Noah asked Austin.

"None of your business."

Noah smirked. "Well, according to Cutler, you didn't stay over at Lakers House, and I don't remember seeing you on our couch. So where were you?"

A ripple of tension went through the air, Austin clearly still pissed at Noah for moving in with Rory.

"Noah," she hissed.

"I have other friends outside of the team, and you four idiots, you know."

"So you were over at a friend's?" Mason added.

"I am not talking about this."

"Was said friend a girl friend or a guy friend?"

"You're an asshole." Austin pinned Noah with a dark look.

"Come on. We're only busting your balls. If you've got a new *friend*, it's all good."

"Fucking idiot," Austin muttered, grabbing his bottle of water and walking straight out of the kitchen.

Rory let out a frustrated sigh. "Did you have to goad him?"

"He's a big boy. He can handle it."

She rolled her eyes at him. "We're supposed to be trying to bring him out of his shell, not force him back in."

"You worry too much, shortcake." Noah hooked his arm around her neck and pulled her in for a kiss.

"How's little bro?" Connor asked Mason.

"He's good. Got a little upset that we had to leave. But Harper will see him weekly at the group sessions. And we're doing the coaching now too."

"He's a good kid."

"He's the best," Harper beamed.

"We need to go out," Noah said. "Celebrate the fact you're back."

"Oh, I don't know about that. I can barely walk—"

"We can hit up Zest or Millers. It doesn't have to be TPB. But it would do you good to get out and join the real world again."

"Yeah, maybe."

It was good to be surrounded by our friends again, and I wanted to hug Noah for trying to make Connor feel at ease. But I could sense his apprehension still.

"We can do a group thing if you'd prefer," Mason suggested.

"Nah, Ella's had him all to herself. It's our turn." Noah grinned. "Besides, the girls will want to catch up too."

"It's not a bad idea," I said. "We could go for dinner, then meet you later?"

"Fine. Let's do it."

"Tonight?" Noah asked.

"Yeah, why not. Might as well get it over with," Connor laughed, but it came out strained.

I stroked the back of his neck, wishing I could fix this for him.

Wishing I could make everything all right. But it was a process, one that was going to take time.

"We can get you a wheelchair if you—"

"I don't need a fucking wheelchair," Connor barked. "I'll manage on my own two feet."

"You mean one foot?" Mason snorted.

"Oh, fuck you. Fuck all of you," he laughed again, his hand tightening around mine.

But this time, his laugh sounded lighter.

It sounded like hope.

CHAPTER 31

CONNOR

I WAS TRYING.

Smart clothes. *Check*. Connor Morgan humor. *Check*. Fake smile and brittle laughter. *Double check*.

It was hard work staying invested in my friends' conversations. Stories and anecdotes from their winter break. I smiled and nodded in all the right places. Laughed along when they cracked a joke. And sipped my soda like I didn't have a care in the world.

But Ella was right. They were my best friends, and they were trying.

Which meant I could try.

I could put on a brave face and spend some time with them outside the house.

We chose Millers in the end. Harper wasn't working

since she was out with the girls, but Kal, the bartender, was a decent guy, and he looked after us.

"Okay, I've got another round of beers, some chips and queso, and some little fried zucchini things Chad is thinking about putting on the menu," he said, arriving at our table.

"Gluten-free?" Mase asked.

"Don't worry, Steele. Chad learned his lesson after making Harper sick. He's extra careful now."

Mason nodded.

"Relax, hotshot. I'll look out for your girl." Kal winked and headed off like he hadn't just laid the gauntlet down at Mason's feet.

Noah let out a low whistle. "He's asking for trouble."

"Nah, Kal's okay." To our surprise, Mason shrugged. "He just likes to give me shit."

"You sure he's not after your girl?" I said, and he flipped me off.

As the conversation continued, it became obvious they were avoiding anything to do with the team or the rest of the season.

"You can talk about it, you know," I said.

"About what?" Noah played dumb.

"Hockey. The team. The rest of the season."

"Nah, we can talk about that anytime. We brought you here tonight to relax." He gave me a reassuring smile, but it did little to ease the knot in my stomach.

"Guys, seriously. I need you to act normal around

me, okay. It was knee surgery. It could have been worse."

"Yeah, we know, Con." Mase tipped the neck of his beer toward me. "We just don't want to rub it in your face."

"You're still my teammates. I'm still a Laker."

"Damn straight," Aiden said.

"So, don't feel like you can't talk about this stuff, okay."

"You got it."

"So, are we going to discuss the other elephant in the room?" Mason asked.

"Austin?" I guessed, and he nodded.

"Where the fuck is he?"

"Had plans, apparently."

"Things are either back on with Fallon, or he got himself a new fuck buddy situation."

"Good for him, I say." Aiden sipped his beer. "Whatever helps him burn off some steam to be ready for practice. We need his head in the game if we want to make it to the playoffs."

Noah and Mason both looked at me, and I let out a heavy sigh. "Seriously?"

"Shit, we're sorry, Con," Noah said. "We just don't want to upset you."

"Been there, done that. Realized there's fuck all I can do about my current situation." I took a drink of my soda just to give myself a way to channel the nervous energy bouncing around me. "Look, it is what it is. I can be there to cheer on the team for the rest of the season and focus on my recovery."

"I'll drink to that." Mase held up his bottle.

"Me too." Noah clinked his bottle.

"And me." Aiden gave me a small nod.

I'd been apprehensive about coming tonight. Worried I wouldn't be able to mask my anguish. But maybe Ella was right. Maybe I didn't need to.

These guys were my friends—my best friends. I needed to lean on them a little if I was going to come out the other side.

"It was a shitshow," I said sometime later. "I made Sara leave, told my old man— Mason?" Following his line of sight, my mouth twitched. "You've got it bad."

"Still can't quite believe she's mine."

"Believe it, asshole." I clapped him on the shoulder, jealousy burning in my veins as he got up and went to greet Harper.

But the second Ella's gaze landed on me, everything inside me settled. Her smile was... fuck, me, it was everything.

She came straight over, a twinkle in her eye.

"You're drunk," I said.

"I had a couple of drinks with dinner. Nothing too heavy." She went to sit beside me, but I banded my arm around her waist and pulled her down on my good knee.

"Hi." I grinned.

"Hi yourself."

"Did you have fun with the girls?"

"The funnest."

"The funnest, huh? How many drinks did you say you had?"

"Oh, hush." She swatted my chest. "Hmm, you smell good."

"You, Ella Henshaw, are wasted."

"Am not. I'm just happy. You make me happy, Connor."

"That's funny because yesterday, you didn't like me very much."

Ella brought her mouth to my ear, giggling. "I liked you when you were fucking me on the couch."

"Fuck," I breathed, a bolt of lust going through me. "Are you trying to kill me, kitten?"

"Death by foreplay, what a way to go." She let out a dreamy sigh. "Where's Austin?"

"He didn't show."

"Oooh, I wonder if he's got a hot date with his mystery girl."

"El, we don't meddle anymore, remember."

"I know. But he's the last man standing. I'll be sad if he doesn't get his happy-ever-after before graduation."

"You know you've been sitting on my knee for at

least five minutes, and you haven't kissed me yet," I pointed out.

"Well, then we should definitely rectify that." She leaned in, ghosting her lips over mine, teasing me.

I gripped her nape and smashed my mouth to hers, swallowing her tiny whimper of surprise. Our tongues slicked together with easy familiarity, the distance between us well and truly gone. In fact, I'd never felt closer to her.

"Fuck, I wish I could take you home and sink deep inside you."

"You can... later. But we should stay for a little bit. We're on borrowed time now." She stared into my eyes —into my fucking soul—and I wondered what she saw.

"We'll all stay in touch."

But I knew it was a fool's hope. Lives changed. People moved on. Still, I would always remember my teammates from my time with the Lakers, my brothers not by blood but by choice.

"You never know. You might all play against each other one day."

Now there was a thought.

"I really want it, El." I tightened my arm around her waist, pulling her back against me.

"I know, baby. I know." She patted my arm, letting her head drop back to my shoulder as we watched our friends laugh and joke.

If college had taught me anything, it was that time didn't stand still. You had to make the most of every moment. Treasure the good times and work through the bad. But I was a lucky guy to get to do it with Ella by my side and a group of friends who I wouldn't trade for the world.

"You're smiling," she murmured, glancing back at me.

"Yeah, kitten. I am."

I had a lot to worry about, yeah, but I also had a lot to smile about.

"Ella, come dance with us," Dayna called, already up, swaying to the music.

"There isn't dancing here," she said.

"There is now. Kal," Dayna yelled. "Turn it up. I love this one."

"Let me guess, she had one or two drinks too."

"We may have gotten a little bit carried away," Ella chuckled, sliding off my lap and turning to face me. I pouted, and she laughed harder. "If I don't go, she'll only make a scene." She dropped a kiss on my cheek. "Enjoy the show, babe."

She gave me a tempting little shake of her ass as she walked over to the girls.

Noah and Mason came and joined me while Aiden drifted to the bar to chat with Kal. Or to warn off any ballsy guys who wanted to shoot their shot with the girls.

"How did we get so fucking lucky?" Noah said.

"I don't know, but I thank my lucky stars every day that Ella gave me a second chance."

"So you two are—"

"Okay, we're okay."

"And last night?" A knowing smirk traced his lips. "Did the two of you manage to—"

"Seriously, Holden." Mase shook his head.

"What? It's a valid question. Sex is an important part of a relationship. If they're not—"

"All you need to know is that all the important parts still work," I said.

"Oh, it's like that, huh?" Laughter rumbled in his chest, but then his expression sobered. "I know you don't want to talk about it, but I've been doing some research, and if you hit the PT hard, there's a chance—"

"Holden," I groaned.

"Just hear me out. There are still twelve weeks until the tournament—"

"Yeah, twelve weeks. That's not six months, Noah," Mason said.

"Yeah, but I read about this guy in Canada who was back on the ice three and half months after MCL surgery and playing for his team after four months."

"It's a long shot," I said, not wanting to get my hopes up. "I've got to sit out the rest of the regular season. Coach will replace me. He isn't going to take a risk playing me in the tournament just because it's my final season."

"Well, he should. You're one of the best D-men we have."

"Was, I *was* one of the best."

Fuck, it hurt to admit that. But that was my reality now. The possibility of being a has-been.

"You'll get there, Con. We're all rooting for you."

"I appreciate it."

It wouldn't change anything. But it meant something to know they had my back, even if my absence from the team could jeopardize their shot at the championship.

"Look what the cat dragged in," I said as Austin slipped in through the back door the next morning.

"Shit, you scared me." He scrubbed a hand down his face. "It's early. I didn't think—"

"Couldn't sleep." I shrugged, nursing my mug of coffee.

"Ella upstairs?"

"Yeah. Mason and Harper are still sleeping."

He gave me a small nod, going over to the refrigerator and helping himself to a bottle of juice. "How was Millers?"

"Good. But we missed you."

He scoffed, "I find that hard to believe."

"Aus, come on."

"It's not exactly my idea of fun playing the seventh wheel." Leaning back against the counter, he ran a hand back and forth over his head.

"So bring your new friend next time."

"It isn't like that," he said, tension radiating from him.

"Is it Fallon?"

"Fuck no."

"Okay, keep your secrets."

"I like her okay, Con. I really fucking like her."

"That's great." His eyes clouded over, and I frowned. "It's not great?"

"I don't know. She's got me all twisted up inside. We have a great time when we're together, but she's keeping me at arm's length."

"Well, don't lose your head over some girl you barely know. The team needs you focused."

"Asshole," he muttered.

"What?" I chuckled. "I'm just saying, I've never seen you like this. And I'm happy for you, Aus, I am. But just keep a level head, yeah?"

There was something about all the things he wasn't saying that made my Spidey-senses tingle.

"Don't tell anyone, okay. It's nobody's business, and I know what you're all like."

"I'll take it to the grave."

"What are we taking to the grave?" Ella walked in in a sleepy daze. She caught a yawn in her hand and mumbled, "Morning."

"You look like you need a strong coffee," Austin said, turning on the coffee maker.

"Yes, please."

"Last night was fun?"

"The funnest," I teased, and she poked her tongue out at me.

We hadn't even fooled around after Harper and Mason had managed to wrestle her into bed. My party girl had partied a little too hard. But she'd been so happy that I hadn't wanted to dull her sparkle.

Still, it was a new kind of low watching another guy half-carry her to bed when that was supposed to be my job. She'd fallen asleep almost immediately, and I'd spent half the night watching her again. Wondering if I'd ever get the chance to propose the way I wanted to.

The ring was tucked away in my bottom drawer, under some of my old jerseys. When I'd been in consistent pain, I'd pushed it to the back of my mind. But now that I was in a better place. I couldn't stop thinking about it—seeing my ring on her finger, talking to her about wedding plans.

It was going to be a long few weeks. Because when I did finally ask her, I would be down on one knee. And that wasn't going to happen overnight. So until then, I had to bide my time.

Ella came and perched on my knee, and I wrapped my arm around her waist.

"And I guess that's my cue," Austin said.

"You don't have to leave at the first sign of PDA every time you're around us."

"And yet, here I am. Leaving. Tell Mase not to be

late for practice." He gave us a salute as he grabbed his water and a banana out of the fruit bowl.

"You're right," I said as soon as he was out of earshot. "He's met somebody."

"See, I told you." Ella grinned. "It's going to be so much fun watching him fall."

CHAPTER 32

ELLA

THINGS SLOWLY RETURNED TO NORMAL. Well, as normal as they could be with Connor unable to attend practice or classes.

I stayed over at his place most nights, forcing myself to vacate his bed every morning to make it to class on time.

He was able to bear weight now, which made getting around easier, but Coach Tucker and the team's physician agreed that he couldn't be anywhere near the facility until he was more stable.

That had hit him hard at first, and he'd spent a few days sulking. But he brushed it off eventually. Especially when his new PT said he could progress to the next level of exercises.

Connor needed something positive to focus on,

small wins to reassure him that he was headed in the right direction.

"Ella, hey." Jordan waved me over as I approached Roast 'n' Go. "How was class?"

"Great. It's good to have a routine again."

"Tell me about it. I swear to God, if Noelle asks me to spend another day lounging around in our pjs, eating nothing but fried goods or candy, I'll scream."

"You sound well and truly over the holiday season," I chuckled.

"Don't get me wrong. I had a great time with her family. But I need my space and my home comforts. How's the invalid?"

"Connor is doing okay. He's—"

"Behind you."

"What? No, he is— Connor," I gawked at him as he came toward us. "What are you doing here?"

"I can't surprise my girlfriend for lunch?"

"Did you know about this?" I asked Jordan.

"Don't look at me," she said, holding up her hands. "I'm as shocked as you are. And no offense, but if you're having lunch with Morgan, I'm going to get my order to go."

"Oh no, you don't have to do that."

"It's all good. I have a ton of assignments to get through. No rest for the wicked."

"Only if you're sure?"

"Of course I am. He looks like he could use some

sugar." She tipped her head toward Connor. "It's good to see you out and about."

"Thanks."

Jordan gave us a small wave and headed into the coffee shop.

"I can't believe you're here," I said. "Are you supposed to be fully walking on it yet?"

"Dev said so long as I watch for inflammation and swelling, I can do a little bit more every day."

"I'm so proud of you." I leaned in to kiss his cheek. "Are you hungry?"

"Starving, feed me, woman."

"Come on." Yanking open the door, I held it open for him, and he went inside.

There was the usual whisper and odd stare. But on the whole, the gossip mill had died down since the semester started.

I knew it bothered Connor that people were talking about his injury, speculating on what it meant for the team and his future with the Flyers, but he'd gotten pretty good at blocking it all out.

"Usual?" I asked him, and he nodded.

"I'll grab a table."

"My hero." I grinned, making my way over to the line.

I ordered a caramel latte and a mozzarella with pesto panini for me and an Americano and a pizzetta for Connor.

Collecting our drinks and table number, I headed

over to him. "Here you go."

"Thanks. How was class this morning?"

"Okay. What did you get up to?"

"Actually, I met with Coach Tucker again."

"You did?" My brows knitted. He hadn't told me about that.

"Yeah. Now I'm able to walk. I want to be there to support the team."

"What did he say?"

"He said so long as Dev signs off on it, I could start attending practice and home games."

"That's great, babe."

"Yeah, it feels good to know I can be a part of it again. Bittersweet, but good."

"I'm happy for you."

"I'm happy now I've seen you." A smirk played on his lips.

"You are such a goofball."

The server appeared with our food. "I've got one mozzarella panini and one pizzetta."

"Thank you," I said, waiting for her to leave. Then I turned my attention back to Connor. "Have you talked to your dad yet?"

"Nope. Until he pulls his head out of his ass, I'm not interested."

"I know he likes Sara a lot, but he's letting this drag out."

It had been almost three weeks since the incident.

"Hmm, yeah." Connor took a bite of his pizzetta. "Fuck, that's hot."

"Well, yeah. It literally just came out of the oven." I nibbled the edges of my panini, blowing on the center, trying to cool it down. "Have you talked to Austin again about his mystery girl?"

"Nope. He's been very tight-lipped about it."

"Do you think they're still seeing each other?"

"It's hard to say now that practice has started back. You know how it gets."

"At least he doesn't have to listen to Noah and Rory going at it anymore." I fought a smile.

"No, he gets to listen to you and Harper."

"Connor!"

"What?" His eyes twinkled with mischief. "Your sex noises are the perfect bedtime soundtrack."

"You are..." I fumed, trying to find the right words.

"Gorgeous. Talented. Amazing in bed?"

"More like vain and conceited."

"You weren't complaining last night," he quipped. "Or this morning."

I pursed my lips, trying desperately to stop myself from blushing, as I remembered the way he'd made my body sing.

It was Connor's new favorite pastime. To find creative ways to make me come, given that he still couldn't apply too much pressure to his knee.

"Keep it up, big guy, and you'll be back to your right hand keeping you company."

"Nah, you'd come crawling back for my dick before it came to that. My girl is needy."

"Con..." Heat rushed over my skin. He was so bad. But I couldn't deny a single thing he'd said because I was a little needy since everything.

His deep laughter drifted over me and made my heart squeeze. I loved that sound more than anything.

And it was all for me.

Two days later, the Lakers had their first game back. The season had officially restarted last weekend, but they'd had a bye week.

"How are you feeling?" Harper asked me as we headed over to Ellet Arena to meet Rory and Dayna. Mason's mom had driven Scottie up from Pittsburgh, so they were joining us too.

"I feel like I'm going to puke," I admitted.

Connor would be there tonight, sitting with the team after being given the all-clear to participate in team activities. He couldn't get out on the ice yet, for obvious reasons, but he was a Laker and would support his teammates as best he could.

"He seemed excited about it, though, right?"

"I mean, yeah. But sometimes it's hard to tell what's real and what's him putting on a brave face."

Harper offered me a sympathetic smile. "It might do him good to be with the team. To feel a part of it."

"Yeah." I zipped my jacket up over my Lakers hoodie, trying to keep the icy breeze out.

"How are things with you and Mason?"

"We're good, thanks. It's so nice to be out of the dorm, but sometimes I worry we moved too fast. I don't want him to regret—"

"Harper, Mason loves you. It's written all over his face every time you walk into the room. Who cares if it's moving fast?"

"I think I'm just in that 'pinch me, is this real' phase."

"Oh, it's real, babe. You just have to trust it."

"Harper. Harper's here," a familiar voice called.

Scottie stood with his mom, flapping his hands excitedly at Harper as she veered toward him. "Hi, buddy," she said, holding out her hand. He high-fived it, then flung himself around her waist.

"It's good to see you too, Scottie," she chuckled, hugging him back.

"I missed you."

"Scottie, let Harper breathe, sweetheart."

He pulled away and said, "Are you and Mason having all the sex now you live together?"

"Scottie!" Melinda grimaced. "I am so sorry, Harper. He's been so excited to see you both."

"It's okay." She crouched down a little. "But

remember what we talked about? It isn't appropriate to ask those kinds of questions."

"I know, but it's in my head, and I needed to get it out."

"Okay, buddy. Come on, let's go inside and get our seats."

"Will Aura be there?"

"Yeah, Rory will be there."

They walked ahead of us, but I didn't mind. Mason's mom was great, and it was so cute to watch Harper and Scottie together.

"How is Connor?" Melinda asked me. "I was so sorry to hear about his injury."

"He's doing a lot better, thanks. He's actually sitting with the team tonight."

"Oh, that's wonderful. Such a shame he's out for the rest of the season. But it's important he still feels part of the team."

I nodded, a ball of emotion caught in my throat. I wanted to check in on him to make sure he felt okay about everything. But Connor had to do this for himself, and I would be there for him after.

The arena was a hive of activity. It was the start of the team's journey to the playoffs, and there was a real buzz in the air, everyone eager to see the Lakers continue their winning streak.

"Harper, Ella, over here," Dayna waved us over.

"Aura," Scottie shrieked with delight.

"Hey, Scottie. It's good to see you again. Excited about the game?"

He nodded. "Number twenty-three, Connor Morgan is out, though."

"Yeah, we know." Her gaze caught mine over the top of his head, and I gave her a weak smile.

"I hope it doesn't screw up the rest of their season."

Me too, kid; I wanted to say but didn't.

Me too.

The game was intense. The Cincinnati U Cavaliers came out swinging, determined to give the Lakers hell.

I was almost relieved Connor wasn't on the ice, getting the stuffing knocked out of him left, right, and center. But my heart ached for him as he sat at the edge of the bench, staying clear of the players as they continually changed the lines.

He caught my eye a couple of times, and the sadness and frustration there hit me dead in the chest.

This was hard for him. To be here and yet, not. Not in the ways that mattered to him.

He cheered along with his team, the fans. Shouted when we lost the puck, and, at one point, even grabbed his crutch and got on his feet when the ref made a poor decision. But he wasn't out there.

Connor wasn't in the thick of it, and I knew it would be killing him.

After conceding two goals back-to-back, the Lakers gained the puck, and Aiden raced down the ice toward the Cavaliers' goal.

"Go, baby. Go!" Dayna yelled. "Take the shot, take the shot."

Aiden marked the goal, but at the last second, he sent the puck curling toward Noah, who had managed to evade the defenseman marking him.

It was a perfect pass. Noah had his stick ready, and with a little flick, he sent the puck careening into the net. The buzzer sounded, and the home crowd went wild.

Connor was out of his seat again, cheering with his teammates.

"He's going to hurt himself," I murmured under my breath.

"He'll be fine," Rory said. "Let him have this. He deserves it."

Noah raced over to the boards and held out his hand for Connor, and my heart swelled watching as the two of them celebrated.

And when the final whistle sounded, and the Lakers won seven to five, every single one of the players high-fived Connor as if it was his win as much as theirs.

We waited for the guys outside of the arena. The crowd had mostly dispersed, but a few puck bunnies hung around to try and catch the attention of the guys.

Rory kept glancing over at them, scowling.

"Don't pay them any attention," I said.

"They're just so... so obvious."

"Well, the guys are no better. It's a cycle that both sides perpetuate."

"True." She nodded. "Oh, here they come."

Aiden moved ahead of his teammates, pulling Dayna straight into his arms and kissed her.

"Whew, did it just get a little hot in here," Rory said.

He flipped us off over her shoulder, and we all laughed.

"Where's Connor?" I asked, searching the crowd for him.

"He's in with Coach Tucker."

"Is everything okay?" I chewed on the end of my thumb, my stomach curling with nervous anticipation.

"Think he's getting an earful for not staying in his seat," Mason said, Scottie already glued to his big brother's side.

"He's not hurt, though, right?" I asked.

"Relax, El. Your guy is good."

That eased my nerves a little. But it was seeing him

come through the doors that made my shoulders sag with relief.

I didn't wait for him to reach us, closing the distance with hurried strides. "Hi," I said, searching his face for any signs of his mood. "Everything okay?"

"It will be," he said, lowering his face to kiss me.

Somebody wolf-whistled, but it didn't deter him as he deepened the kiss, sliding his hand in my hair and his tongue into my mouth.

"I love you, Ella Henshaw." The intensity in his voice made a shiver run through me.

"I love you too. Do you want to go home? I think everyone's going for dinner to celebrate, but we don't have to go."

"We can go."

"Yeah?"

He nodded. "And then I want to go home and make love to my girl."

"Sounds like my idea of heaven." I leaned up to ghost a kiss over his mouth.

"Dinner and orgasms. You're an easy girl to please." He grinned before attacking me with his mouth again. Covering me with big wet kisses. But it was perfect.

He was perfect.

And despite the road ahead, I knew we'd be okay.

CHAPTER 33

CONNOR

"How does that feel?" Dev asked as I worked through his exercises. Hamstring curls, calf raises, heel raises, he'd put me through my paces this morning.

Every day I felt stronger, though. The pain was still there; only it was like background noise now. Irritating, but if I focused enough, I could drown it out.

It helped that I'd been allowed to sit with the team during the game. But I couldn't deny being there watching them fight for the win against the Cavaliers had stirred something inside me.

It was too tight, though. Even if I pulled a miracle out of the bag, Coach Tucker had made it pretty clear I was out for the season.

It had hurt hearing the words, the finality of them. But I had bigger things to think about.

"In a couple of weeks, you'll be ready to start some gentle exercise. Swimming, biking, so long as you keep it low intensity. No jogging yet, though. Not until we assess how things go without the brace."

"Which will be when?" I couldn't wait to get the damn thing off.

"The typical guidance is at the end of week ten."

"Okay, I can live with that."

"Just don't get to thinking you're Superman and push yourself too much too soon. And stay clear of the ice."

"Yes, boss." I smiled, ignoring the lingering pit in my stomach. I hadn't ever gone so long without playing hockey. Or at least putting my skates on and getting out on the ice.

But I had to accept my fate and focus on the things I could control.

It had become my mantra over the last few weeks. Ever since I watched Ella walk out on me.

I never wanted to be in that position again, and I'd made a promise to myself to do whatever it took to ensure that never happened.

"So I have a question... but it's kind of personal."

"Jesus, Connor." He blew out a long breath. "I don't get paid enough to give you sex advice. You can ask your doctor—"

"Come on, man. Help a guy out," I said. "We're managing, but I want to know when I can... get creative again."

"College guys," he muttered under his breath. "Always thinking with their dicks."

"So is that your way of giving me the green light?"

"You know your own limitations, Connor. You've got to watch out for pressure on the joint. Flexion should stay under ninety degrees."

"I think I've got it, Dev," I chuckled at the serious look on his face. The guy needed to lighten up a little.

"Just take it easy. There's no rush. Everything will come eventually."

"That's the plan," I said, exploding with laughter as his expression morphed into one of utter disbelief.

"Go, get out of here. And try finding some decorum for our next session."

"You'll miss me when I'm gone."

"Oh, I don't know about that. My next client is a seventy-year-old retired football player with enough stories to make your college days look pure and innocent." It was his turn to laugh. "I'll see you next week. And don't do anything I wouldn't."

I grabbed my crutches and gave him a small salute and went in search of my girl.

"Oh my God, Connor," Ella panted as I fucked into her.

Dev might not have given me the green light for

everything I wanted to do to my girlfriend, but our session had lit a fire under my ass.

I'd texted her the second I left his office to meet me at the house and to be naked and ready for me.

The sight of her laid out on my bed in nothing but her little black panties had almost made me come on the spot.

"Why does it always feel so good," she murmured through breathy whimpers and moans.

I lifted her legs a little higher, changing the angle, hitting her deeper. She felt fucking incredible, taking me like she was born to do it. "You're so fucking tight, El," I rasped. "I could spend my days watching your pussy choke my dick."

"Connor!" she cried.

I pulled out abruptly and dropped her legs. She glared up at me. "Over you go," I chuckled. "Face down, ass up."

"It's a good thing I love you and your magical cock." Ella got into position, giving me a sexy little ass wiggle.

Grabbing onto her hips, I lined up my crown and slammed inside her. "Fuck," I groaned.

"Oh, God. God..." she shrieked.

"Babe, you gotta keep it down. Austin is due back any minute."

"So hurry up and make me come, hotshot."

My fingers dipped beneath her body to find her clit, and I applied enough pressure to send her wild.

"Yes... oh, God, yes."

"You were saying?" Laughter pealed out of me as I pushed her body toward the edge.

I was close, too, that familiar tingle at the bottom of my spine building and building as I thrust into her over and over.

"I'm coming. Oh fuck, I'm coming..." Her legs began to tremble, her walls rippling around my dick as I chased my own release.

"Fuck, Ella. Fucking, fuck." My fingers dug into the soft swell of her hips as I came hard, filling her up, marking her from the inside.

"Hmm." She flopped down on the bed, laying her cheek on her arm as she twisted to look at me. "That was nice."

"Babe, you're killing me here. The sex we have isn't nice. It's fucking life-altering."

"Alright, stud." She wore a dreamy, sated smile.

"Wait until Dev gives me the green light to fuck you *however* I want."

"Connor," she groaned. "Please tell me you did not talk to your physical therapist about our sex life."

"What?" I shrugged, grabbing her some tissues to clean up. "It's a valid question."

"Oh my God." She threw her hand over her eyes. "You are unbelievable."

"Unbelievably prepared. I've got a whole list of positions we can start working our way through."

"It's a good thing I love you," she murmured, removing her arm to look at me.

"Here, I need to take a leak." I handed her the tissues.

"So thoughtful." Ella rolled her eyes as I pulled on a t-shirt and some sweats. It was a tricky task, but I liked to try and be self-sufficient as much as possible.

"Bring me some snacks," she called after me.

I paused at the door and glanced back. "Don't worry, kitten." I smirked, unable to resist one last joke. "I have something you can snack on later."

The body was an amazing thing. Eight and a half weeks ago, I felt like I might never walk properly again. Today, I walked out of Dev's office without my crutches or knee brace.

"Looking good," Noah said as he stood. "How does it feel?"

"A little weird, but okay."

"I guess that's to be expected." He fell into step beside me. "You've done amazing, Con."

"Yeah, it feels good."

"Just in time for Valentine's Day too. You got any big plans."

"Maybe," I gave him a cryptic smile, and he snorted.

"Oh, it's like that, huh?"

"Yep."

"Fine, keep your secrets. I'm a bit bummed we have

a game on the fourteenth. It's my first Valentine's Day with Rory."

"You can still see her and do something after the game or on Sunday."

"Yeah, I guess. Everything's just a little bit tense. We're so close, Con."

"You'll do it. The team is looking strong. As much as I hate to say it, Leon has stepped up to the mark. He's looking good in defense."

"He's no Connor Morgan, though." Noah winked. "Rory mentioned you'll be back in classes soon?"

"Yep, starting Monday."

"That's great, man. And the meeting with the Flyers' first-year coordinator went well?" I nodded, and he added, "It's all coming together."

It was.

Ella and I had started a shortlist of neighborhoods we wanted to check out when we visited Philadelphia in a few weeks, and she had already contacted a few places about possible internships.

The future was ours; all we had to do was reach out and take it.

My Valentine's Day plans would go somewhat to making that happen. At least, I hoped they would.

"You want to get something to eat from TPB? Or we could hit up Millers," Noah said as we walked to my truck.

"Actually, I need to head home. My dad is visiting."

"He is?"

"Yeah."

Noah hesitated with the keys in his hand. "You want to drive?"

"You can give me one last ride," I chuckled.

I'd been given the all-clear to drive, but I promised Ella I wouldn't rush into it. Besides, I kind of liked having Noah chauffeur me around.

We climbed into the truck, and Noah fired her up. "Your dad finally come to grovel?"

"Something like that."

Things had been tense since I set him straight about my relationship with Ella. But it was time we cleared the air, so I'd invited him to Lakeshore to talk. Part of me was surprised he had accepted, but the other part knew he would come around.

"Hopefully, the two of you can sort out your differences," Noah said.

"Yeah, I'm hoping we can."

My father wasn't a bad person. He was just a little misguided and stuck in his ways. And I was determined to get him to see how amazing Ella was. Because they were both important to me, and I wanted them to get along. But he had to make the first move and apologize.

"Did Coach talk to you about traveling to away games with the team yet?"

"Yeah, he said I can start traveling next weekend with you."

"Fucking A. We're so close, Con. None of us want to do this without you."

"Thanks, that means a lot."

Noah nodded. "On or off the ice, you're still a Laker. And we're going all the way, baby."

He beeped the horn at a group of students wearing Lakers hoodies, and they all waved.

"You're fucking crazy." I fought a smile, but his excitement was infectious.

"Just hyped for the rest of the season. Oh, looks like you've got company," he said as the house came into view. "You need me to come in with you?"

"Nah, I got this. Say hi to Rory for me."

"You got it. Text me later and let me know how it goes."

"I will." I shouldered the door open and climbed out, muttering under my breath, "Here goes nothing."

CHAPTER 34

ELLA

Excitement fluttered in my stomach as I approached the guys' house. I wanted to surprise Connor. He'd finally had the brace removed and didn't need to rely on the crutches anymore.

It was a huge milestone.

One I thought we should celebrate.

So I'd grabbed some food to go from one of his favorite restaurants and put on something nice for him and headed over here. But when I turned the corner, and the house came into view, I drew up short.

Ted's car was parked in the driveway. A million questions ran through my head, none of them good.

What the hell was he doing here, unannounced?

It had been weeks since the incident, and he hadn't tried to mend any bridges.

Had he come to try and persuade Connor to see sense?

A shudder went through me. I couldn't just stand out here, hoping he left soon, but I didn't want to see him either.

The decision was made for me when the front door opened, and Connor followed his dad out of the house. The two of them chatted for a minute before Ted pulled his son in for a hug.

Well, then.

I guess they'd finally cleared the air.

I didn't know how to feel about that, but old insecurities rushed to the surface.

Calm down. You don't know what he wants yet.

For all I knew, he was here to apologize and put things right. But Connor hadn't mentioned his visit. Surely, if he wanted to make amends, he would want to apologize to me directly. Or maybe he only came to fix things with his son, and he was never going to accept our relationship.

Dread churned in my stomach as I watched Ted climb into the car and wave at Connor as he backed out of the driveway.

I waited for the car to disappear down the street before approaching the house. "Hey," I said right as Connor was about to go inside.

"El, what are you doing here?" Guilt shone in his eyes, and it hurt.

God, it hurt so much.

"Was that your dad I just saw leaving?"

"Shit, yeah. Uh, he wanted to come and clear the air." He ran a hand down his face, his expression telling me everything he wasn't saying. "Make amends, you know."

"That's nice. I thought I'd surprise you. I got takeout." I held up the bag. "But if it's a bad time…"

"What? No, of course, it isn't. You just caught me off guard, is all."

That flicker of guilt didn't leave his expression, though.

"Is everything okay with your dad, I mean?"

"Everything's fine, babe." He pressed a kiss to my head. "Come on, before the food gets cold."

Connor ushered me inside, following me into the kitchen. I grabbed some bowls and cutlery to keep myself busy.

He was hiding something. And I had a pretty good idea what it was.

"You didn't tell me your dad was coming."

"Uh, yeah. He said he might visit. I didn't want it to be a big deal."

"Right." I turned away, forcing myself to take a calming breath.

Connor just wanted to protect me from the truth. I got it. But it didn't hurt any less.

"El, babe." He came up behind me. "I don't know where your head's at right now, but—"

"I'm fine." I turned around, smiling at him. "I'm

happy for you."

"El, it's not—"

"It's fine. We should eat before the food gets cold. We've got a lot to celebrate. The brace is finally off. You can walk unaided now. And you've made up with your dad. It's a good day." As I said the words, my heart tumbled.

I didn't want Connor to be at odds with his father. Of course, I didn't. But I didn't want Ted constantly whispering in his son's ear, either.

I was a good person, and I loved Connor with everything I had. It would have been nice to think that one day, Ted would see that.

Ted's visit lingered with me. And by Saturday, I was still ruminating over Connor's vague responses when I called him out on it.

"Ella, babe, you've got to stop this," Dayna said as we sat in Ellet Arena, watching the team warm up. "If Ted doesn't like you, that's on him. Connor loves you."

"Yeah, but I don't want to always be this bone of contention between them, you know. One day, he might be my father-in-law."

"Yeah, I could see how that might be a little awkward. But a lot of people don't like their in-laws. It's like a rite of passage or something."

"You like Aiden's mom."

"Yeah, Laura is pretty awesome." She gave me a wistful smile, but then her expression turned serious. "Look, it's Valentine's Day. Connor probably has some super romantic date planned once we get out of here. You can't let Ted be the third person in your relationship."

"Yeah, you're right."

I'd just been feeling extra insecure ever since watching Ted and Connor hug outside the house.

"Speaking of Connor..." Dayna nudged my shoulder and pointed to the team's bench. Connor stood with Coach Carson, the two of them deep in conversation. He wasn't dressed in any of the protective gear, but he did have his Lakers jersey on.

His gaze found mine across the arena, and he smiled.

"There is not an ounce of doubt that he loves you. The way he looks at you." She let out a dreamy sigh. "It gives me butterflies, and I'm in a very fulfilling relationship of my own."

"Okay, okay, I'll stop complaining. If Rory and Harper don't get here soon, they're going to miss the start of the game."

"They'll be here."

Sure enough, two minutes later, the girls appeared, looking a little flushed.

"Where have you been?"

"It's a long story," Rory said. "What did we miss?"

My brows furrowed at her dismissive answer, but before I could ask what was wrong, the team's fight song blasted through the speakers, and the crowd went wild.

"That was close," Dayna said after the second period ended. "They could have used Connor in defense. Leon is good, but he doesn't quite have the coverage Con does."

"Where is Connor?" I asked, noticing he was no longer with the rest of the team as they filed off the ice.

"Perhaps he went to the bathroom," Rory suggested.

"Yeah, maybe."

The crowd dispersed around us, people taking a quick bathroom break or replenishing their drinks and snacks. I glanced over at the team's bench again, my gaze snagging on a woman moving down the aisle.

"That's strange," I said.

"What is?"

"I'm sure I just saw Connor's mom. I must be seeing things." I searched the crowd again, but there was no sign of her.

A sinking feeling went through me. Surely, Connor wouldn't ambush me, and not tell me that his parents were attending the game tonight.

It was Valentine's Day. He'd promised me a romantic dinner after we got done here.

"El, what's wrong?" Rory asked as I tried to stem the rush of emotion inside me.

"Nothing, I'm fine. Just a little tired, is all."

I sat quietly while the three of them dissected the team's gameplay. By the time the players filed back onto the ice, I was a bundle of nervous energy again.

The Lakers didn't warm up again, though. Instead they formed two parallel lines from their entrance onto the ice.

"What is—" I sucked in a sharp breath the second I saw him.

Connor was on the ice.

He wasn't skating, but he was walking precariously down the middle of the lines.

"What the hell is he doing?" Panic clung to every syllable as I clutched my throat. "He's going to slip. He's going to—"

"Shh," Rory said, gripping my hand. "He's going to be fine. See."

He looked steady. Strong and focused as he reached the end of the lines and high-fived Noah and Austin.

Then he scanned the crowd and landed right on me. Crooking his finger, he beckoned me onto the ice, but I couldn't move.

"Hmm, El, I think that's your cue."

"But what... I don't... oh my God."

Blood raced in my ears as my heart crashed furiously beneath my rib cage.

This was happening.

In front of the entire arena, this was really happening.

"Oh my God. I can't." I stood and sat down and stood again.

A rumble of laughter started to rise in the arena as I kept my stupid, idiotic boyfriend waiting.

"I'm going to kill him," I breathed as the girls finally nudged me out of my seat.

"Go easy on him," Dayna winked at me as I stumbled down the stairs to the plexiglass.

"Someone help the girl out," the announcer said over the PA system, and my cheeks burned brighter than the sun.

A steward directed me to an entrance onto the ice and helped me navigate my way to Connor.

"What the hell are you doing?" I seethed, unable to tear my eyes off the man standing before me.

"Hi, El." He crooked a grin.

"Connor!"

"I had plans, babe. Big fucking plans, and then I had the accident, and everything got so fucked up. I didn't want to do this if I couldn't get down on one knee and do it properly. So I waited. And fuck, baby, it almost killed me.

"Because you, Ella Henshaw, are my sun. You are

the stars and the moon. You are the love of my life, and I want everyone to know it."

"Connor," I gasped as he pulled out a ring box and sank down on his good knee.

"Ella Henshaw, I want nothing more than to spend my life with you. Will you marry me?"

The silence was deafening.

I was sure I had stopped breathing, but I felt the moisture of tears rolling down my cheeks. Felt the gentle caress of Connor's fingers as he reached for my hand.

"What do you say, kitten, want to grow old with me?"

"Y-yes. Yes, I'll marry you, you big idiot." I grabbed his shoulder and tugged him to his feet. Connor wrapped me into a hug, and my heart felt fit to burst.

"She said yes," the announcer cheered, and I threw my head back, laughter bubbling out of me. "You're crazy," I said.

"I know it's a little dramatic." Connor's eyes twinkled with amusement. "But I wanted everyone to know that you're mine, El."

He took my hand in his and slid the stunning princess-cut ring onto my finger.

"It's perfect," I said, a fresh wave of tears falling.

"I may have had a little help," he admitted.

"Who?" I asked, admiring the ring.

"Rory and Dayna and the guys."

"They all knew all this time." He nodded and the realization hit me. "Christmas Day. You were going—"

"Yeah." A shadow passed over him. "I had it all planned, and then everything went to shit."

"Oh, Connor." I threw my arms around him and kissed him, and the crowd went wild again.

So much made sense now, and instead of just admitting the truth, he'd kept it from me. Letting me believe it was just a reaction to the surgery. Because he wanted me to have this moment.

Connor wanted me to have the fairy tale.

"I love you," I whispered the words onto his lips. "I love you so much."

"I love you too, the future Mrs. Morgan." His eyes lit up. "Fuck, I like the sound of that."

So did I.

More than he would ever know.

"Come on. We should probably get off the ice before Coach blows a gasket."

"How did you get Coach Tucker to agree to this, by the way?"

Connor looked at me and smirked. "I'm out for the rest of the season. Seemed like the least he could do."

"Congratulations."

Indigo and cyan confetti filled the air as Connor and I entered Millers.

"Thank you." I hugged Rory first, then Harper, and Dayna. "I can't believe you all knew."

"Let me see it." Harper took my hand in hers, and the three of them all swooned. "Your man did good."

"So good," Dayna said. "It's a perfect fit too."

"I hear you two helped with that."

"We may have had something to do with it."

"Ella, oh, sweetheart."

"Mom?" I whirled around to find Mom and Margo standing there. "What are you—"

"We were there, sweetheart, in the crowd. Connor invited us to come. Got us tickets and everything."

"He did?" Glancing around, I searched for my fiancé, but he was busy talking to the guys.

"He wanted us to be there for your special moment. Oh, sweetheart, I'm so happy for you." She pulled me into her arms.

"You are?" The words spilled out.

"Don't look so surprised, Ella," she tsked. "I know your sister, and I haven't always been Connor's biggest fans, but we were only worried about you."

"I'm glad he pulled his head out of his ass, Sis." Margo grinned.

"I'm so happy you're both here. Did Jonah come?"

"He's around here somewhere. But I think Connor wants you." She pointed over to where he stood.

"I'll find you later." I made my way over to Connor,

hesitating when I realized he was now standing with his parents.

So I had seen his mom in the crowd.

"Oh, Ella, sweetheart. Congratulations." Helena wrapped me in a hug. "I am so happy for you both."

"Thank you."

"Ella." Ted gave me a curt nod.

"Dad," Connor warned.

"Ella, I owe you an apology." Ted stepped forward. "I'm not proud of the way I treated you over the holidays, and for that, I can only apologize. I only want the best for my son, and well, I can see now that it's you. Congratulations, sweetheart."

We hovered awkwardly until I took a leap of faith and hugged him. "Thank you, Ted. I promise you can trust me with his heart."

"I have no doubts." Ted pulled away, fiddling with his tie. "Yes, well. Enjoy the celebrations. It's on us."

"What—"

But Ted was already leading his wife toward the bar.

"What did he mean? This is on them?"

"They wanted to contribute, so I let them." Connor shrugged. "It's the least he could do. That's what I invited him to Lakeshore for—to talk about the engagement. I didn't mean for you to see him."

"Always with your secrets," I tsked.

"Hopefully, this one was worth it, though."

"Oh, it was. It definitely, definitely was." I looped my

arms around his neck and moved in closer. Not caring one bit that we were surrounded by our friends and family.

"To the future," he said.

"No, not the future." I smiled against his lips. "*Our* future."

EPILOGUE

ELLA

I*f someone had told* me in my freshman year that by senior year, I would be engaged, looking at apartments in Philadelphia, and interviewing with major publishers for internships, I would have laughed in their face.

But here I was. About to embark on the next chapter of my life with the man I loved more than anything in the world.

"The team sure knows how to travel in style," Dayna said as we entered the hotel lobby, where the team was staying for the Frozen Four tournament and joined the check-in line.

After winning their regional final, the Lakers had secured their place in the tournament, and our small town had mobilized to come and support their team.

"Harper, Rory," I called, spotting them as they entered the hotel, lost in the sea of indigo and cyan jerseys.

"God, this place is crazy," Rory said, looking a little starstruck.

"Wait until we get in the arena. You think Ellet Arena is big, the PPG Paints Arena holds almost twenty thousand people, and it's a sellout."

"I'm so excited for them," Harper said. "Although Scottie is disappointed he couldn't come. But Melinda was worried it would be too overwhelming for him."

"At least they'll get to watch it at the center," I said. The RCC, where both Harper and Mason volunteered, was showing the game on a big screen for all the kids and their families.

"I can't believe we won't see the guys before the game," Rory pouted.

"I kind of get it." Dayna scanned the crowd. "They'd be completely swarmed. How does Connor feel about everything?"

"He's just happy to be with the team, supporting them."

Connor's injury was barely noticeable now unless he pushed himself to the limit. Something he tried to avoid because he didn't want to jeopardize things with the Flyers.

We'd visited their facility a couple of weeks ago and met with the coaching staff to talk about Connor's recovery. It was also a chance for us to look at some apartments.

We hadn't made any decisions yet, but I no longer got a pit in my stomach whenever I thought about the future.

I glanced down at my ring finger and smiled.

Engaged.

It still didn't feel real—even though we'd talked about the kind of wedding we wanted. I didn't want to make a big fuss. Just the two of us and our closest friends and family. But we planned to wait until we were settled in Philadelphia. Maybe next spring or early summer after the Stanley Cup playoffs.

There was no rush; we had all the time in the world.

"Thank God, we're almost there," Dayna said, pulling me from my thoughts. She was nervous.

We all were.

The team had made it this far.

Nobody wanted to go home without the trophy.

The arena hummed with frenetic energy, the noise almost deafening. But there was something infectious about it. The crispness of the air. The heavy anticipation. The ripple of excitement.

It was easy to see why people fell in love with this sport. There was no feeling in the world like it. I couldn't even imagine how the team felt down on the ice warming up.

This was it.

One shot.

No going back.

If they didn't win this game, they would return to Lakeshore U losers.

But I had a good feeling.

Music blasted out of the speakers, lights whizzing around the ice and over the full-capacity crowd. It was something else.

And sitting right there, on the Lakers bench, amidst it all was Connor.

Even though I knew he'd made his peace with things, my heart still ached for him.

Sensing my anguish, Rory grabbed my hand and squeezed gently. "He's okay," she said.

"Yeah, I know."

Coach Tucker leaned down to whisper something to him, and Connor nodded. My brows furrowed as I watched him get up and—

No.

I clapped a hand over my mouth as he joined the other players on the ice.

"Oh my God," Rory breathed as the crowd went wild.

The announcers were saying something, but I couldn't hear over the roar of blood in my ears.

Connor was on the ice.

He was *skating* on the ice.

"What the hell is he doing?"

"Look," Dayna pointed to the jumbotron, and my eyes teared up.

It was Connor's stats. It moved to another player, and I lost my breath. But then senior players started a lap of honor around the rink, and Connor was right there among them, waving at the crowd as he passed the Lakers section.

"Jesus, I'm a mess," Dayna said, wiping her eyes.

I wrapped my arm around her, hugging her tightly as she watched Aiden on the precipice of his penultimate or final game of his Lakers career.

"I'm so proud of him," she said.

And I smiled.

"I know exactly how you feel."

CONNOR

The roar of the crowd as I did another lap of the rink was deafening. But it was when our fight song blasted across the arena that I realized the magnitude of this moment.

It felt like the entire population of Lakeshore had made the journey to Pittsburgh to support us. A swathe of indigo and cyan cut across one section of the arena like a silent battle cry.

As I slowed down and skated toward our team's bench, I searched for Ella in the crowd. She had no idea Coach Tucker had requested that his senior players do a lap of honor tonight.

And I'd had no idea that he intended to include me in that until ten minutes ago.

My entire college hockey career was reduced to this single moment.

But it was worth it.

All the pain and heartache and tears. Even though I wanted more than anything to go out on the ice tonight and play for my team, I'd made my peace with the fact that it wasn't going to happen.

I couldn't risk my entire career with the Flyers for the chance at a last few moments of Lakers glory.

But to get to go out on the ice with my teammates and acknowledge the last three and half years of my life was something I would be forever grateful for.

"Thanks, Coach," I said, exiting the ice.

"I know things didn't turn out the way you hoped, son, but you are a part of this team. And it's been an absolute pleasure coaching you over the last four years, Connor." Coach Tucker squeezed my shoulder. "Now, I want you to sit tight and keep your eye on the game. You see anything that isn't working. I want to know about it."

"Yes, sir." I gave him an appreciative nod.

Coach beckoned the team in, ready to deliver his final pep talk before the game commenced. "This is it," he said. "Every minute of practice, every hour spent in the gym, every day you sacrificed the normal college experience to play hockey, it all boils down to this.

"But win or lose, I want you to know that I am proud to call myself the head coach of the Lakeshore U Lakers. Aiden, son, take it away."

Aiden cleared his throat, running his eyes over every single one of us. "I think Coach Tucker pretty much covered everything I have to say. But I will add this. Coach might not care if we win or lose, but I find myself disagreeing with him there. Because I don't know about you all, but I came here to win. I came here to go all the way."

The guys all nodded.

"So let's raise the fucking roof and let them know we didn't come to play around. We came to take that trophy home. Lakers on three."

"One, two, three, Lakers."

The team dispersed, and the first line moved into position. Aiden glanced back at me and gave me a subtle nod.

"Go get 'em, Cap," I said. "Go get 'em."

ELLA

I rocked on the balls of my feet, trying to see over the gathered crowd. It had been almost ninety minutes since the final whistle blew, and the Lakers won their semi-final game.

We were going to the finals, and everyone wanted to congratulate them.

Dayna insisted we push our way to the front of the crowd. But security had stopped us from going any further.

When the doors finally opened, and our guys appeared, looking as hot as hell in their gray suits, the crowd all cheered.

"Oh my God," Rory laughed. "This is— wow."

It was infectious, though, and before long, we were all cheering and clapping too.

There was a strict code of conduct for the weekend, and the guys had to board their bus to take them back to their hotel, where we hoped to join them later. But as it was, we couldn't wait that long.

Connor spotted me almost immediately.

"Shit, don't do it, Morgan," Ward Cutler yelled. "You know what Coach said, anyone caught—"

"Fuck the rules." Connor marched straight up to the security fence and cupped my face in his hands. "Hi." He grinned.

"Hi. Aren't you supposed to be—"

His lips crashed down on mine, stealing my words and my heart.

Another cheer went up as Connor kissed me like he might never get another chance.

When he finally pulled away, I was breathless and a little weak in the knees.

"Let's go, Morgan," Coach Walsh called.

"Coming, Coach." He fixed his eyes back on me. "I'll see you later at the hotel."

"You will." I nodded.

"Wear something sexy. Or better yet," he leaned in, whispering, "don't wear anything at all."

"Connor." My breath caught, butterflies taking flight in my stomach.

"I love you, Ella Henshaw."

"I love you too.

"Today. Tomorrow. And all the fucking days after that." His eyes crinkled with laughter. "In fact, what would you say to marrying me sooner rather than later."

"How soon?" My heart careened against my chest.

"Morgan, let's go," Coach Carson yelled again.

And my ridiculous boyfriend started backing away.

"Connor, how soon?" I demanded.

He couldn't just say that, then disappear on me.

"Soon," he mouthed. "Before graduation."

"You're crazy."

"Crazy about you." His eyes lit up. "Is that a yes?"

"I'll think about it."

"I'll wear you down."

I didn't doubt that.

But the truth was, I didn't need to be asked twice. I already knew my answer.

He probably did too.

PLAYLIST

Rush – Lewis Calpaldi ft. Jesse Reyez
I Looked Into Your Eyes – Sky McCreery
House Of Cards – Alexander Stewart
Half A Man – Dean Lewis
It'll Be Okay – Shawn Mendes
Drunk Text Me – Lexi Jayde
Better Off Without Me – Matt Hansen
Never Knew A Heart Could Break Itself – Zach Hood
Hurt The Ones I Love – Reagan Beem
Falling Apart – Michael Schulte
Atlantis – Seafret
Holding On To Letting Go – Scott Quinn
All For You – Cian Ducrot

ACKNOWLEDGMENTS

Oh, Connor... you demanded a full story and who knew it was going to be such a hard path to your HEA. I hope you enjoyed getting into our lovable rogue's head as much as I loved writing him!

Jen, thank you so much for holding my hand through this one. I appreciate your insight and enthusiasm for these characters so much.

To my team: Kate, my editor, and Darlene and Athena, my proofreaders, thank you for continually working around my crazy schedule and tight deadlines! To all my Promo and ARC Team members, thank you for your continued support. And a special shoutout to my audio producer Kim over at Audibly Addicted for bringing this series to life - I'm so excited to hear Connor in all his glory.

And, I say it every time but a huge, huge thank you to all the readers, bloggers, bookstagrammers, and booktokkers who have supported the series - your continued support means everything.

Up next is Austin, our grumpy goalie. Are you ready?

Until next time...
L A xo

ABOUT THE AUTHOR

RECKLESS LOVE. WILD HEARTS.

USA Today and *Wall Street Journal* bestselling author of over forty mature young adult and new adult novels, L. A. is happiest writing the kind of books she loves to read: addictive stories full of teenage angst, tension, twists and turns.

Home is a small town in the middle of England where she currently juggles being a full-time writer with being a mother/referee to two little people. In her spare time (and when she's not camped out in front of the laptop) you'll most likely find L. A. immersed in a book, escaping the chaos that is life.

L. A. loves connecting with readers.

The best places to find her are:
www.lacotton.com

Printed in Great Britain
by Amazon